BLOOD GAME

JEFFE BOATS

Copyrights and Disclaimers

Copyright © 2025   Dr. Jeffery J. Boats   https://jeffe.boats

Cover design and production by Miblart,
        part of the Mibl Group of brands: www.miblart.com

Editing by Rebecca Lloyd

Chapter opening illustrations created by the author from
        free stock imagery of night skies

Published and distributed by IngramSpark, part of the
        Ingram Content Group: www.ingramspark.com

First printing: February 2025
                e-book ISBN: 979-8-9918999-1-8
                paperback ISBN: 979-8-9918999-4-9
                hardcover ISBN: 979-8-9918999-7-0

For my father,

John M. Boats,

whose love of
smart action heroes
inspired me
to create my own.

CHAPTER 01   The Flash Op

Eight years before…

    I hadn't planned to jump off the roof of a three-story building. That's not the sort of thing you plan. They say your life flashes before your eyes in moments like that, but mine didn't. There was no time for it. The truth is, I barely had enough time to regret how I got there.

    The evening began simply enough. Another routine training exercise in the big city. Four of us in a dark unmarked car, earpieces crackling with the faint sound of static, waiting for Control to code in and start the briefing. A brisk November wind provided the only other sound, whistling past our car and blowing littered paper in swirls. The sun was down, but the streetlamp on the corner was unlit. In other parts of Philadelphia, pedestrians weaved their way home through rush hour traffic, but the sidewalks were empty in this part of town. Criss-crossed and padlocked doors barred entry to the boarded-up shops.

    I sat shotgun with a black leather toolkit at my feet. Like my colleagues, I wore grays and blacks, a Smith and

Wesson CS45 concealed inside a light jacket. One deep breath, then another. My hands curled into fists in my lap, and my toes twitched secretly in my shoes.

I was team leader tonight, but it was a team of Control's choosing. We were five months into intensive training at The Farm, and for some of us, graduation loomed near. For the rest, perhaps a position at Langley as an analyst or a support person, but that was no one's goal.

Battle sat behind the wheel, eyes closed, meditating. That wasn't his real name of course—no one here went by their real name. "Sean" had been my choice from the short list of suggested names. Battle must have hated all his choices and insisted on a nickname. Tonight, he'd be the wheelman except for emergencies. Marco and Donna sat in the backseat holding their own toolkits, and Donna's rifle lay low in the seat between them. She was our best sniper, and I was wondering whether long arms would be necessary for tonight's "flash op" when the static finally crackled to life.

"Yankee, three, niner, zero. Copy?" Control said.

"Bravo, two, eight, two … go," I responded into my headset, and instantly the world came into focus. I had a new problem to solve.

"You've all read the dossier on Biko Ojoola and his suspected terrorist cell. We just intercepted a text message from him to an unknown recipient. Message reads 'I'm coming for it now.' Recipient is geolocated. Satnav feed incoming."

Battle made a few taps and swipes on a tablet mounted on the dashboard, displaying a map of the northside of Philadelphia. Location markers indicated the positions of Ojoola and the Recipient. Battle pointed to a spot on the grid to indicate our position.

"Ojoola was spotted leaving his apartment 40 seconds ago, on foot. Appears to be heading toward the Recipient. Any action must be plausibly deniable. Any termination must seem accidental. Break out the oars and paddle."

The others looked at me. Control's mention of "OARS" was an acronym: Observe, Assess, Report, Subdue. In this training exercise, it was my call whether and how we would carry these out. One immediate observation, that I kept to myself, was that Battle found our position on the map too quickly. That suggested he'd seen it before, and possibly practiced. While this sort of thing would raise a red flag in a real, life-or-death situation, it was something I'd frequently noticed in other training exercises. It merely gave away, to anyone observant enough, that he was in on it. It wasn't Battle who was being evaluated tonight. I set that aside and called out the play.

"Battle – you drop off Marco a block behind Ojoola, and he'll be the eye. Marco, you'll call it in if he talks to anyone, stops anywhere, or is involved in any dead drops." By the time I'd said this, Battle had already turned at the first intersection. "Then drive me and Donna here," I said, pointing to a parking structure across the street from the Recipient's location. "Donna will take a godspot position on the upper deck."

Donna nodded as Battle announced he'd spotted Ojoola. Seconds later, we reached Marco's drop-off point. Battle turned onto a side street less than a block behind Ojoola, slowing rapidly. With practiced ease, Marco slipped out of the car fluidly, despite the car never fully stopping. Battle put the pedal back down the moment his door closed.

"Target acquired," radioed in Marco. "Negative contacts."

Battle turned the next corner sharply and sped down a side street. I couldn't help but watch his eyes. The map on the tablet rotated ninety degrees with every jarring turn of Battle's wheel, yet he knew the city without ever taking a single glance at it. Did he grow up here? Does he have photographic memory? A better explanation was that his briefing included my most likely strategies. Was I being evaluated on my predictability? As I mulled over the possibilities, he glanced over.

"Stop staring at me," he said, eyebrows tensing.

We swerved into the unattended parking garage, stopping for a moment as I slid out of the car with my toolkit in hand. The car continued up a parking ramp. I might have a minute to think before Donna was set up.

"Battle, after you drop Donna, make sure the roof is clear and then swing back in support of Marco."

I looked across the street and saw the Recipient's three-story building. It was over a hundred years old judging by the faded brick and crumbling mortar. It stood like a ghost of prosperous times past. Old Philly, once thriving, now forgotten.

The main floor of the Recipient's building was a small hardware store, darkened, its sign flipped to "CLOSED." The second story was also dark, no details visible from the ground. A black metal fire escape ran up one side of the building with a landing at each floor. On the other side, an alleyway barely wide enough for a car separated it from the adjacent building.

A faint squeak of feedback accompanied Marco's voice as he reported. "Ojoola's E.T.A. now 5 to 6 minutes. Still no contacts."

A faint glow came from the third-floor windows. The Recipient was surely lurking up there, and I awaited confirmation from Donna. I opened the toolkit and took out a keygun. The metal fire doors at each fire escape landing should house standard deadbolt locks. I chose the corresponding probe from the master set, and inserted it into the keygun barrel. It clicked into place as Donna's voice sounded in my earpiece.

"In position," she said. "Third floor is a single, large room. I see one grey-haired man working at a table. There's some sort of electronic device. That might be a brick of C-4. It's a bomb. I only see one bomb, but my vision is partially obstructed."

"What else is in the room?" I asked. "Is he alone?"

"I see no other people. Black handgun on worktable. Filing cabinets. Computer on a table in the background. Wall full of hanging tools and electronics components."

I pocketed an upload prong and a radio-controlled explosive primer from the toolkit. Seeing no nearby pedestrians, and with still no sign of Ojoola, I darted across the street. The old metal of the fire escape squeaked and groaned beneath my feet, as though begging me to turn back.

"What are you doing, Sean?" Donna asked.

"Creating a diversion. We need intel."

I climbed to the second-floor landing, ignoring the stench of week-old garbage wafting from the dumpster below. The fire door had the deadbolt I'd expected. I inserted the keygun probe into the lock, and gently squeezed the trigger. Nodules on the probe sprung out vertically within the keyhole, prodding the inner lock mechanism to learn the correct shape to take. The faint clicking of the probe taking form was nearly inaudible. In a few seconds, when the clicking stopped, I turned the handle of the keygun clockwise, and the lock opened.

I cracked the door a few inches, waited a beat, and then closed and relocked it. I extracted the keygun and reset it while quickly climbing toward the third floor.

"He's moving, Sean. The Recipient. He grabbed his gun and is moving to the side of the room. I'm guessing toward stairs."

"Good. Keep telling me where he is. Do you see anyone else?"

"Negative. He's alone." The tone of Donna's voice told me she now understood the maneuver. A lone bombmaker would respond to an intrusion himself. If he'd had a guard nearby, out of view, then certainly the guard would react. We now knew he was alone, and that the third floor was temporarily unoccupied.

The third-floor deadbolt popped as easily as the previous. My pulse thundered in my ears as I hurried inside. Spotting a small laptop computer, I inserted the upload prong into its USB port. The prong was a DARPA innovation, needing only thirty seconds to upload the entire contents of the machine. I left it to its work and turned toward the bombmaker's table.

The bomb was a work of art. It had a tetryl acid-based primer, common for C-4 munitions, and its wiring seemed deliberately complicated, involving multiple diodes and switches, and possibly a collapsing circuit. It had not yet been activated.

"Recipient's still on two. I don't think you have long, Sean."

"Ojoola's two minutes away, tops. He's on his phone now. He's double-timing it."

I took the radio-controlled primer from my pocket, and carefully turned the C-4 brick over. The tar-like smell of the plastique was unmistakable. A heavy sweat chilled me, as though I were breaking a fever. With effort, I inserted my primer and resculpted the brick bottom as smoothly as possible. The right ultra-high frequency radio signal could now detonate the bomb at any time of our choosing.

At that moment, the "upload completed" light blinked on the prong. I yanked it immediately.

"He's coming back up, Sean!"

I hustled back to the fire door and closed it behind me. I used the keygun to relock it.

"Ojoola's 10 seconds away! Don't let him see you!" Marco shouted. The loud blast in my earpiece froze me for a moment, my shoulders tensing and hands shaking as my nerves jangled. I looked down the fire escape and saw so sign of Ojoola, but Marco's warning made it clear I'd never get to bottom without being seen. The only choice was up.

I stepped up onto the fire escape railing and pulled myself up onto the edge of the roof. I then crouched low behind the small border ledge surrounding the flat building top. From behind cover, I watched Ojoola arrive. He went straight for the fire escape.

I kept low, moving around the perimeter of the roof, to minimize the sound of my footfalls to anyone on the floor below. The gravel atop the black tar roof crunched beneath my feet, and I worried Ojoola would hear the sound from the fire escape. I hurried to the other side of the building and looked over the edge. There was no fire escape, but the next building was only two stories tall and about ten feet away.

"Battle, pick up Marco. Then pick me up on the other side of the adjacent building. Then we'll swing back for Donna and regroup."

"Already got Marco," Battle replied. "What do you mean, the adjacent building?"

I stood on the edge, looking down, remembering my lessons on parkour rolls to break a fall. The farther I jumped laterally, the better the landing angle would be for absorbing the impact with a shoulder roll.

I took one last deep breath and made the leap. Donna blurted a curse in my ear as she watched, then muttered a silent prayer of gratitude when I landed the roll well and brushed myself off.

The Recipient's building had no windows on this side, and Donna reported no opposition on its roof, so the getaway was assured. I walked to the other side of the adjacent building and calmly descended its fire escape.

My guard remained up as my shoes reached the pavement. Battle's car was still incoming, so I kept to the alley. I peeked around a corner of grimy brick and saw the same glow as before from the hardware store's third floor, and no other lights. A faint flickering above me, accompanied by a dull buzzing, indicated that the streetlights were finally switching on.

My mind churned with strategy. The next logical step would be to follow Ojoola and the bombmaker as they left and react to any other new intel from intercepted communications. I was still weighing options when Battle pulled up, with Marco riding shotgun and Donna already in the back.

Battle's eyes fixed on mine, and his glare bored into me like a drill. I climbed in the back and found my retrieved toolkit on the floor. I buckled in, ready to talk about next plans, but before I could speak, a voice crackled in all our earpieces.

"Clean escape. Op closed. Return for debriefing."

Donna's eyes widened almost imperceptibly at the sound of the voice. Marco spun around in his seat to look at us, and mouthed the words "was that…Crayburn?" I slowly nodded and could only guess that my astonished expression matched his.

The voice belonged to Richard Crayburn, Deputy Director of Operations. The car fell deathly silent. Whatever we had just done, right or wrong, we did it in front of the DDO.

Still eight years ago...

Battle's hands were angry fists strangling the steering wheel as he turned off Allegheny Avenue and drove toward the highway. This time he looked at the navigational display a few times, and didn't take off his earpiece like the rest of us. I thought about putting mine back on to see if I was missing anything, but thought better of it.

The scenery became more familiar on the highway. A mirage of city lights from across the Schuylkill shimmered upon its wind-blown ripples. I'd seen this many times on the way home from graduate classes at Drexel. Tonight's flash op had taken place in a part of Philly I'd never seen before. We were leaving as quickly as we'd come. The hardware store we'd used was clearly a legitimate business during the day, but it was a front. The Company owned a number of buildings scattered throughout the area. The space above the store might have been a safehouse once. Or a data collection center. Or an interrogation room.

I settled back into my seat and looked down at my hands. I had been subconsciously picking at the dead skin of my thumb cuticles. I slid my hands under my thighs to stop it, and glanced around to make sure no one had noticed. Marco unwrapped a piece of nicotine gum that I could smell from the backseat. Donna stared listlessly out her window. I caught Battle eyeing me in the rear-view mirror.

"This is all on you, hotshot," he said, before breaking off his stare to focus on the road. "Let's see you explain your way outta this one."

I looked over at Donna. Her expression drooped as she looked down and away. For the briefest moment, her lips pursed and her eyebrows raised momentarily above the bridge of her nose. Microexpressions revealing feelings of sadness and fear. She was afraid for me. And Battle was irritated with me and doing his best to act enraged to the point of violence. I'd seen his act too many times to be fooled. But it was clear they knew something I didn't, and that was worrisome.

A half-hour passed before we arrived at The Farm. We drove through a metal gate which slid shut behind us. The main building loomed in our headlights. It had once been a wide Amish-style barn, built long ago and later fortified, and still appeared as such from a distance. Inside was a two-level open-design set of offices, communications stations, and classrooms. The rest of our indoor training took place in the "Meat Locker," a long warehouse fifty yards beyond the dormitories, so named because it had once been used for slaughtering livestock.

Groups of people walked into the main building as we parked. Dimly visible in the background, and well beyond sight of the road, the shooting ranges and obstacle courses were obscured by darkness. The tactical driving course and the demolition pit used for munitions lay empty and quiet.

The main building provided the only light nearby, and we all walked toward it. The quartermaster stood inside the door, collecting our weapons and tools as we entered single-file. I stepped inside and looked up, the starry night replaced by the sturdy timbers of a sloped roof. A single ceiling-mounted floodlight shown down on our group of trainees sitting among several rows of wooden folding chairs. They faced a projector screen and a lectern.

I was the last of my group to reach the chairs. Control was handing out debriefing packets. As I approached, hand held out, he stepped around me to hand packets to the three remaining trainees behind me. Two of them were Ojoola and the Recipient, but the third I didn't recognize. The third man took his folder and started toward the chairs, but then spun around quickly and stepped up to me, poking me in the chest with his folder.

"I studied my role for days, and you didn't even get to me," he said. "Tell me something, genius…who do you think hired these guys?" He slapped the folder against his leg as he turned and skulked toward his seat.

Control's hand clamped down gently on my shoulder, and I jumped slightly.

"This way, Sean." He steered me toward one of the closed, private rooms. I didn't bother glancing back at the trainee class in their chairs. I knew the drill. I had messed up, and my dressing down would be the initial part of the debriefing. Not a one of us had managed to avoid this room the whole six months.

I stepped into the soundproofed room, and Control closed the door as he followed. He walked over to the front desk, where his Mont Blanc pen and clipboard were at the ready, and the usual camera fixed on my isolated seat was already recording, probably already displaying me on the screen before the class. But this time we weren't alone. DDO Crayburn was already seated next to the camera, arms crossed, nostrils flared.

"Let's begin with what you did right," Control said.

"I feel good about Donna as the godspot in that high position." I said, and thought a bit more as Control scribbled on his clipboard, and Crayburn glared at me, unfazed. "Assigning a teammate to the eye position feels right, though I wonder if I should have switched Battle and Marco's roles."

Control nodded, still scribbling. "They're both capable, hard to say. On limited information, you should just go with your gut. Use your judgment."

Crayburn snorted, eyes never leaving me, one corner of his lips dipping low for a moment. Disdain. He unfolded his arms and leaned in, slapping the table. "Judgment?! Now let's talk about where you fucked up!" He stood up quickly, kicking his chair backward in the same motion.

I felt, for a moment, like I was in a surrealist painting. Maybe a Picasso, where people had two eyes on the same side of their head and the background didn't make sense. I couldn't speak. Why was Crayburn even here? And why was he so angry about one training exercise? He turned his gaze at Control for a moment, and I thought I noticed the slightest nod.

"I didn't follow the money," I said. "It's always about the money."

"No shit you didn't follow the money," Crayburn said, leaning back in. "Tell me, genius, who do you think hired those guys?!"

I glanced at Control for a moment, wondering if I was hearing what I thought I was hearing. He'd been only a few feet away when the third man had said the same thing to me, almost verbatim. He looked down and away for a moment, his pen hand rising up to wipe the corner of his mouth with his wrist. He knew that I knew.

My shaming had been planned from the start, coordinated by a number of people, probably including

Battle, and I could only guess who else. The clues had been there, but their miscue as to who was to deliver the "genius" line was the mistake that laid all others bare. Had the deck been stacked the whole time? Was my failure part of the plan? The entire plan? All I could think to do was to play their game, just a bit wiser than the moment before.

"My plan was to have Donna watch Ojoola and the bombmaker. We were going to regroup at her position and await further comm-intel to try to determine their motives and plans."

"You set off a silent alarm. Deliberately! You think they're gonna just go on with their original plan after that?"

"Yes, because it would seem like a false alarm, and everything else would seem normal."

"Because everyone always reacts logically, right? That's your judgment, is it?" Crayburn threw his hands up, like a lawyer playing for a jury. He turned to Control, pointed to him, and then pointed to me. "Fix this," he said, and then stormed out of the room, slamming the door behind him.

I watched DDO Crayburn leave and turned back to see Control stepping over to the camera and flipping a switch. The red LED disappeared, indicating the camera was off. Control walked around the table, clipboard in hand, and grabbed a folding chair. He brought it over and sat next to me. He sighed deeply, eyes forward, before turning to face me.

I looked down at his clipboard, and saw it contained my personnel folder. My birthname appeared at the top in block letters: VALE, THOMAS JAY. I looked upon my true name with a sense of dread.

"This is just between us now," he said. "Can I call you Thomas?"

"Thom," I said, and I couldn't help a nervous chuckle. "Nice to meet you, sir."

"Bill," he said, and he shook my hand. "You know, in the olden days, this is the point where I'd offer you a cigarette."

He started flipping through my file, as though he needed to examine it one last time. The top sheet spelled out my vitals. Six-foot-two, two hundred ten pounds, no eyeglasses or distinguishing marks, et cetera. Page two summarized my marksmanship scores, martial arts progress, language proficiencies, and various other tradecraft scores and ratings.

Control already knew it backwards and forwards, but he flipped through the file a little more anyway. I felt grateful for the delay. It gave me time to process.

It was over.

I'd worked so hard to qualify for the clandestine services, and it wasn't going to happen. My chest felt weighed down by an anvil, and yet I felt a sense of relief. Months of tension left my face, and its release triggered tears to fall from the corners of my eyes. I slumped in my seat as I wiped my face dry with a sleeve.

"Breathe," he reminded me.

An unseen force within me propelled me to my feet. I paced back and forth, eyes on the floor, counting my steps. Eventually, I just leaned back against a wall and waited for the discussion that I knew had to happen. The discussion I had hoped would never happen.

"We know, Thom. We know."

"How?"

"A lot of things. Your slightly awkward gait, for example. You know, the funny thing is, when you're training or on an assignment, you're smooth as silk. You read people like books and react to them as though you're really in tune with them. But the second you go off-duty, that gait comes right back. Your face goes expressionless, and you barely react to anything. You don't make eye contact with people."

He was right. I couldn't keep up the act all the
time. It was exhausting. Years of calculating my way
through social situations and stepping up my game when
duty demanded it. Since high school, I'd been living half
of my life on red alert. You can't live like that all the time.
No one can. And here I was in a program where they're
always watching, always analyzing.

"And look at your fingers, Thom."

I didn't have to look. My fingers had numerous
tiny cuts on them, particularly near the thumbnails, where I
had nervously picked at them in moments where I had a lot
on my mind but no physical stimulation.

"I believe that's called stimming, right?"

"Yes, sir."

He paused a moment, measuring the silence, and
then, finally, dropped the bomb.

"How long have you known you're autistic?"

When I didn't answer immediately, he began
flipping through my file again. Even from a distance,
upside down, I recognized many of the documents. A birth
certificate, my college transcripts from St. Bonaventure, a
thick packet with what looked like my family tree on the
cover page, undoubtedly full of cross-referenced and
annotated interviews taken discreetly during my
background check.

"Thomas Jay Vale, of Kill Buck, NY. High-school
graduate at sixteen. I don't suppose the schools in a small
town, back then, would know how to deal with you. Then
four years at SBU, math and physics, nothing but praise
from your professors. Research fellowship to Drexel. And
a year ago you turned twenty-one and applied. That's
when we noticed you, and we were intrigued...."

"I was never officially diagnosed," I interrupted.
"But I've known since junior high school. They used to
call it 'high-functioning Asperger's Syndrome,' but now
it's just ASD."

"You're on the spectrum," he nodded. "And now you've been officially diagnosed, though of course these records are classified. You know, there's nothing about it in your medical history. Nothing at all except a few interviews with your family. I can't show them to you, but…I'll just say that most of them mentioned you were quirky and weird, and kept to yourself. Some of them said you were the smartest person they'd ever met, and the rest … spoke unkindly."

"I don't talk to my family much."

"Good for you."

I walked back over to Control and turned my chair so I could sit facing him.

"What finally gave it away, sir?"

"Donna." He sat up, and his hand rose slightly as he adjusted himself, palm up at a right angle to the forearm. A gestural emblem, suggesting he wanted me to stay back. He was about to level with me, and he knew I wouldn't like it. I reclined back in my chair and crossed my arms, a distancing emblem calculated to put him at ease.

"Part of her training. I ordered her to seduce you, five weekends ago. I'm sure you remember the evening. Her report mentioned the difficulties she had. How hyper-sensitive you were to touch at first. How she overcame your shyness. And how dulled your sense of touch was after a hot shower, how long it took afterward to build you back up for…performance."

I nodded and grinned. "She didn't seem to mind."

"Well, it was your sensory issues that made us re-examine your behavior. You like warm baths and take a lot of them. That's unusual for a guy. Comforting behavior, right? Calms you and dulls your sense of touch. Helps you maintain emotional control. That's when it started to come together. But I have to say, I'm damned impressed it took us this long to notice. You have a remarkable act."

"Thank you, sir."

"But I hope you understand the position this puts us in. There are certain aspects of fieldwork, of being a targeting officer. You've merely been approximating them. And there are deficiencies in your behavior, and physicality. Thom, I'm sorry."

That last word hung in the air and echoed in my head. The last year of my life flashed before me in a stream of images. Hand-to-hand. Marksmanship. Improvisational acting. Asset collection. Infil/exfil ops and targeting. Class after class, op after op, and always at least average for my class, often well above average. None of it mattered.

"What's going to happen to me, sir?"

Control tossed the clipboard onto a neighboring table. He leaned in and lowered his voice a bit.

"That's the thing, Thom. We don't know. Crayburn and I agree this isn't the place for you. In his mind, because of your academic background, the default would be to make you an analyst. But between you and me, you're way too damned good at tradecraft to just hang like a spider in some corner of Langley. And the way you see things, the way you think, it's not just different. It's valuably different. For instance…why did you open the second-floor fire door tonight?"

"Like he said. To set off the silent alarm."

Control smiled. "You've never been there before. There were no external signs of an alarm system. You didn't have time to peer into any windows, and you wouldn't have seen anything if you had, I made certain of that beforehand. Donna didn't scope anything." He paused for emphasis. "How did you know?"

"I couldn't be certain, sir. But it was clearly a legitimate business, and still operating in a neighborhood like that."

"Go on."

"It was closed and had no bars on the windows or lockable gate in front of the main door, like most of the other businesses within several blocks. Alarm system, then."

Control smiled wider and chuckled. He reached over and patted me hard on the shoulder as he got up, and I stood up with him.

"That's what I'm talking about, Thom. Observation. Tactics. Where you fall short in predicting other people, you excel at seeing everything else. I've been talking to some colleagues in the Pentagon. War gaming. Simulations. Data mining. Resource allocation problems. Game theory."

"If I wanted to do math, I'd go back to Drexel and do math!"

"Maybe you can do it all. You know what I like best about my job? The few rules I have—they bend easily when I need them to. And I don't think you belong in a moldy old room in the basement of the Pentagon, either."

He pulled out a blank piece of memo paper, wrote an address on it, and handed it to me.

"There's a car outside. The quartermaster put all your personals in it, and the driver will take you back to your apartment. Take a few days to come down from this. And then Monday morning, 9am, come see me at this address."

"Your office?"

"Pancake joint, you'll love it. Never plan your future on an empty stomach."

He walked me out of the room. The other recruits had already cleared out and the building was empty and dark. He clapped me once more on the back as I pushed open the door, but once I stepped outside, I was alone. My car and driver were forty paces ahead, taillights glowing, exhaust puffing in stagnant air.

In the pure darkness, I looked up and could just make out the faint glow of the Milky Way. Ursa Major. Cassiopeia. My favorite constellation, Orion, hung front-and-center in the Fall night sky. Every star from my childhood memories were there, watching me. Every one of them, as always, hanging exactly where they belonged. I wondered how they must feel.

CHAPTER 03

Still eight years ago…

The next thirty-six hours passed in a blur. I might have slept, but it wasn't really sleep. I know for a fact that I didn't eat or open the blinds in my apartment. Call me to the witness stand, make me swear any oath you want, and I'll testify I have no idea what the weather was like that Saturday.

Sunday morning, the sun stung my eyes on my walk to campus. My Drexel hoodie covered all but the brim of my ballcap. My favorite food truck was parked right where I needed it to be, and I ravaged two of the best cheesesteaks this side of Campo's.

And then I just kept walking. Past the trainyard. Over the Market Street Bridge. Past the Mütter Museum, City Hall, and a dozen historic sites. Edgar Allan Poe's house was closed for lunch hour, or I might have popped in for the free tour. A strange urge filled me, telling me to see everything one last time. But that was silly—I wasn't going anywhere.

Five intense months of training for international espionage. Before that, a year of part-time language, culture, and general fitness training. But I wasn't going anywhere. Nowhere except back to my graduate studies at Drexel, to study more applied math, write a dissertation, and end up just another college professor. Either that or take a big pay cut and ride a cubicle at a three-letter agency, analyzing all the things I'd rather be doing.

I kicked a stray stone a block down from the Liberty Bell Center and felt relieved when it narrowly missed a parked car. I looked around as the big bell slowly came into view, cordoned off from the tourists and selfie-takers. It looked about the same as when my family had come on vacation, a dozen years before. I smiled at the memory of Mom badgering a passerby until he finally agreed to take our family photo.

I thought about Dad, the ex-Marine, with his hand on my older brother's shoulder as he talked about patriotism and serving our country. He never touched my shoulder like that. He barely said a word to me two years ago when he drove me to Philadelphia to help me move in. I hadn't seen him since. I'd never told him about being a CIA recruit, so at least I didn't have to tell him I'd failed.

I noticed a man in sunglasses and a thin jacket walking in front of the Liberty Bell and watched him for a few seconds. He seemed to look around at everyone and everything but the bell itself. The jacket was a little too large in the shoulders for him. I looked down at his shoes and noticed the hems of his pantlegs sagged almost completely over them, but less so on the left ankle.

Shoulder holster. Ankle holster for a right-handed shooter. Undercover cop or fed.

I glanced around and noted all the sightlines before I even realized I was doing it. I wondered for a moment if he was walking a standard post or if he was there expecting some specific trouble. And then I thought better of it and just turned around.

None of my business. Not anymore. I wasn't going anywhere.

I ducked into the next seedy bar I saw, which didn't take long. It was a dark and narrow recess, as though dug out of the side of its building. It was lit by TV screens, bare lightbulbs over the bar, and willpower. It was empty except for one bartender and a couple tables of twenty-something guys in ballcaps.

I pulled my hood down and sat on a loose barstool. The bartender came over and I double-taked. She looked exactly like Donna. Same height, same skin tone, similar face. Only the hair was different—long African-beaded braids rather than Donna's closely-cropped style.

"What'd'ya need?" she said.

My mind wandered back to a passionate evening. At the Farm, we were effectively sequestered from the outside world. On off weekends it was common, if not expected, for recruits to make the most of their R&R together. Drinking, gambling, and lots of adventurous sex. I myself hadn't partaken often, but the memory of my ice cube raising goose bumps on Donna's quivering skin leapt to mind. What do I need, she asked?

"How about a Citywide?"

"One special. Anything to eat?"

I shook my head, and she turned away for a minute. The bar mirror gave me a view of the table behind me. Their table chatter had picked up, and the loudest of the group was looking my way. I scanned them quickly looking for signs of concealed weapons and estimated their heights and weights. I was stronger and at least four inches taller than any of them.

"Hey, you! You're blocking our view!"

I pictured the guys at the table in my mind, but

didn't look at them. There were six televisions in the bar, all showing the Eagles game, and I wasn't blocking any of them. The waitress was still at the other end of the bar.

"Hey, twinkletoes! I'm talking to you!" the mouth of the group said, and the others laughed.

Stupid locals. Mr. Mouth was building up his confidence. Any moment now, he'd be coming over to prove himself in front of his stupid friends. I slid forward in my chair an inch, subtly shifting to ready myself for quick movement. I kept my head down as the barkeep returned and set a shot of Jim Beam and a can of PBR in front of me.

"Thanks," I said, pulling out a twenty and a five. "Actually, three more, please, and keep the change."

"Four total?"

I whispered, "They're for the table behind me."

In the mirror, I saw Mr. Mouth getting up. One of his laughing friends gave him a swat on the back as he headed my way, rolling up his sleeves.

He never saw my punch coming. I barely saw it coming. My spinning roundhouse drove his nose back into his skull and his body back into his friends. It was one-quarter training and three-quarters hatred of the dozens of bullies I'd known all my life. His friends pushed him back onto his feet just in time to get a face full of barstool as I brought it down on him. He collapsed into a pile at their feet, fragments of wicker and wood clattering around him.

"Anyone else?! Plenty of stools left!"

I didn't give them a chance to answer. I turned and sped out the door, wanting to put as much distance as I could between me and the fool who picked the wrong guy on the wrong day.
I walked as quickly as I could, looking back over my shoulder, until I was a block away and sure I wasn't being followed.

I'd just gone from zero to sixty in two seconds, and it felt good. Too good. I wasn't going anywhere, but there was no going back, either. I pulled the slip of paper Control gave me out of my back pocket and looked at the address.

Tomorrow morning. I'd be there. No going back now.

CHAPTER 04   Any Given Thursday

Present day…

I abandoned the safety of my vehicle and kept my head down as I moved briskly toward the bright lights. The pervasive cameras followed my every move. They were expecting me, or at least they should have been. My mission was to escape with the money, and as usual, it would be unwise to bet against me.

It was a typical Thursday night as I stepped onto the main floor of Rivers Casino in Pittsburgh. The security guard waved me through. I paused several steps inside. The poker room lay to my right, but my normal ritual was to first walk slowly around the perimeter to acclimate to the clatter and bustle.

The humming of slot machines gave way to sporadic shouting and cheering. I walked through an aisle of blackjack tables and passed a standard assortment of gamblers. The hopefuls, the tourists, the beaten-down addicts, the happy drunks, and a few bitter drunks. The nickel slot machines were as loud as ever, their steady drone punctuated only by the boisterous melody of the occasional winning spin. Some vacant machines were playing music to attract customers. An old lady was cursing her machine in some language from the old country.

By the time I got halfway around the floor, to the much quieter buffet area, I felt acclimated. The bright lights and cacophony no longer overwhelmed me. I was ready.

I arrived at the Poker Room a few minutes later. The young blonde behind the podium seemed unfamiliar. New girl, perhaps. She pretended not to see me, busily swiping left and right on her phone. I cleared my throat, and she looked up in annoyance.

"What game you want?"

I was about to answer when the room manager spotted me and rushed straight over.

"Tommygun! Punchin' the clock! Lookin' for some action? The seventy just started, still got room. The two-five-ten PLO is goin' in the back. You want some of that?"

The "seventy" referred to a $70 buy-in tournament, No Limit Hold'Em with $1,200 up top, give or take. Not worth my time. I'd normally want the PLO – Pot Limit Omaha – for a number of reasons. Because it's a more popular variation in Europe, but still growing here, so most American players aren't good at it yet. Because wherever it runs, it's the biggest game in the room. And big games attract big gamblers with big bankrolls, whose big ambitions are paired with mediocre talent.

"Just some one-three tonight, please," I said. "But if you could keep me near the PLO, that'd be great. Maybe I'll jump in if it looks good."

"No prob, Tommygun! Got a new table startin' up. Get some chips and go to twelve, in the back."

I walked through the room, winding around tables, toward the cashier. Seemed like a bigger crowd than usual for a Thursday. The seventy looked ripe with tourists and the regulars were licking their chops. I peeled fifteen hundreds off my walk-around roll of five large. The cashier filled three rows of a plastic rack with $5 red chips and ran one along the edge, demonstrating they were twenty full. She put eight $25 greens in the fourth row and ten $100 blacks in the fifth.

I pocketed the greens and blacks on my way to the table. The greens were in case I ran bad at first and wanted to top off without leaving the action. The blacks were in case I saw a good spot at a high-stakes table. The room manager and I had an arrangement. He'd quietly let me jump the waiting list, and I'd kick him back 10% of my winnings.

My friend Sammy sat to the left of the only open seat. He smiled and waved me over, patting the empty seat as though he'd been saving it for me all day.

"Professor! Always a pleasure! How's the good doctor feeling today?"

"Same as always, Sammy. And you?"

"I'm blessed by the best," he said, lifting the gold crucifix from its chain and giving it a kiss. "Now don't get too out of line tonight, young sir! I'm an old man, and my heart can't take it!"

I loved Sammy. He was one of the few people in my life who could always make me laugh. He was sixty-five years old, going on twenty, and he looked about ninety. That was the trap. He was easily one of the best players in the room, but he only ever played the lowest stakes. He liked it down in the trenches, where he could win almost every time and leave you with a smile as he left with your money. And every once in a while, he'd drop a real head-scratching pearl of wisdom on you.

Every poker room in the world has a Sammy.

"How's the ant farm coming?" he asked. Sammy referred to my online poker experiment. My "bots," computer-automated players, played online at some of the lowest levels of PLO. Little bots playing a game for little stakes – my little "ant farm."

"Breaking even, collecting good data," I said. "Too early to tell if it'll help at all."

Sammy was also one of the few players in the room who knew I had a Ph.D. After I finished at Drexel, Control pulled some strings with the department chair to get me a five-year contract at Carnegie Mellon, lecturing precalculus and calculus for the social sciences. Of course, Sammy had no idea about the rest of my job, nor did anyone else in my life. The other half of my time was spent assisting agencies under the Homeland Security umbrella. Mathematical modeling of global political environments, tactical strategies for war time or peace time, optimal response to terrorist events, pandemics, natural disasters, et cetera. Whatever they need, no questions. At Carnegie Mellon, only the former and current chair knew what I was really up to, and how I'd gotten the job.

But to look at me, you'd only see a thirty-something dressed like a teacher. Untucked dress shirt over khakis, unimpressive haircut. Just another poker room degenerate.

"It's magic time!" Sammy announced as the cards finally started flying. I called over a waitress, gave her two red chips, and had her bring me a Corona. It was merely a prop. Talking to Sammy with a fruit-garnished bottle in front of me would make me look like a "fun player," disguising how tight I actually played.

After an hour of patiently folding rags after rags, a new dealer slid the button in front of me and dealt me the jack of hearts and jack of diamonds. Red fishhooks on the button. Time to play. The "under the gun" player limped, and action folded around to the hijack position, two spots to my right, where Zombie Joe set out four reds with a firm thump on the felt.

"Twenty," the dealer said. The limper wilted in his chair, so I knew he wasn't sticking around. Zombie Joe loosened the collar of his stiff white shirt. He'd probably driven straight here from his funeral parlor in Dormont. He'd left his jacket and tie in the car tonight. His eyes were as puffy and bloodshot as ever. Probably hadn't slept for days.

It was a good spot to isolate him with a three-bet. I grabbed a bunch of reds in one hand and pushed them out.

"Raise, fifty-five," the dealer announced.

Sammy and the big blind folded immediately, and the limper gritted his teeth before flicking his hand into the muck. Joe looked sideways at me as I thought about the range of hands I'd put him on. He grabbed a large stack of chips and laid them out in piles as though counting out chips for a raise, but then put them back into one large stack. He was chip dancing, again and again, all the time watching me, trying to get a reaction. He finally called.

"Heads up," the dealer said. He burned the top card and set out the next three cards for the flop: five diamonds, eight of clubs, three of diamonds.

Joe showed no microexpressions or postural shifts as he watched the flop, nor did his breathing change or neck muscles twitch. He just extended his left hand and tapped the felt with two fingers, indicating a check. I waited only a few seconds before setting out a continuation bet of $70. I expected him to fold, but to my surprise he quietly slid chips out to match mine.

"You ain't got shit," he said, staring me down.

The dealer set out the turn: the nine of diamonds. Zombie Joe peeked under the corners of his cards before cupping his hands together and shoving the rest of his chips toward the middle.

"All in," the dealer announced. The entire table sat up at attention as Joe looked away. His messy shove gave me time to think. He was representing the nut flush – two diamonds in the hole, one of them an ace. I took my first swig of beer in a while and stroked my chin.

"What's taking so long, smart guy?" Joe asked, suddenly leaning in my direction. "Thought you'd blow me off the hand with a few big bets? Trying to figure the odds? Want to borrow a calculator?"

Sammy couldn't hold back a laugh. "One thing I can promise you, Joe. Tommy don't need a calculator."

Joe's peek at his hole cards suggested he didn't have two diamonds, as he'd remember a hand like that. Peeking suggested he had off-suit cards and was checking to see if one of them was a diamond. His draw hadn't come in yet. I took another swig of beer and shrugged. I flipped one chip out to commit to a call.

"Goddammit," he grumbled, finally showing his mood. "What do you got? Aces? A set?" I turned over my pocket jacks, and he grimaced and shook his head. He turned to the dealer. "Gimme an ace or a diamond, one time!"

The river was the deuce of clubs, a total brick. With a vulgar curse, Zombie Joe stood up and threw his cards at the dealer before stomping off toward the exit. His ten of spades fluttered face up onto the felt. The dealer remained calm and professional as he searched for Joe's other card. He had to call over the manager when he found the missing ace of diamonds on the floor. Standard procedure.

Eventually, the dealer shoved all the chips from the center my way, and I tossed two reds back at him, partly a tip, partly an apology on Joe's behalf.

"That's right, Tommy. Way to keep it classy," said Sammy.

"Nice hand, big tipper!"

The voice came from behind me, and I instantly recognized it.   My teaching assistant Dante knew where I'd be on a Thursday night, and he'd dropped in on me many times. I told the dealer to deal me out for a few hands. I stood and gave Dante an obligatory fist bump as we walked toward a quiet corner of the room.

"I almost feel bad for Joe," Dante said. "He should have just jammed all-in over your raise. You'd have folded."

"I had pocket jacks."

"I know you, Doc. You'd have still folded. God bless the fishes, though, am I right?"

Dante knew my game well. He'd paid his way through college by out-hustling the hustlers in the Michigan card rooms. He was twice the player I was. We'd talk strategy over lunch some days, and I'd heard a lot of stories about growing up in Detroit, and some of the struggles he'd faced as a young black scientist-in-the-making, the first in his family to go to college. He wasn't just a good teaching assistant—he'd become a good friend.

"You didn't come all the way down here to just railbird me, did you?" I said.

"Nah. I was thinking of jumping into the seventy tonight. You see all the tourists? I swear I counted at least four of them with nametags from a convention. Easy pickings."

"Don't you have a seminar in the morning?"

"Yeah, all morning," he said, adjusting his Tigers ballcap. "I won't stay here too late. That reminds me…Doc McKenzie's got your papers for tomorrow, since I won't be around."

It made me smile to hear he'd been talking to McKenzie. Dante was getting to know all the right people. A visiting scholar from Waterloo was in town, leading the combinatorics seminar in the morning and giving an invited symposium in the afternoon. Maybe Dante would be invited out to lunch with the research group, or better yet, the post-symposium dinner. Maybe he was getting close to finding an adviser. I was rooting for him.

"Well, I won't hold you up then. Registration closes in ten minutes."

"Run good, bro," Dante said, and gave me another fist bump before heading into battle.

CHAPTER 05 — Hail from a Clear Sky

The chiming of my cellphone alarm woke me the next morning. My gambling roll was still lying out on the nightstand. I'd gotten in way too late, too tired to bother with accounting. It had been a good night. I hit the snooze button and stole another half hour of sleep.

I dragged myself out of bed at half past seven. The first light of the day seeped into my second-floor studio. I drew back the curtain of the bedside window and saw a dark grey, overcast sky, typical of mid-October Pittsburgh. The aromas of cinnamon, pastries, and espresso wafted up through the vents, coming from the coffee shop and bakery below. Mr. Sobczak had been baking since 3 o'clock. A truck from the nearby grocery would soon pull up to buy his breads wholesale.

The studio was a completely open-design, the bathroom being the only walled-off area in one corner of the level. In the other three corners were a living room, a kitchen and dining area, and the bedroom, all within sight of each other. It had originally been another level of workspace, decades ago, when the building was a much larger bakery. In present day, I lived on the second and third stories and had put a lot of work into renovating them.

I threw on a bathrobe and trudged sleepily up an old, iron-wrought, spiral staircase to the third floor. Long ago, the third floor had been a windowless storage room, half the size of the first and second floors. The other half of the level was a rooftop terrace. I'd had the wall to the terrace knocked down and replaced with floor-to-ceiling windows, giving the room natural light. This was where I spent most of my time. It had a small workout area and a room-length desk with several computers and a lot of workspace.

I continued outside onto the terrace. The brisk morning chill woke me up a bit more. Hints of red and orange colored the clouds in the east. I leaned against the covered outdoor hot tub in the center of the terrace and enjoyed the color of the sky and the ambient noise of morning traffic on East Carson Street, thirty feet below. Hedges around the roof's perimeter buffered the street noise and gave me a bit more privacy. It had been well worth the effort of lugging carloads of soil, one bag at a time, up to what eventually became my peaceful sanctuary.

I decided I was too tired for my usual morning workout. A long hot shower later, the glow from my phone caught my eye. Dante had texted a reminder:

<<Dr. McKenzie has your papers>>

I dressed and went down to the café. The whirring of coffee machinery grew steadily louder as I descended the back stairs. I walked through the bakery kitchen and out into the coffeeshop, where Mr. Sobczak was waiting on a customer. He looked my way and smiled, gesturing that he'd be with me in a moment.

"The Buzz" was what it said, in pastel-colored letters over the double doors. The tables were mostly empty in the mornings, but from mid-afternoon through closing they'd be half-filled with college students, fueling

their studies with caffeine. A different artist's paintings
adorned the walls each month, price tags underneath. Indie
rock poured gently from the speakers.

"You want latte?" he asked me. "And chocolate
croissant?"

"Yes, please. Thank you."

"Take me minute. Marina is making ambulance
today."

He always beamed with pride when talking about
his daughter Marina. He was a first-generation Polish
immigrant, and the way he gushed about America, the Land
of Opportunity, you'd think he was still fresh off the boat.

Marina would usually be making coffee and tending
the register in the morning, freeing him for more baking.
But she was an EMT and had apparently been assigned a
graveyard ambulance shift. The place felt quiet and empty
without her. On many nights, I'd seen her return after long
daytime shifts to take care of the café until closing. She
was the hardest working person I knew, and her father had
a lot to be proud of.

No sooner had I stopped wondering where she was,
when I heard the backdoor burst open, and in she scurried.

"Sorry, Dad!"

She entered the café while tying on an apron,
coming in at the perfect time to see me flinch as her father
started the espresso grinder. I could see her giggling but
couldn't hear her over the loud machine. She covered her
mouth and made a dismissive wave with her other hand as
the noise suddenly cut off.

"I'm sorry," she said. "You just get this really cute
look on your face whenever that happens."

Mr. Sobczak handed her the finished latte and the
croissant, and she carried it over to me.

"What's today? Just precalc?"

"Yeah," I said, "and maybe I'll drop by the Friday
Symposium. Pretty good speaker in town."

"Mom's making pierogis and city chicken tonight. You should come by."

"We'll see."

"We'll see," she parroted, in a silly overly-baritone impression of my voice. "No really, Thom, come over."

She handed me my breakfast while walking with me toward the back door.

"How was your shift this morning?" I asked. The look of amusement on her face was revealing—she had lied to her father about actually having a shift.

"Well, just between you and me," she whispered, "some mornings I just want to sleep in."

"I can relate."

I left her at the backdoor, got in my car, and drove off through the morning rush hour. At a stoplight, I couldn't resist the urge to check email on my phone. I saw a message from my handler, Avery Hamlin, and decided against opening it until I got to campus.

My latest work for Hamlin had been a language processing project, to improve the algorithms that sort through intercepted messages. But I hadn't heard from him for weeks. In that moment, I realized it had been years since the last time I'd gone more than a few weeks without a job from some three-letter agency or another. Not that I minded the break.

By the time I parked in the faculty garage, I still had nearly an hour to settle in and prepare for class. I read Hamlin's email and was surprised it didn't mention any recent projects. It was just a pat-on-the-back of sorts, telling me to expect a briefing on a new assignment soon.

Students walked briskly across campus, buzzing like bees as they weaved around my leisurely stroll toward Wean Hall. There was a communal tension among them. Fall mid-terms were looming.

Ahead of me, coming the other way, I saw "Fair Emily," the latest facial-recognition and machine learning experiment of the Robotics Institute. Fair Emily roamed the mall freely, though her programming team was always monitoring nearby. She crawled on six legs like a giant metal insect and spoke to passersby from a centaur-like chest and head protruding from the front. I'd often wondered whether the designers made her look horrifying on purpose.

"Good morning, Doctor Vale," it said in a sweet but tinny voice. "Are you sad today?"

It always asked me that. It didn't merely recognize faces—part of its program was to interpret facial expressions and predict emotions and mood. Its funding came from the Department of Defense, with the hope that its algorithms would help front line soldiers identify enemy combatants amidst civilian populations. Fair Emily always interpreted my unemotive face as sadness. I had stopped answering it months ago.

I entered Wean Hall, the main mathematics and science building. Only a few steps later, I came face-to-face with my department chair, Tucker Burgreen. He and his usual crowd were standing their usual post in front of the espresso bar just inside the entrance. He stopped in mid-sentence when I caught his eye, and just glared at me. Rigid cheekbones, downturn of one corner of his lips, dead eyes. Disdain. These weren't microexpressions. They were full, open expressions, the kind that wouldn't be more apparent if they were phosphorescent. He despised me and didn't care who knew it.

I gave him a polite nod and walked past. He disapproved of my joint position between Carnegie Mellon and Homeland Security. As far as he was concerned, my office belonged to someone who would bring in grant money for him, and anyone else was beneath his contempt. But he'd never reveal my secret to anyone. For one thing, it might cause some of his mid-seven-figures DoD funding to dry up. It might also make it harder to fire me when my contract was up, assuming he couldn't find an excuse to do it sooner.

I walked up one flight of stairs and passed by my office on the way to the faculty lounge. Rick McKenzie was there, as usual, sipping his morning coffee and gazing out the window at the traffic and pedestrians on Fifth Avenue. As a retired Professor Emeritus, he was entitled to a small office shared with other Emeriti. No one had ever actually seen him in it.

"Good morning, Rick."

"Morning," he said, turning to greet me. "Your papers are on the table. Dante says hi."

"I didn't know you two were talking."

"Well, yes," he said. "He's a good kid, Dante. Bright as hell. Has some very original ideas."

"I'm glad to see someone taking an interest in him."

McKenzie took a last drag to finish his coffee. He looked down and away and his shoulders drooped. He was very troubled. I walked over to a couch and gestured that he should join me. He glanced back at the door, and satisfied we were alone for the moment, sat down next to me.

"Dante's in trouble," he said. "Burgreen trashes him every chance he gets. He made it clear in a recent meeting that he thinks Dante is a waste of an assistantship. He's pressuring the scholarship committee to take it away so it can be given to someone…'more promising,' in his estimation."

"What's he talking about? Dante's brilliant."

"When a guy like Burgreen looks at Dante, do you think brilliance is what he sees first?"

It took me a moment to understand. I'm so damned naïve sometimes.

"He can't just get rid of someone that fast, can he? That's what we have the committee for."

"Who do you think appoints the committee?" McKenzie said. "I'll give you a hint. It's the same guy who signs off on all the budgets and expenditures around here. You want a little extra travel money, or to bring a big speaker in from the other side of the world? Takes Burgreen's approval."

It's always about the money.

"You remember Iris? Grad student a few years back, from Normandy. Remember her?" He waited for me to nod before continuing. "She came to his holiday party, about three years back. She didn't like where he wanted to put his hands. Wouldn't follow him into his bedroom. She's working on her Ph.D. somewhere else now, I hear."

I felt sick to my stomach.

"So yeah, I want Dante to talk to as many combinatorics guys as I can find," McKenzie said. "Somebody with a lot of support takes him under their wing…then he'll be fine."

McKenzie patted me on the knee, like an old man who just explained the meaning of life to his grandson, and used my knee to propel himself up. He crumpled his paper cup and tossed it in the trash as he walked out of the room.

I just sat there a while looking out at the same view McKenzie had been enjoying. I wondered how many other things he could see that I couldn't.

My phone vibrated to remind me of my class in fifteen minutes. I hurried back to my office, shuffling through Dante's papers, noting his remarks and thinking about how to adjust today's class content. I grabbed a textbook and some whiteboard markers.

Amidst the confusion of the loud hallway outside my classroom, I said hello to a few old students as they darted by, while holding the door open for some current ones. I sat my materials on the front desk as a few more students filed in. The classroom chatter quickly dwindled. I straightened the pile of graded papers with few raps on the desk, and looked out at the class, ready to hand their work back.

A familiar face was sitting front row, center seat.

It was Control.

CHAPTER 06   A Seat at the Table

The sight of my former training officer, sitting in the front row of my class, surprised me enough to make me stop in mid-sentence and double-take. My students didn't seem to notice, uninterested or oblivious to the new face in the crowd.

Bill Tamm, whom I'd once known as Control, was a physically unimposing figure, short and trim, and impeccably dressed in a designer suit with a red kerchief in the pocket. He was also now the Director of Special Activities in Eastern Europe. That opened a lot of possibilities for why he was here. I hadn't seen or heard from him in nearly eight years. I doubted it was just a social visit, but whatever it was, it couldn't be anything urgent. He felt no need to interrupt my workday. He nodded curtly, as if to say, "carry on."

I couldn't help but hurry through my usual coverage of inverse trigonometric functions. The class let out ten minutes early. After the last of the students asked their out-the-door questions, Control and I were finally alone.

"Just passing through?" I asked. "Need to brush up
on your trig?"

"It's good to see you again."

"You too, sir."

"Let's walk. They still have those food trucks over
by the gym?"

We went back to my office so I could drop off my
things and made casual small talk along the way. He asked
me about Fair Emily as we passed it in the hallway. He
told me how he'd spent most of his time jetting back-and-
forth between Washington and Frankfurt. That he'd
forgotten what a great city Pittsburgh is and asked how I
liked it. He was probing, trying to get an emotional read on
me as we talked. I didn't mind. That's what we do.

"You're always welcome to visit, but…I'm
guessing you're here on business."

"Yes, Thom. You seem like you've kept fit. Kept
up on the rest? Feeling sharp?"

"Razor sharp, sir."

"You've never been to Czechia," he said, and then
continued since he didn't need my verification.
"Something's come up, rather suddenly. Two weeks ago.
It suggests major funding to a known terrorist group. And
it seems to involve a high-stakes poker tournament. I
thought of you."

My mind raced through all the information I'd read
in the online poker forums, YouTube vlogs, and podcasts.
There was only one event matching his description.

"If it's in Czechia, you're probably talking about
the European Poker Championships. They hold it every
Fall, in Rozvadov."

"That's the one. What do you know about it?"

"Well, the first thing is…it's not one tournament,
it's a lot of them. Like three dozen tournaments, maybe.
I'd have to look up the schedule to be more precise.
Mostly Texas Hold'Em, but plenty of PLO and other

games. Good mix of low buy-ins and big buy-ins. Kind of like what they do in Vegas every summer, but not as big."

"It starts the day after tomorrow," Control said. "And you're going."

I met his eyes for a moment. I wanted to make sure he was serious. If he wasn't, he had me fooled. He nodded, and I started searching through web pages on my phone for a few seconds, finally calling up the tournament schedule. I held out the phone so Control could look on.

"Let's keep moving. You can make your plans later, Thom. Come on, let's get some falafel at the food trucks." Control was consistent, I had to give him that. Never make an important life decision on an empty stomach. I'd wondered more than a few times how someone who was constantly eating could maintain a distance runner's build. Control was a mystery to me, in many ways. I suppose that, in his line of work, calling someone a mystery is the highest form of flattery.

We walked on. I started thinking about the three-week schedule, and all the juggling I'd have to do to take care of my classes. I'd be asking a lot of Dante.

"Plan for two weeks," Control said, seeming to read my mind. "I'll take care of Burgreen. The rest is on you. Can you handle it? If you can, then I'll break the proverbial seal."

"Let's hear it," I said.

We arrived at a grove between several buildings, not far from the food trucks. It contained a stylish stone platform, artistically designed with a geometrically interesting border, and tiled on top with seemingly random numbers. It was my favorite art piece on campus—very Carnegie Mellon. It also happened to be the perfect place for a soft-spoken conversation to go unheard and uninterrupted. We climbed some stairs and stepped onto it. We were afloat on a sea of numbers.

"What do you know about al-Alrasid?" he started, and he was clearly unsurprised when I shook my head. "New group, in Arabic it means 'the balance.' Operating out of Saudi Arabia and/or Yemen, as far as we can tell. The usual recruiting videos with the usual shitty production quality. Hasn't made much of a splash yet.

"Except…al-Alrasid might be responsible for last month's market square bombing in Dubai. They're claiming it. I'm sure you saw it on the news. Two tourists dead, several others injured. What didn't make the news is that one of the injured was a Mossad officer. Could be a coincidence. Could be this upstart group somehow has knowledge of foreign intel officers. They're a 'group of interest' now."

"And some of them play poker?"

Control couldn't help a laugh. "Highly doubtful. But they have a growing list of suspected supporters. I'm sure you haven't heard of any of them, small potatoes mostly. But there's one guy, name of al-Karchi. Oil and finance guy, nine figures, Dubai. He's a big fan of al-Alrasid, judging by his wire transfers to them. Over a million so far. Thought he was being discreet, channeling through dummy holdings, but we tracked every last penny. He's become a 'person of interest.'"

"There's a lot an upstart group can do with a million dollars," I said. "9/11 was funded for half that much."

"So, imagine the interest we took when he wired two million, two weeks ago, with no real attempt to hide it. Half of it was a direct transfer through Swiss banking, the other half was crypto. But he didn't transfer it to anyone in Saudi Arabia or Yemen. He sent it to a software engineer in Istanbul. Name of Soner. Kadri Soner."

"Who's he?"

Control shrugged and shook his head.

"Nobody. He's absolutely nobody. No one's ever heard of the guy. No record of any kind. And believe me, the last few weeks, I've had our Istanbul station on this guy like white on rice, checking up on everything, watching him, intercepting his comms as much as possible. He's as clean as a priest's sheets. Except that, well, obviously he isn't."

"What do you think he'll do with two million dollars?"

"Well, I can tell you the first thing he did. He booked three weeks at Casino Rozvadov, for the entire length of the championships. Not just one room. Thirty-four rooms."

"Seven hundred fourteen nights total. Wow."

Control chuckled. "I'd forgotten about how you do that. Yeah, sounds like a helluva party. And you're crashing it. We've already booked you a room and wired $25,000 in your name. Your mission will be to gather intel on Soner and al-Karchi and whatever operations they're involved in. Who else is involved? Who's in charge? What are their objectives? Assess the threat. Report everything. Follow the money."

I felt a slight twitch in my eyelid when he mentioned following the money, and surely Control picked up on it. His way of reminding me of a past mistake, lest it become a repeated mistake.

"I'm starving," he said. "I know you're going to have a thousand questions. You organize them in your head while I get us a couple sandwiches." And he walked off toward the trucks. Just left me there, reeling.

My own shadow falling across the number tiles caught my attention. The sun was high and merciless upon my neck and the top of my head. A cold wind blew from the west and carried the scent of dead leaves and yesterday's rain. My world was spinning. I could hear the sound of a flute from the Fine Arts building. I could feel and hear my heart pounding. My legs were shaking, and I wished there was a place to sit down, but the platform was bare, leaving me no choice but to just stand there, and take it.

After eight years, I was finally being offered a clandestine ops mission.

My mind flashed immediately to the night I was dismissed from the Farm, but I had to dismiss those thoughts quickly. They didn't matter anymore. The despair of my goals being quashed. Years of being relegated to data analysis and game theory. I saw Control in the distance in front of the food truck. He'd be back in two minutes, maybe three or four if I was lucky. I couldn't breathe.

I looked down at one of the tiles. It was the number eight. I tilted my head, and it was an infinity symbol. I took a deep breath, and then another, and another, and another. It was an eight again.

Eight.

"So, let's talk it through," Control said, returning, offering me food.

"You said you wired the money in my name. What's my cover?"

"You won't have cover. You're going as Thomas Vale, an amateur American player who's ready to take a shot at some big games."

"But sir…"

"No 'buts,' Thom. That's how it's going to be. This is strictly recon, gathering intelligence, and leaving and reporting. You will not initiate aggression. I have other people for that."

I turned and paced away, at least as far as the platform would allow. Traveling under my own name limits my options. Or at least, it limits what I can do without inviting the danger of reprisals from an enemy, or the danger of being burned. The latter danger bothered me more—if my identity was burned, any clandestine ops potential I might have would be over before it started.

"I do fit the profile," I conceded. "I'm 30 years old, a child of the internet. Science or tech background. Good physical condition."

"Excellent physical condition, by my estimates. You look like you live in a gym. Won't that make you stand out?"

I shook my head and assured him I'd fit right in. I explained further that pro poker players aren't like the ordinary, disheveled players you see in typical low-limit card rooms. Most of them spend a lot of time working out, and many meditate or do yoga. Pro poker players in the new generation don't fit the Doyle Brunson or Amarillo Slim mold. Nowadays, they study like scholars and train like athletes, and most of them even have coaches.

"Information on the principals," I said. "Dossiers, maps, resources."

"You'll get a standard redpack in the car tomorrow morning. Be ready for a driver to pick you up at oh-four-hundred. Redpack will be in the backseat, sealed. He'll drive you to Andrews Air Force Base."

"Tech?"

"You'll get that on the tarmac at Andrews. Phone and laptop, with all the usual extras. Remember to bring plenty of pocket litter for both."

"You said you had other people. Do we have agents in place? Do I have a team?"

Control looked down and shifted his stance.

"We have minimal support for you," he said. "I'm working on finding you a partner. There are complications. I'm pulling some strings. Give me twenty-four hours."

It was then I realized this venture was his personal project. Control had undoubtedly been talking to station chiefs in Saudi Arabia and Turkey, and maybe elsewhere. He was putting something together on the fly, without any committee approvals, and probably without the knowledge or approval of the CIA Director or SAC Director. That explained why someone like me, disqualified from the Farm as a potential liability, could get a covert op. Because the people who would say "no" were unaware of it.

"Compensation," I continued.

"We wired you the twenty-five large. Whatever's left when you're done is yours. If you go bust, I'll see what I can do. But…don't go bust."

"Small arms?"

"No, Thom."

"I've kept up."

"I know you have," Control sighed and pursed his lips. "I'm going to be frank with you. I need you reined in on this one. You're my personal recommendation for this HUMINT op, and I need you to stay on the reservation."

"Why me, then?"

"Because it's tailor-made for you. Because I think you can handle it. And mostly, it's because I meant what I said to you eight years ago. Your math isn't your only asset. You know, I've seen reports of some of the work you've been doing the last half-dozen years. I can tell you that it's saved thousands of American lives. It's helped further our interests in many other ways, too. Everyone you work with says you're one of the most creative and insightful people they've ever met. But that's all they see when they look at you. No one who matters thinks you can be trusted in the field."

"Do you think that's a fair assessment of me?"

"Fair?" Control laughed. "That's a word that means whatever the people in power say it means. You should know that by now. 'Fair' is for whining children and umpires. Never expect fairness from anyone in power. They think you don't deserve a chance. I need you to prove them wrong."

I just stood there, blank. I was being praised while simultaneously slapped in the face. But I knew an opportunity when I saw one. "Count me in, sir."

CHAPTER 07 — Arrangements

Dante knocked on my office door just before three in the afternoon. I was in the middle of shutting down the office version of my "ant farm" and aggregating the week's data for future analysis. I beckoned him in. I seized up for the briefest of moments as he flicked on the light. I hadn't even noticed that the day was overcast, and I'd been working in dim natural light.

"PLO again?" he laughed. "You ain't solved that shit yet?"

"Not even close," I said, "but you'll be the first to know."

Dante looked sharp in his usual sweater, khakis, and high tops. I imagined him dressing the same back in the day, when he was a Catholic prep school valedictorian. There was a hint of chalk on his fingertips, which meant he'd been up to the chalkboard in the seminar room. And that suggested he'd been presenting solutions and maybe some original ideas there. It was a good sign. It probably explained the sunny expression on his face. He looked like he could beam with pride, except he was trying hard to play it cool.

"How was the seminar today?"

And just like that, 'cool' flew out the window, and Dante's infectious smile breached containment. He told me all about the combinatorics topics they were exploring, some of which, I had to admit, were a little beyond me.

At one point, Dante had asked a question of the visiting speaker, and the speaker had been stumped by it, standing in silence in front of everyone for several minutes. Eventually the speaker shrugged and said he'd have to get back to him on it. In math-speak, that essentially translates to "I'm intrigued." I gave Dante an obligatory fist-bump. He had clearly impressed someone very impressive. To a mathematician, "I don't know" isn't an embarrassment, it's the first step on an intellectual adventure. Mathematics research is like solving a puzzle no one else has ever solved before. The harder the puzzle, the better. It's a peculiarity of mathematicians that "difficult," "interesting," and "fun" are often synonyms. When Dante stumped the guru, he hadn't embarrassed him, he'd impressed him.

"You're going out to dinner with them after the symposium?" I asked.

"Yeah. Doc McKenzie said he'd spring for me, which is really nice of him. I hear they all split the bill evenly, and it can get pretty big."

"It certainly can, but don't sweat it. Just make sure to sit near the profs you'd most like to work with. But don't talk shop at dinner, just be social. Get to know people."

Dante nodded like he was taking mental notes. His eyes shifted down and to the left, as if he was sifting through some memories, and then the corners of his eyes dropped just a bit.

"I don't even know what to say. Most of those profs, I got nothing in common with them."

"I'm probably the worst person to give advice on socializing, but I think I get where you're coming from. You're afraid you won't fit in. You're worried maybe you don't belong, right? I get it. But you know, everybody's an outsider until they break in. An old friend was trying to tell me that today. Don't let them decide what you deserve, Dante. Go get what you deserve."

Dante nodded, and his gaze turned toward the window. He stared outside for a while, contemplating, looking as though he might be seeing beyond. His face looked ten years older for a moment. But just as quickly it was gone, and his infectious smile returned.

"You get the grading?" he asked.

"Yes, and actually, I need to talk to you about the class," I said. "I'm going to need a lot of help actually."

"How much?"

"I have to go out of town tomorrow, for…I'm not sure…but maybe as long as two weeks. I've spent a lot of time today writing lecture notes and finishing the mid-term exam and key. Do you think you can teach the class until I get back?"

"Me?!" Dante leaned back in his chair, eyes widened. "I've only led recitations."

"You're a good teacher. I know you can handle it. But I know it's asking a lot, too."

"Where you going for two weeks?"

"A workshop near Prague. Short notice, I know. But it could be really important for my career. I can't pass it up."

He nodded. "I get it. Yeah, I got you, no problem. Let me have those plans and I'll be ready on Monday."

I passed them over to him, and he tucked them under one arm as he headed for the door. In the doorway, he turned and looked at me sideways. He stroked his chin for a moment thoughtfully.

"A workshop near Prague? Two weeks in October, huh?" He paused pointedly and smirked. "Run good, bro."

*　*　*

That afternoon, it took a second soup-bowl-sized latte before I felt properly wired. I brought my empty bowl up to the counter of the 61c Café in Squirrel Hill and flipped an extra dollar into the tip basket. It felt like treason, hiding out from the Sobczaks, who would happily give me all the fancy coffee and treats I could eat. But I needed to be away from interruptions, to put my thoughts together. I'd ordered the first latte with my mind swirling like a maelstrom, lightning bolts crackling within a tornado of anxiety. The caffeine was helping.

I spent two hours on my laptop in the window of the café, occasionally distracted by the passersby on Murray Avenue. I knew I'd be given an information packet to study, or a "redpack," shrink wrapped and probably stamped "Eyes Only" and closed with a red seal. It would be exceedingly thorough. I would be expected to study it and later relinquish it before leaving friendly ground. A digital version might be downloaded into a secret drive in the phone or computer I'd be issued.

But I'm a scientist, and scientists like to do their own research. I spent most of the time looking at maps of the areas around Rozvadov, reading about the nearby cities and their attributes, and learning about Czech culture and history. Most of the information would be useless during the mission, but it served to put my mind at ease. With a little more lead time I might have tried learning some basics of the Czech language, but that was infeasible given the time crunch.

By the time I walked back to my car, all the headlights and streetlights were on. The pedestrian traffic was thick, with gangs of students and families beginning

56

their weekends at a favorite dinner spot. The aromas
wafting from numerous ethnic restaurants battled in a kind
of tournament where there could only be winners. The
clock with Hebrew characters above the Jewish
Community Center chimed 7 o'clock, and I drove down the
hill as several well-dressed Hassidic families walked up it.

Several highway minutes later, I was driving
through Pittsburgh's south side—my neck of the woods. I
hung a right just past The Buzz and swung around to park
behind it, my garage door opener sliding the chain-link gate
open and closed. As I pressed the key fob to lock the car
doors, it suddenly occurred to me in a flash: what if that
was the last time I ever drove that car?

What if I never came back?

I shivered in the cold breeze as it whistled between
brick buildings over the low din of the early-evening
Carson Street bar hoppers. The air didn't smell of diverse
ethnic foods here. This place smelled like good pizza, but
with undertones of week-old garbage in dumpsters. I
looked up at my third-floor terrace. From ground level, all
I could see was a row of hedges, which would probably
seem strange to anyone who ever stopped and looked up.
But no one in a city ever looks up. Another shiver passed
through me, and I decided I would feel better when I got up
to the roof.

I walked around to the front of the building, and
stood on the street corner for a minute, people watching. A
cloud of exhaust from a passing bus hung in the cold air,
refracting the light from neon signs across the street.
Beyond the neon, bar patrons were riveted to the Penguins
pre-season opener, against the Flyers down at the Igloo.
Raucous full tables of loud-talking, hard-drinking steel
town men enjoying the end of their work week.

I turned and walked into the Buzz. Even on a
Friday night, most of the tables were full with groups of
students who were reading and comparing notes. Marina

was behind the counter. She looked up from her own book as I entered and saw me walking toward the back stairs. She bounced over and intercepted me before I could get to them, and threw her arms around me, giggling.

"You hate this, don't you?" she said.

"No. It's…nice," I said.

"Just you, me, and the med students. You missed dinner. Again."

"I'm sorry. Something came up."

"Can I get you something?" she asked, letting go. I shook my head, and she went back to the counter to accept a mug one of the patrons had brought back. I stood alone near a table for a minute, watching her take coffee orders from customers who'd just walked in.

She'd just graduated high school when I met her six years ago, slinging coffee for her family's business, working toward college. But college didn't happen because the business was failing. Mr. Sobczak was behind in rent payments to the building owner, and that owner was losing money because he couldn't lease the rest of the building. I bought the entire building at a good price and struck a deal with the Sobczaks. Their rent would be one dollar per month plus the property taxes, and in exchange they'd give me all the coffee and food I wanted. The move had worked out wonderfully for all of us.

Now Marina had grown up, and things between us were getting complicated.

She was only getting busier as I watched, so after a few minutes I exchanged a quick wave with her and headed upstairs. I breathed a sigh of relief. I just didn't have time for it tonight. In less than nine hours, I'd be in a car heading for Washington, and I had preparations to make.

I packed a suitcase quickly, emphasizing the types of clothes young poker professionals tend to favor. Business casual, mixed with some good jeans and stylish hoodies. A pair of swim trunks and some workout clothes.

I packed one good suit, just in case, though I didn't expect any formal occasions.

Upstairs, I shut down the home version of my "ant farm," and pulled several flash drives out of a desk drawer. One of them had records of the apps, notes, and phone numbers normally kept on my phone. Another had a complete backup of all my academic files. I plugged that one into my work laptop and updated it with the new files from the last few weeks.

These drives gave me the appropriate "pocket litter" for the equipment I'd be provided. In the olden days, if an operative wanted to pass inspection as an ordinary civilian, he'd better have the sorts of things in his pockets an ordinary civilian might carry. Nowadays, pocket litter is more about digital footprints. I was going to be issued a phone and laptop with special drives that would evade the detection of anyone outside my fold. But if the normal drives on those devices didn't have files and apps appropriate to my person, it would be obvious under inspection that something wasn't right.

An unexpected sound from downstairs jolted me to attention, and my right hand slid instinctively under the desk. My Glock-19 was in a holster, attached with Velcro to the bottom of the drawer, and it slid with practiced ease into my hand. But I then pushed it back, realizing that the startling sound was merely my door opening, and the identity of the intruder was obvious, and not a threat.

"Thom? You around?" Marina called.

"Up here, come on up!" I took a deep breath and realized I was already on edge.

Marina had a habit of just opening my front door when I forgot to lock it, sometimes remembering to at least knock lightly before coming right in. I'd been meaning to talk to her about that. Somehow, whenever I'd tried to broach the subject, something about her warm, caring, brown eyes had gotten in the way. But tonight, I felt tired and stressed, and I didn't want to be around anyone. The next few weeks were going to be hard enough.

"I can't get over how cool this place is, cuz like, there's no walls," she called out, still downstairs. "I remember when this whole place was an empty storeroom." I could hear her clomping around on the hardwood downstairs in her Doc Martens. "Why's there a suitcase on your bed? Don't you play poker on Friday nights?" Clomp, clomp, clomp. "You hungry?!" Clomp, clomp. Before long the clomping finally reached the spiral staircase, making it shake. She was walking up the stairs slowly, and something smelled delicious.

"Mom saved you some pierogies and city chicken…" And she stopped in mid-sentence, mouth agape. "Wow!"

I only then realized she'd never been up to the third floor, at least not since I'd moved in. Come to think of it, neither had anyone else since the last of the renovation work had been finished, over four years ago. The last time she'd been in this room, it had belonged to her father, and it was a dank, empty storage room with one blackened window, lit by a single lightbulb hanging in the middle of the room.

Now it was my home office and my sanctum, impressing its first guest. Marina stared at the wall of windows, which reflected our own images back at us now that night had fallen. Her hair swooshed behind her head as she looked back-and-forth around the room, and in her long café apron, she reminded me of Cinderella arriving at the ball.

"Set those down and we'll finish the tour," I said. I flicked the lights off, leaving us with only the glow from a screen saver and the ambient city lights.

"Thom? Where are you?"

I took her hand and led her several steps in the dark to the glass door, and we stepped out onto the terrace.

There was a little more light here, and as she looked up and around, I could see that her wide eyes had unnaturally dilated pupils. A few extra buttons of her blouse were undone, compared with minutes before in the café. Her hand gently squeezed mine.

"This is amazing! Do you ever come out here and just look at the stars?"

"On clear nights, sometimes. You can see all the big ones, and sometimes a planet or two. Too much light pollution to see a full sky."

"I've never been camping or anything. What's a full sky like?"

"The stars are so abundant and full that you know you could never count them. Like grains of sand on a beach. Like God made art out of infinity."

"I want to see that someday."

I told her about my childhood home, back in Kill Buck, New York, seventy miles from the nearest city. In the Appalachian foothills, far from any lights and surrounded by forest, my parents' house sat at the base of Eagle's Hill. On Summer nights, my brother and I would climb to a small clearing at the top, where we could lay on our backs and stare up at eternity.

"I like to soak in the tub at night," I continued. "When the jets are going, the city noise fades away, and I can stare up at the sky, and I don't feel anything."

"I'll have to bring a swimsuit next time," Marina said. "Or better yet, maybe I won't."

Her hand was trembling. She pulled herself close to me, and her embrace—it felt like warmth and peace. She kissed me so softly on my collarbone, it was like the touch of a feather.

"Marina…I have to go away tomorrow. I'm going to Czechia for a couple weeks."

She looked up at me, and her face was blank and expressionless, pale smooth skin barely lit by distant streetlamps. She looked away quickly.

"Oh my God, I just realized. I left the café unattended for like, ten minutes."

"Marina, I'm sorry."

"The suitcase. Of course. Yeah, you gotta pack, and get all focused, and stuff."

"Marina…"

"Just…let me know when you get back, okay. Be safe."

"I will…"

She was gone. I stood alone atop my sanctum, safe from love. I didn't want to think about her. I didn't want to think about anything. I had enough on my mind already. I looked through the glass wall into my home office and saw only darkness except for faint light coming up through the spiral stairwell. Beyond that light, Marina was downstairs, serving customers, reading a paperback, and hopefully not crying. What the fuck was the matter with me?

I flipped open the top cover of the hot tub and started the jacuzzi jets. I stripped and got in. The churning water enveloped me, quieting the city clatter and numbing my senses. I looked up through the steam and imagined where Orion and all my other favorite constellations would be, if only my night had been clear.

    I hadn't really slept when my alarm went off at 3:30am. I showered and shaved with urgency. A large red suitcase sat by the door, packed with everything I'd need, but that wasn't much besides my clothes and digital pocket litter. I looked around for any last-minute pieces of extra flair and decided to throw in a Pittsburgh Pirates ballcap and a copy of an Ian Anderson book on card counting.

    I carried the suitcase down the back stairs, listening to the clanking of giant mixing bowls and a wet slap of dough plopping down on a counter. A lively polka streamed from Mr. Sobczak's antique transistor radio, tuned to a local AM station. His heavy breathing as he kneaded almost drowned out the music. He didn't see me, and I thought about trying to sneak a cup of stale coffee leftover from yesterday's brewing, but decided against it. He would hear me and insist on making something fresh. I slipped out quietly instead.

    A small, black limousine was parked in the side street, quiet and in the shadows, like a predator waiting for passing prey. Its headlights clicked on, and the motor started as I stepped outside, closing the back door softly behind me. Its tiny trunk popped open. I walked through a cloud of exhaust and loaded my suitcase. I got in and scooted to the middle of the backseat.

The plexiglass separator slid down, and the driver turned to look at me. It was the man I knew as Marco from back at the Farm.

"Long time no see, Sean," he said. "Or I guess I can call you Thomas now."

"Marco! Good to see you're still kicking. I hope the years have been kind."

"Not the word I'd use, but I'm still here. How've you been?"

"Busy. Always busy."

"Well, that reminds me."

He frisbeed my redpack back to me. It was shrink wrapped in cellophane and bore a round red seal, upon which was printed in white block letters: "Eyes Only: Vale, Thomas J." A clipboard, mechanical pencil, and several manila folders lay within. They'd been ordered up by some officer at Langley, or perhaps by Control himself. They'd been assembled by research librarians from different sections, reprinted on thin extra-flammable paper, and bound together only hours ago. No one in the process would have more than partial knowledge of the project, and only the bookbinder and the courier knew its destination.

"Whatever you're into, you got yourself a thick one," Marco said. "Happy reading. You eat yet?"

I shook my head.

"Hope you don't mind if I stop for gas and fast food halfway. But I'll leave you to your homework. We'll be at Andrews in four-and-a-half hours. Wheels up for Ramstein in five."

He raised the plexiglass, and the limo started forward. For a moment, it had sounded like Marco was coming along on the mission, but I knew that was unlikely.

He was acting as a courier at the moment. Perhaps he'd
been a targeting officer at some point in the last eight years.
Perhaps he would be again in the future. I knew better than
to ask, and I knew he would extend me the same
professional courtesy.

We turned onto the highway and sped east, still
hours before the first hints of sunrise. The limousine cabin
was dark except for tiny track lights on the floor near the
doors. I put my head back and thought about trying to get a
little more sleep, but I was too curious about the redpack. I
switched on an overhead reading light and tore open the
wrapping.

The first two folders were dossiers on Soner and al-
Karchi. I skipped past those for the moment. The next
folder gave a floor map of Casino Rozvadov and its
attached hotel, as well as a map of Rozvadov itself,
highlighting key buildings and all the other housing for the
large tournament crowd. Some key casino personnel were
mentioned, including its owner, Goran Urusov.

I'd read plenty about Urusov on the poker forums,
where he was quite famous, and universally well-liked. A
talented player himself, he occasionally sat in and played
against his guests. He'd been the designer and part-
financier of the casino at the start, and now owned it
completely. His original plan had been to create the
greatest poker room in the world, celebrating the game and
its players, and then build a casino around it. Many
professional players, if asked, would tell you he'd
succeeded.

The thickest folder contained information on
Czechian history and culture, and some key phrases with
pronunciation guides. It was much more thorough that
what I'd gleaned from the internet, and included
information on specific buildings in the area, contour maps,
and information about the German-Czechian border not
available to the public.

There was no sign of what I'd been hoping for – support personnel. No mention of a partner, or agents or assets in place. Control told me to give him twenty-four hours. I'd be at Ramstein Airbase in Germany by then. Wherever he was, I hoped he would come through.

I set the bigger folders aside and opened the first dossier.

Kadri Mustafa Soner, the main principal, was thirty-two years old. The top page went on to give his vitals in great detail. Born in Ankara and lived there all his life, up through four years at Ankara University. Played club soccer in his youth and showed talent. Graduated with a first in software engineering. Left a graduate program in computer science to start his own business, which failed within its first year. Worked increasingly lucrative consulting jobs ever since.

Soner's net worth was unknown, but mid-six figures was given as an estimate, not counting the two million he'd just received. Unmarried, no kids, living in Sisli, one of the nicer districts of Istanbul. Worked high-paying jobs in countries including Albania, Bulgaria, and Saudi Arabia. The speculation was that he'd met al-Karchi during one of his Saudi jobs, though that could not be confirmed. Fluent in Turkish, English, Arabic, and probably Russian.

I sifted through a collection of candid photographs, most of them black and white. He was a little on the chubby side, but had a thin, pinched face adorned with wire-framed glasses. He didn't look happy or at ease in any of the pictures. In all of them he was walking, and rather quickly by the look of his forward lean. He looked like a man who knew he was being hunted.

In one of the pictures, he had a small flip-phone to his ear, and his eyes were shifted up and to his right, but not seeming to focus on anything. He was probably lying to whomever was on the phone.

I flipped through some of the following pages, skimming through his financial portfolio and bank account information, medical records, phone records, credit card usage, and maps of every place we knew he'd visited in the past two weeks. At first glance, nothing stood out. Closer inspection showed that his smart phone usage had dropped to almost nothing in the last two weeks. He hadn't used his credit card at all. He'd gone cash only and was using a burner phone, possibly several of them.

I flipped back to the largest picture of his face and clipped it to the clipboard. I committed his features to memory, and poured over every nuance, hoping some stray crease or blemish could be a window into his soul. He was highly intelligent and was doing an excellent job of being careful. He knew he'd be under the magnifying class at Rozvadov and forced out into the open. He just didn't know who was coming for him, or how many of us.

But he was the one with all the advantages. He knew what his plans were. He knew who he'd made them with. He knew what was at stake. And he had millions of dollars at his disposal.

I had twenty-five large and a picture of him on a clipboard.

I switched over to the other dossier. Sheikh Nassif Muhamad al-Karchi, aged fifty-two, and filthy rich. Net worth currently estimated around four-hundred million dollars.

First son of an oil sheikh who died three years ago. Educated at Oxford, earning firsts in civil engineering and economics. Fluent in Arabic, French, and English, and probably more. Inherited a small fortune, built it up into a gigantic one. Petroleum processing, investing, crypto currencies, and a small-percent-ownership in a credit card company. Extensive family throughout the Middle East. No kids. Married to a French wife of fifteen years, née Veronique Thioux. Home address is a multi-level penthouse atop one of the taller skyscrapers in Dubai, not quite a thousand feet up. Personal helipad, and a butler doubling as his personal pilot. By all reports, he isn't there half of the time, traveling frequently to look after business interests. Veronique is always with him, always in full burka and hijab.

The rest of al-Karchi's dossier was mostly general information and mentioned his links to al-Alrasid. Several pages of political analysis laid out the case for why he would support them. The short version was that al-Alrasid's mission was to use highly focused cyber-attacks and terror attacks to destabilize Western markets, as a balance against sanctions the U.S. had made against certain Islamic countries. Successes by the group could prove very helpful, financially, for al-Karchi and a number of other rich Saudis. Follow the money.

My eyes felt tired from all the reading. I sat back and thought about al-Karchi and his family. A man of such wealth, taking one foreign wife and giving her no children. That couldn't have sat well with his father, the original sheikh, now deceased. How close could al-Karchi be with the rest of his family? His dossier didn't mention any close relationships. Was he the "black sheep," so to speak? I put one of his older pictures on the clipboard and looked at him and Soner together, trying to imagine the nature of their relationship.

I yawned and decided to close my eyes for a minute.

*   *   *

I was twelve years old, and every time the crowd roared, the white-knuckle grip on my clipboard tightened. Floodlights shone down from tall poles all around the football field. The chants of the cheerleaders could barely be heard over the feet of the crowd, shuffling and stomping on the high metal bleachers. It seemed like half the town was in the stands, and we were all on our feet.

"Complete! Eighteen yards from Matt Vale to Cory John. First down, Warriors!"

Before the P.A. announcer could finish, I had already marked down another pass attempt and completion on my stat sheet. My big brother Matt, the All-County quarterback, had the Salamanca Warriors on the move. With less than thirty seconds to go and only one timeout left, they were down 21-20 but driving again. Tonight's game was to decide which team would advance to the District Championship, played in the Buffalo Bills' stadium.

"Did you see that one, T.J.!?" My father looked down at me for a moment, and I nodded, writing an 18 in the pass yardage box. His hand was clamped down on my shoulder like a vice grip.

The ball rested at midfield as the teams quickly lined up without a huddle. Matt's voice echoed off the nearby school building as he barked out an audible.

"Hustle it up, Matty!" Dad yelled, over the crowd. I turned and looked up at Mom. She was taking a long pull from a metal flask, and she looked at me warmly. Her breath smelled like cigarettes and peppermint.

The scoreboard read nineteen seconds at the snap of the ball. Matt faded back, moving in the pocket, and spun out of a tackle from a blitzing linebacker. The crowd quieted, as though holding its collective breath, as he scrambled one way, then another, looking for a receiver to come open. Finally, he drew back and fired downfield to his favorite target, who made a diving catch between two defenders.

The crowd erupted. Shrieks and Indian-style whooping filled the night air. The bleachers shook under my feet. I seized up. My whole body tensed. The bright lights above seemed to shake along with the bleachers. Noise and noise and noise.

"Vale to John for 24 yards! Timeout, Warriors!"

Mom's arm wrapped around me, pulling me in close.

"It's okay, T.J." she said, rubbing my back. "Exciting game, eh? How many yards has does Matt have now?"

"Two hundred seventeen."

"What's his passer rating now?"

I had to think for a few seconds. "A hundred and six point six."

I looked up at Dad, who was high-fiving some other football fathers, and in between, clapping so hard it must have been hurting his hands. Down on the sidelines, Matt was being swarmed by his teammates. I wondered how many college scouts had just watched him have the game of his life.

"Cole Powless comes on for the field goal try!" the loudspeakers announced.

"Three for seven," I said. "Powless is only three-for-seven this year outside 40 yards."

Dad looked down at me.

"Naw, we got this. Matty's going to Buffalo!"

"It's forty-two-point-nine percent…"

"That's enough, you little…" And he swallowed the last word, while backhanding the clipboard from my hands. It clattered on the bleachers and tumbled down beneath them into pitch dark. He glanced at Mom, and then turned back to the game. I looked up and saw Mom having another long pull from her flask.

I climbed down through the opening and had just enough light to see the support bars. I lowered myself down to the concrete. It was too dark to find my clipboard. The cheering wasn't quite as loud down there, and I could see the chain link fence behind the stands, separating the stadium area from the parking lot.

"It's good!!! Powless from 43 yards! Final score: Warriors 23, Huskies 21!"

I fell to my knees as the pounding on the bleachers rumbled like thunder above me. I covered my ears, but it didn't help. My eyes squinted, my hands balled into fists, and my body started rocking. It sounded like a stampede, and I realized that some of the crowd was rushing the field. The thinning crowd allowed a little more light to come in, and I finally saw my clipboard several feet away. I grabbed it and ran out from under the bleachers, leaning back against the chain link fence, my entire body shaking.

I looked up and tried to find Mom, but the floodlights above made it impossible to see anything but moving shadows. I walked in the direction of the exit, and when I got to the end of the bleachers, I turned and climbed back onto them. I had to fight through a crowd of happy spectators heading for the exit. Eventually I saw my parents and waved them down.

I sat and waited a few minutes for them to get to me. Mom took my hand and pulled me in for a hug. Dad was laughing and talking to Cory John's father. It was the happiest I'd ever seen him. His normally stern, cold eyes were glassy, holding back tears of joy. His rigid, soldier-like walk had faded away. He glided as if floating on air.

We walked together to the parking lot, where Mr. John waved and went his separate way. Dad unlocked the car doors remotely as we approached, and he turned around to take another look back at the stadium. His eyes then fell down upon me, and his smile vanished.

"Get in the car," he said.

* * *

I snapped awake at the sound of heavy traffic. Morning light poured brightly through the window. I looked outside and saw a bridge and a familiar park. We were traveling east on the 495 near Washington, D.C.

The plexiglass divider rolled down, and I saw Marco observing me in the mirror.

"Think fast," he blurted, and I reacted just in time to catch the cold, wrapped, English muffin sandwich he flipped back through the opening. "I'd have woken you up for breakfast, but…you just looked so peaceful back there."

Marco drove us through two security checkpoints, around the base perimeter, and eventually up to a silver mid-sized jet. The morning Sun reflected brightly off its hull. The slight blur of heat refraction near its engines suggested that pre-flight warm up was underway. It was a sleek machine, reminiscent of a Falcona, but undoubtedly modified and enhanced for supersonic travel. The cabin entry door hung down and served as a boarding staircase, awaiting me.

"Good luck," Marco said. "And try not to fall asleep in the middle of your mission. Looks bad in the report."

"Take care of yourself," I said, getting out. "Smart ass."

It took a moment for my eyes to adjust to the sun. I heard the trunk pop open behind me, and I held my redpack up as a makeshift sun visor as I watched another car pull up behind us. The passenger door opened, and out stepped Control. He carried a laptop case by the handle, its shoulder strap dragging on the tarmac. He pointed at my redpack with a smirk on his face.

"Spies always wear sunglasses. Didn't anyone ever tell you? How do you get out of The Farm without learning that? Someone oughta fire your instructor."

"Or promote him," I said.

He took off his sunglasses and squinted for a moment. He looked past me at the jet, and raised an arm to give it a wave, and then held up two fingers toward it. He handed me the laptop case, and I slung its strap over my shoulder. I handed over my phone in exchange for the new one he provided.

"Okay, Thom, all jokes aside now. We're a little pressed for time, so let's get down to business. I shook a few trees. I found you a partner, and we've got a man in place at the casino."

I breathed a sigh of relief. "That's welcome news, sir."

"And we have some new intel in the last twenty-four hours. Our boy Soner has been in Prague the last three days. We're not sure how he got there. Somehow he evaded our surveillance until he popped up on our radar at a hotel. Soner…he reserved the entire fifth floor of an expensive hotel for three days, and he paid for it all in cash—up front. He's got at least three or four dozen people in his entourage, it's hard to say."

"Did they trash the place?" I asked.

"I don't have information on that," Control said. "So, my guess would be negative."

"Then it's business, not pleasure." Whatever Soner was up to, it involved a lot of people. A lot of payroll. Some of the two million must be for personnel. And not just to pay for their hotel rooms, but to pay for their services as well. But what services?

"Vans from the casino have been showing up at the hotel every half hour," Control continued. "Every van picks up two men, two women, and four big, black trunks."

"What's in the trunks?"

Control shrugged. "I'm a bit curious about that myself. Whatever they're bringing to Rozvadov, they're bringing a shitload of it. Let me remind you, that's less than two miles from the German border."

I stood there thinking for a moment, trying to imagine what an organization like al-Alrasid would want to deliver close to the border of a Western country. Particularly, a country with one of the larger Western economies, which hosts a number of American military bases. But I quickly dismissed those thoughts. It's never a good idea to jump to panicked conclusions. Better to just gather facts and see where they lead.

"Well, I'm glad you found me a partner, since Soner's bringing a small army. Who is he?"

"She," Control said, "is waiting onboard. Sondra. I called her off R&R for this, so don't expect warmth and enthusiasm. But I needed someone good, and she's good."

"You mentioned an agent in place?"

"More like an asset in place, but yes." Control fished a black and white photograph out of his suit pocket and showed me. It was a handsome older man, perhaps mid-forties, thin, clean-shaven and well-groomed. "This is Anton. He's a host at Casino Rozvadov, serving the highest of high rollers. He's been helping us out for years. Very well connected. A fixer. He'll coordinate your comms with our Prague office."

"Anything else?"

"That's all, Thom," he said. "Good luck. Report as often as you can. And remember…this is intelligence gathering only. No aggressive actions."

I retrieved my suitcase from the trunk. I started walking toward the jet, but then turned back and held up one finger.

"One quick question. What does the SAC Director think about this mission?"

Control's eyes widened and his lips parted slightly, in a momentary microexpression of surprise. But he recovered smoothly and quickly, pulling his sunglasses from a breast pocket and putting them back on in one smooth motion.

"I'll be sure to ask him next time I see him," he said. "Play it safe, Thom." And with that, he got back in his car, and it drove off quickly.

An officer in uniform awaited me at the boarding stairs. He took my suitcase for storage. I walked up the stairs with the redpack under one arm and ducked slightly as I entered. The cockpit door was already closed. Once inside the cabin, the ceiling was just high enough for me to stand straight up.

The left side of the cabin had a long couch-like bench stretching most of the way back, and the right side was lined with tables and low cabinets. Several reclinable swivel chairs surrounded a small round table at the far end, and one of the seats was occupied. The shades were open on most of the windows along both sides, and soft lights ran along the ceiling, down the center.

A brigadier general sat on the bench near the front of the cabin, going over something on a tablet. A warrant officer sat on each side of him, observing whatever he was showing them. The general looked up at me as the entry door clanked shut, and his eyes narrowed as he grimaced. His eyebrows knitted as he went back to his tablet.

One of the warrant officers indicated, with his thumb, that I should head to the back. The other warrant officer stared down at the floor, jaw clenched, shoulders and biceps flexing. He was making a point of not looking at me. I turned and walked toward the back of the cabin, wondering what had offended him.

The plane shuddered slightly as it prepared to taxi. I found my way to one of the swivel chairs before the plane started moving. The cabin lights dimmed as I buckled in.

I looked across the table and saw a redpack, still sealed, sitting on the edge of the table next to its owner. She was dressed in army fatigues and boots, laying as far back as the chair would allow, hands folded across her belly, with her hat pulled down over her eyes. Her steady breathing suggested she was asleep, but as the jet finished taxiing and the engines grew much louder, she lifted the brim of her cap for a moment to peek at me.

We rocketed down the runway and were airborne, ascending quickly. I glanced over, and looked for a name on her redpack, but her red seal was completely blank. We climbed for ten minutes. By the time we leveled off, we were farther up than I had ever flown before. The sky was a darker shade of blue than normal for daytime, and the clouds looked like a puffy white quilt spread over shimmering blue. My best guess was that we were cruising at ten or eleven miles up, moving faster than sound.

The woman finally sat up as the cabin lights came back on. She shook off a yawn and lifted up her cap for a moment, running her fingers through hair that was trimmed so short it was nearly a crew cut. She rotated her chair to face me, and leaned forward, hands on knees. She looked me up and down, and then locked eyes with me. Her face was impassive and expressionless, and she said nothing. She raised one eyebrow.

"Me first, huh?"

She nodded so slightly it was barely perceivable.

"Okay, but first I want to know something," I said, gesturing toward the front of the cabin. "What're those guys so pissed off about?"

Her eyes closed for a moment, about twice the duration of a blink, and she looked down. One side of her jaw tightened as she turned to look at them, and her right hand involuntarily clinched in a fist. But then a wry smile crept across her face, hiding all signs of shame and anger, and she looked me in the eye again.

"Oh, General Clark's just pissed we're going to make him late for the ballet tonight."

"Which ballet?"

"I don't know. He probably doesn't even know. I think for him it's all about the tutus."

"How does he look in them?" I asked.

"Better than those other two," she countered, laughing.

She seemed a little more at ease, and that made me feel more at ease. She stood up, yawning again, and walked around the back of the cabin, stretching her arms and back as she did. She was tall for a woman, just a few inches under six feet, and while her baggy fatigues hid her figure, there was a clear strength and sturdiness to her. I guessed her to be in her mid-thirties. Martial artist, judging by the stretches. Apparently, she really had been sleeping up until I arrived. I wondered how little sleep she was going on. I wondered how much lead time she'd had before being sent to this jet, for this mission.

"Control told me you were pulled off of R&R. Sorry about that."

"Control?" She said, amusedly. "Jeezus, kid, you're greener than broccoli. His name is Bill, and he's a professional shyster. But he's got your six when you need him, and that's what matters."

"I'm Thom, by the way. With a T-H."

"Pleased to meet you, Thom with a T-H. I'm Sondra, with an F-U."

She kept pacing angrily around the back of the cabin, but she wasn't stomping. She moved with the agility of a jungle cat, all grace and pride and hunger. Her eyes flared, but then quieted as she turned to speak to me again.

"I'll try not to hold it against you that Bill called me off a month of R&R for this. I know it's not your fault. Besides, when we're done, now he's giving me two months. So, fair enough, I guess."

She sat back down in her chair and grabbed her redpack off the table. She looked like she was about to open it, but then slapped it back down on the table and swiveled toward me.

"I'll do my homework later. I want to hear your version first."

I leaned in and started telling her. I watched her eyes as I recounted everything I knew about the operation, looking for reactions. She didn't seem to have any prior knowledge of the principals, but her eyes flared slightly at the mention of al-Alrasid. I guessed that, at a minimum, she'd been briefed on them recently.

By the time I finished, she was sitting back in her chair. Her arms were crossed, but not tense. She stared past me at nothing in particular. Deep in thought. After a few minutes, she started nodding confidently.

"I get it," she said. "Makes sense Bill would send you. And now I know why I'm here."

"Why are you here?"

"Because he probably told you something like 'no aggressive action, unless,' right? Well, that's who I am. 'Unless' is my specialty."

She picked up her redpack and tore it open. I left her to her reading and booted up my new laptop. Over the next hour, I plugged in one flash drive after another, installing hundreds of folders full of documents and mathematical software. The laptop had a special uploading protocol, enabling me to backdate the files as I loaded them. By the time Sondra finished reading through her redpack folders, the laptop looked as though a math professor had been using it for years.

I placed my right thumb over the thumbprint reader and struck the "Fn" and "Q" keys simultaneously three times. The main screen disappeared in a blink and stayed black for about ten seconds. Finally, a new screen with a solid maroon background appeared. I had entered the secret "ghost drive," which had a completely different arsenal of software and internet capabilities.

At the moment, only my thumbprint would give access to the secret drive. Anyone else's print, or the absence of one, and those same keystrokes would erase the drive's contents permanently. I slid the machine across the table, and Sondra looked up from her reading. Without missing a beat, she put her own thumb over the reader and held down "F7" for a few seconds, and then slid it back to me. She now had the same access.

The usual arsenal of software was installed. A dark web browser, audio and video enhancement software, voice match and vocal stress detectors, et cetera. Out of all the tradecraft software, what impressed me most were the language translation algorithms, designed to hear speech in one language and translate it in real time into any other language. They were still a bit clunky, missing words or occasionally mistranslating, but they were getting better all the time.

A folder marked "Info" contained a digital version of the contents of my redpack. The ghost drive on my phone had a similar folder. It was still my duty to memorize as much of the redpack as possible, of course, but it was comforting to know I had some back-ups.

Out the window, and down through a break in the clouds, jagged edges of land penetrated the crashing sea. The northern coast of Iceland, I guessed. Halfway there.

Across the table, Sondra reassembled her folders. She rapped them on the table twice, to straighten out the pile, and then set them down. She looked over at me with the faintest trace of a sneer on her face.

"What did Bill tell you about me, exactly?"

"All he told me was your name, about two minutes before I boarded."

"Sounds like him," she said. "Well, it seems I'll be playing the role of 'girlfriend' on this escapade. Gives me an excuse to be there and keep an eye on you."

"It plays," I said. "Lots of pros and amateurs go there alone, all business except maybe the occasional party. But some of them bring girlfriends, or boyfriends, or whatever."

"How common is that?"

"Some of these guys live like rock stars," I explained. "They travel gig to gig, except instead of playing music, they gamble. It's kind of like how some married rock stars travel with their family, or maybe their wives and kids visit them on the road now and then. These pro tournament players have to go where the action is, and they bring the important parts of their life with them."

Sondra took in what I was saying, all the while scanning me. She was calculating. I was a variable in her equation, and she was measuring me in her mind. Toward the end of my explanation, she involuntarily looked down at her redpack, and then looked quickly away.

I'd seen that classic tell a million times before. The "chip tell." When the dealer lays down a card that suddenly improves a poker player's hand, sometimes he can't help but glance at his chips for a moment, because he's so eager to make a bet. Sondra had looked down at her redpack in the same way. Something I said made her feel better about something she'd read.

That's when I knew—one of her redpack folders was specifically about me. Control, for reasons I could probably guess, had decided it was important to explain me to her, in detail. But he hadn't felt the need to explain her to me.

This wasn't really my mission.

It was Sondra's mission.

I was just her asset.

But that was okay. Control had been honest with me from the start. He'd told me that no one who mattered trusted me in the field, and that I had to prove myself. Alright, then. I decided, there and then, I would do exactly that. I would prove myself. Whatever it takes.

"So, what does a poker girlfriend do, anyway?" Sondra said.

"I have no firsthand experience at that," I said, "but from what I've seen on the popular vlogs…you pop in once in a while to say supportive things to me, and the rest of the time you blow all my money on slot machines and the spa."

Sondra half-chuckled, half-snorted. "Maybe you're not so green after all, kid."

CHAPTER 10   Anton

The sun set about ten minutes before our wheels screeched across the landing strip in Ramstein. It felt like lunchtime. I started to get up, but Sondra gestured that I should stay. She slid her redpack into a burn bag, and then slid the bag over so I could do likewise. I sealed it. The bag and its contents would be destroyed later.

The three uniformed officers in the front deplaned as soon as the jet finished taxiing. A few minutes later, two military police officers boarded and walked quickly toward us.

"Sir. Ma'am. We have orders to escort you to the mess. Your car should be arriving within the hour. Let's get you some chow first."

Sondra and I gathered our bags from storage and followed the MPs. We hopped in the back of their jeep. Sondra's green canvas sack looked like it belonged in the jeep, but my big red suitcase stuck out like a sore thumb. It might as well have had pretty pink bows on it. The MP who hadn't spoken earlier took one look at it and whispered something inaudible to the other, who smirked.

We drove off the tarmac and past several buildings until we reached the mess hall. It was a long building, capable of serving hundreds at a time, but it was mostly empty now. Sondra and I settled down across from each other at an empty bench style table. The lead MP left us for a minute. The other MP stood against the wall about 20 feet away, watching. He mostly stared forward, but a few subtle eye motions told me he was listening to something in his earpiece.

The lead MP soon returned. With him came a man wearing an apron over fatigues and carrying two trays of food. Fried chicken, biscuits and gravy, green beans, a heap of mashed potatoes, and a carton of milk. It reminded me of a school lunch, only a lot bigger.

"Thank you," Sondra said.

The MPs both stood against the wall as we ate. It occurred to me that part of their job was to keep us away from the soldiers. No contact at all, not even standing in the same chow line. I glanced at Sondra, and she looked through my eyes as though she could see straight into my mind.

"Just eat," she said, "And then we'll hit the head. I'll need to change before we go."

It was delicious, or maybe I was just starving. It was after 7 o'clock in the evening, local time, yet we were having lunch. A normal traveler would have jet lag to look forward to, but because we'd be keeping poker hours, I'd barely feel it. Poker pros often sleep until noon or into the afternoon, because the best games usually run in the late evenings and well past midnight. Lunch in the evening and dinner after midnight is par for the course. My normal routine was quite different, usually waking up around 6:00am in Pittsburgh, but that translates to noon in Rozvadov. Perfect.

Sondra pushed her tray back. She had finished it all, and I wasn't even half done.

"Take your time," she said. "I'm going to need a while. And I'm going to see if I can fit everything into one suitcase. It'll look better." She got up and grabbed both of our bags, and the lead MP walked with her to the women's room and stood outside as she entered. I felt relieved that I had nothing embarrassing in my bag, since she'd undoubtedly be going through it all.

I kept eating, trying not to be conscious of the other MP, who stood guarding me. Like on the jet, I was the only person not in military attire. I wondered how much he knew. Surely, he didn't know the details of the operation. But he knew I wasn't Army, and he knew his orders were to keep us isolated. He probably knew we were intelligence of some kind.

The MP's stare was unwavering, and I consciously resisted digging at my cuticles or any other stimming actions. I took a packet of sugar from a nearby condiment tray and neatly tore open the top. I set it on the table, nearly upright, leaning against the tray. It was an old superstition of mine, and my shoulders untensed as my nervousness left me.

Ten minutes later I finished the dinner, and the sugar packet fell over as I stood up holding the tray. The MP watching me, with a hand gesture, indicated I should just leave it on the table. I set it down and paced a little, stretching. Out of the corner of my eye, I saw movement near the bathroom, so I turned to look.

My jaw dropped.

Sondra walked out, pulling my suitcase on wheels behind her. If not for the suitcase, I wouldn't have recognized her. Long, blonde hair cascaded over her shoulders, and her fatigues were replaced with black leggings and a flowing zebra-striped blouse which hung off one shoulder. With a tiny, stylish handbag under one arm, she glided gracefully on low black heels, which made a slight clack on the tile floor with each step.

She reached the table and handed off the suitcase to me.

"Sondra, you look…"

"Shut up."

One of the MP's touched his earpiece, and I could tell the other was listening to the same message. After a few seconds, they looked at each other, and the main MP beckoned us to follow them. The car was ready. We walked outside, and a mid-size rental sat idling with its trunk open. We thanked the MPs after they gave us basic instructions for departing the base. Sondra insisted on driving since she knew the area.

As we drove through the exit gate, I opened the glove compartment and found the rental papers. They were made out in my name, prepaid, and the rental had been leased in Frankfurt, which made sense – that's how an ordinary person would have flown into the country.

I also found a passport and opened it to see Sondra's picture. "Sondra Sampson," aged 34, from San Diego. An alias, obviously, and probably one of many. She was a non-official cover operative, and if she were compromised, our government would not claim her.

"San Diego's nice this time of year," I said, handing her the passport.

"Yes, it is."

"So, Sondra…remember that night we met? Where was that again…at the blackjack table at the Rio, right?"

"You told me to hit on soft eighteen, and I was like…whaaat?"

And for the next few hours, on the roads from Ramstein toward Czechia, we invented an entire relationship. We'd met on a Vegas vacation five years ago, had a long-distance relationship for years, and she'd just moved to Pittsburgh six months ago, leaving one retail job for another.

She told me a little about her family, but of course she was making it up and keeping things deliberately simple. In that, I had a bit of an advantage. I wasn't undercover, so I just told her about my real family. Why not? If she really wanted to, she could find it all out anyway.

I told her about growing up in Kill Buck, New York, and how my father had been the postman. I told her about what had happened to my Mom and my brother. About graduating at sixteen, and then years of studying, studying, studying. About my job at Carnegie Mellon, my amateur poker, and the rental properties I owned. Before long, she could rattle off all the public aspects of my entire life. She would easily withstand scrutiny and pass as someone who really knew me.

The car's clock ticked past ten in the evening, and we slowed down and pulled over on the side of the highway.

"You're the man, here," she said. "Rental's in your name. You drive us across the border."

"How far?"

"Five minutes to the border, give or take. Then about three klicks to the casino."

At the border, the line wasn't long and moved quickly. The guards took our passports and ran them over a scanner, inspecting them closely. He asked us some basic questions, and upon hearing we were going to the casino for the EPC, just patted the car and wished us luck. He'd already heard the same story from a hundred other cars.

With the border in the rearview mirror, the glow from the casino already lit the darkness ahead. I pulled up slowly into the valet circle. Two attendants came out to greet us. One took my keys and a five-euro tip, and a similar tip went to the other, a porter, who put my suitcase and laptop bag on a small cart. He was about to take it to the front desk when a third figure intervened. Anton.

"These are old friends. I'll handle them from here," Anton said, and the porter bowed quickly and left. The valet drove off with the car. I glanced at Sondra and noticed a release of tension in her shoulders. Her eyes, for the first time all day, seemed to warm. Anton tossed a small duffel bag onto the cart next to our luggage, and then looked at Sondra, with a brief smile and recognizing eyes. He turned to look me over for a second, before saying, "Let me show the lovely couple to their room."

As we approached the front doors, the mellifluous tones of the slot machines greeted us. They sound about the same anywhere in the world. Sondra and I walked behind Anton as he steered the cart through the front lobby and down a long hallway. "No smoking" signs hung on the wall near every entrance, in English, French, and Czech, but the heavy odor of smoke made it clear that these signs were mere suggestions. The walls were decorated with a blue and gold motif, adorned by paintings in ornate frames and car-themed murals and mosaics. Through the occasional gateway poured the lights and sounds of the gaming area we were circumventing. It sounded very full and very loud.

Eventually we arrived at the hotel. Anton took us up to our third-floor room and handed us two keycards after opening the door with one of them. He wheeled the cart into the middle of a spacious room. It was thickly carpeted and beautifully decorated in a motif of white and gold, with a four-post king bed, a business desk, a sitting area with a table, chairs, television, and a comfortable-looking couch. From what I could see of the bathroom, it was the size of some living rooms. The large walk-in closet suggested it was common for guests to be wealthy and have very long stays.

"How was Bulgaria?" Anton asked Sondra, as the door closed.

"Rough," she said, "but it's over. Was on my way to R&R, then this popped up. How's the family?"

"Great. Same same. Mara sends her love."

Upon hearing the name "Mara," Sondra's eyes lit up.

"So, I should open the bag now, then," Sondra said, smiling. She looked over at me as she grabbed the duffel bag and sat down near the table. "I should have mentioned before, Thom. This is Anton. We've worked together many times."

I took my suitcase off the cart and set it on the bed, while Sondra unloaded the duffel bag onto the table. She pulled out a Sig Sauer P226, with a silencer attachment and five full 0.38 clips. A variety of melee and throwing knives. A steel-cable garrote. Lock picking tools and a keycard magnetic override. A Nagra-CCR, which is a microphone and recorder that looks like a credit card. A fiber-optic snake camera. A pair of thin-framed stage glasses with a high-density pinhole camera concealed in the nose bridge. Two TEC torches. A standard first-aid kit. And finally, a brown paper bag with a grease stain near the bottom.

"You're a prince, Anton."

"Mara remembers how much you like her *trdelnik*."

"Well now I'm glad I came."

Anton turned toward me, and his expression turned serious again. The blush response I noticed in his eyes at the sight of Sondra quickly disappeared. As he looked at me, his business demeanor returned, as if looking at me reminded him he's a player in a tough, dangerous business where every new person you meet could be your last.

"I've already swept the room for bugs, as a routine precaution," he said, "but considering the size of the opposition, you should operate as though this is a denied area and use covcom protocols."

"How big is the opposition?" I asked.

"Unclear. But big and getting bigger. If I may use your computer?"

I took the laptop out and set it on the desk. I struck the key sequence to open up the ghost drive and stepped aside. Anton sat down and typed some addresses into the dark-web browser as we looked over his shoulders. By the time he was done, two browser windows were displaying real-time video footage of the front casino lobby and rear hotel lobby.

"Have you tapped into the security cameras?" I asked.

"No, that's beyond my expertise. These are discreet cameras I planted myself two days ago. Now watch. Should be any time now. Watch the rear lobby."

We watched the cameras for a few minutes and didn't see very much. Both cameras, in my estimation, gave nearly complete visual ranges of the lobbies, though distorted slightly at the edges, due to a fisheye effect.

Then, on the rear lobby camera, a couple walked in, arm in arm. A porter followed with a cart, and two big, black trunks were on it. Judging by the effort the porter was making, the trunks were very heavy. They stood at the counter for a few minutes, checking in. Eventually they left the lobby, with the porter in tow, presumably heading to their room. Moments after they left, a second couple walked up to the check-in desk. Two identical trunks sat on their cart, pushed by another porter.

"I believe that's twenty-eight couples so far, and fifty-six trunks," Anton said. "And I think they still have a few more coming. We've dedicated four of our shuttle vans. We've been bringing them in from Prague all day today."

"Can you roll back the footage on these?"

"If you want, but I've already been making notes today. I've written down the arrival times. I'll cross-reference those with check-in times later and try to compile a complete list of these…two trunk people."

"That would be really helpful," I told him. "Especially if you throw in their room numbers, too." Anton agreed.

"What about Soner, and al-Karchi?" Sondra asked.

"Kadri Soner checked in early this morning, but no one has seen him since. He appears to be the only opposition with a car. He came alone, and didn't bring any trunks, just a suitcase and computer bag, almost exactly like yours, actually. He hasn't left his room all day, as far as I know. He ordered room service twice."

"Working on his computer," I guessed aloud. "A software engineer who's connected to a known al-Alrasid supporter. That's why we need to use covcom protocols. We have to assume he's setting up a 'man in the middle', or at least trying to."

Sondra nodded at my assessment. I was suggesting that Soner could be rerouting cell signals to and from the local tower through an intermediary device of his own. If successful, he'd have a record of all cell phone activity within several square miles. Any texting done on the premises would need to be in code-speak, on the assumption that everything was being intercepted and recorded.

"Now…Sheikh al-Karchi, he's a different sort," Anton continued. "He arrived by helicopter around noon, with his wife and two bodyguards. Very formal and affluent Arab-style garb. I'm not sure exactly where they flew in from. He's the biggest high roller here, by far, so I've been taking care of him myself. He's spent most of today playing baccarat in a private, high-limit salon. I've noticed nothing peculiar. Very pleasant fellow, actually."

"Bodyguards with him at all times, I'd bet," Sondra said.

"Of course. His wife, Veronique, does not set foot in the high-limit salon."

"What's she like?"

"I couldn't say," Anton said. "My impression is she does not speak without the permission of the Sheikh. I have not heard her voice, and I don't even know what she looks like." Sondra looked away with a sneer on her face upon hearing this, and she cracked her neck while subconsciously eyeing the gun. Anton shifted his stance and cleared his throat.

"I shouldn't want to go missing for long. I'll leave the charming couple to settle in."

And with a quick bow to Sondra, Anton left.

Sondra walked to the bed and opened my suitcase. She had made room in it for her canvas bag, which she extracted and swung over her shoulder in a smooth motion.

"I've been here a few times for R&R," Sondra said. "It's like a palace, you're going to love it. Why don't you go take a tour and get the lay of the place? Play a few hands and see who you see. Start blending in."

"You coming?"

"Not tonight. I need to wash the road off of me and clear my head a bit."

I nodded as she closed the bathroom door behind her. I looked over at the table, and its assortment of weaponry and trade tech. I felt a little envious and couldn't help but wonder if I was completely out of my league. I was trained in every bit of it, but that's not the same thing as having experience.

Curiosity got the better of me, and I opened the brown bag. It contained about a dozen, thin, bracelet-shaped pastries, "*trdelnik*" apparently. They smelled like cinnamon, sugar, and walnuts.

"I counted those!" came Sondra's voice from the bathroom.

CHAPTER 11   Lay of the Land

    The sound of the gaming floor grew to a crescendo as I walked toward the action. Coming the other way, I recognized two semi-famous poker vloggers as they passed. The pervasive noise of the slot machines made it difficult for me to eavesdrop on their conversation, but that wasn't the goal tonight. My only goal was to learn my way around the premises, preferably without being memorable.

    I walked around the perimeter hallways at first, stopping to take a few selfies in front of the sporadic artworks, as any tourist might. Past the front lobby, I found the spa, which offered Thai massages in addition to the usual assortment of services. Several unmarked doors followed, which I knew from my redpack study to be access points for casino security.

    The noise of the games and people in the main hall struck me like a wave crashing on a shore. I found my way to the first available slot machine chair, closed my eyes, and gave myself time to acclimate. Several slow, long breaths later, I opened my eyes and looked around. The blue and gold motif of the pillars and chandeliers was mesmerizing. The patterns of gold trim and the dome-shaped ceiling made me feel as though I was inside a giant Faberge egg.

My pocket vibrated. I checked my phone and saw that Sondra had texted.

<<Dazzled yet?>>

<<Awesome>> I responded.

I got up and made my way toward the other side of the hall and found the "TV table." While all the other poker tables lay in the rooms beyond, the TV table was in the main hall to make it as big a spectacle as possible. A thirty-foot-wide giant screen took up the entire wall behind it. Daily tournament action would be broadcast on internet streaming services, hole cards showing, on a 30-minute delay.

I left the main hall and entered a long lounge area, at the end of which was the buffet. Open twenty-four hours a day, and gratis for gamblers, it was the most impressive selection of world cuisine I'd ever seen. I kept it simple for the moment, grabbing a slice of pizza to go, but I looked forward to putting the attending sushi chef to the test in the coming days.

An archway just before the buffet led to the high limit room. A well-dressed attendant, part host, part security, stood in front of the arch. I was tempted to peek in and see if al-Karchi was still playing, and to get a look at his personal guards, but thought better of it.

Half the lounge was cordoned off to serve as an "overflow room" during the larger tournaments. The usual lounge goers were compressed into a smaller area. I took a bite of pizza and eavesdropped on a table of high-rollers. Several bank-wrapped bundles of American hundreds lay on the table. They were playing some sort of card game that I couldn't identify, with at least two hundred thousand dollars in play. They paid me no mind at all, and I kept walking.

At the next table, several men were watching an American college football game. They were shouting what sounded like Russian at the screen while pounding their table with fists. A four-liter "giraffe" of a local beer sat on their table, half-drained, wobbling next to an empty one. Each blow to the table threatened to knock them both over.

Toward the edge of the lounge, overlooking the poker hall, three Arab men in matching tan suits sat at a smaller table, leaning in and speaking in hushed tones. And finally, two tables beyond them, an Arab woman in a burka and hijab sat alone at a small, bare table, watching over the vast poker hall. I wondered whether she could be "Veronique," and was careful not to look directly at her as I took in the scenery and situation.

The lounge overlooked the poker hall, ten feet below. Its chalet-style slanted roof stretched out well over a hundred feet. It looked like it would make a most pleasant white noise during a heavy rain. Chip girls and waitresses bustled between nearly one hundred tables, about one-third of them hosting action at the moment. They would all be full tomorrow. I scanned the room, looking for Soner, or any other familiar faces. I saw none.

"Hey, you there, American!"

I froze for a moment, then turned to see one of the Russians pointing at me.

"You! You American, yes?!"

I nodded. The entire room, including Veronique, was now staring at me.

"Who you like this game?!" He was pointing to the screen.

I shrugged. "I don't really follow college football."

The Russian looked disappointed and irritated. "Sorry, next time I ask your husband!" His table mates roared with laughter, and within seconds they were back to ignoring me. I was staring at them like a deer in headlights, but quickly snapped out of it. I calculated that the best course would be to skulk off angrily, to avoid any further attention. In my peripheral vision, I could tell everyone else in the lounge was still watching me.

I walked down a short flight of stairs to the poker hall. The tournament podium was near the front of the hall, currently empty. The cashier's booth was in the back. I walked past all the tables, looking around and recognizing several famous poker professionals. The acoustics of this room were much friendlier to me, and there was almost no smell of smoke.

"Vale, Thomas Jay," I said to the cashier, showing my passport. She examined it and typed something in her computer. Her head rocked slightly back, and her eyes showed recognition as she found me in her database.

"You have twenty-five thousand American."

"I'd like to withdraw five thousand Euros, please"

She nodded, tapped her keyboard briefly, and then cut out chips. A video screen behind the cash games podium showed thirty games running, mostly 2-5 Hold'Em or 1-2 PLO, with sizable waiting lists. There were a few high stakes games secluded to the corners of the room. I recognized several players at those tables from poker television shows.

"We can seat you right now at 5-10 uncapped Hold'Em, sir," she said. "Or we can text you when a seat opens…."

"5-10 is good," I said. She pointed out an open seat at the end of a nearby table. My first cards floated across the felt to my spot as I arranged my chips before me in color-sorted stacks. A quick glance around the table revealed I had the shortest stack by far.

I pulled the cards in and peeked under the corners, seeing an ace and an offsuit eight. I flicked them back to the dealer. This was a bigger game than I was used to, so I'd be playing conservatively, even in good position. Tight play also had the virtue of giving me more time to just look around.

I barely played any hands for the first hour, but was still up about 100 Euros, having won a few small pots with aggressive continuation bets. Most of the time I scanned the room for Soner but had no luck. Veronique remained perched in her seat up in the lounge, overlooking the action. From a distance, it was unclear at whom or what she was looking. I was careful to never look her way for more than a second or two.

Most of the tables were echoes of mine. A symphony of European poker clichés, punctuated by the occasional impeccably-dressed Asian. Across from my dealer sat two German players in thin sweaters and jeans, the only players talking at the table. On my right, a baby-faced kid with messy blonde hair poking out of his hoodie, bobbing his head rhythmically, the hood bulging on the sides from some unseen pair of noise-cancelling headphones. On my left, a young swarthy player was constantly on his phone, an unlit cigarette hanging precariously from his lower lip as if by sheer willpower.

Directly across from me, an old man with wavy white hair leaned forward over his chips, like an ancient dragon sitting atop its hoard. He had, by far, the biggest stack at the table. Several gold necklace chains disappeared into a nest of grey chest hair, and he had three large gold rings on each hand. Each time I entered a hand, he glared at me before acting. I half expected him to yell at me to get off his lawn. He was a loose player, but shrewd, turning on the aggression at all the right times. The whole table, in fact, seemed solid. I was swimming with the sharks.

<<Having fun?>> Sondra texted.

<<Yeah, not much to see yet. Buffet looks good.>>

<<Don't make me wait up too long, sexy loverboy! XOXO>>

I chuckled at that text. Sondra was getting into her role, texting like a girlfriend, just in case somebody somewhere was intercepting and recording.

It was nearly two in the morning when a premium hand finally came my way. Black aces in the hijack position. Time to party. Two players limped in for 10, and I raised to 40. I got calls from the button and in the small blind. The old man, in the big blind, exhaled deeply. He glared at me, a bit longer than usual this time, and then announced a three-bet raise to 160, his first pre-flop raise in hours. His confident voice had a thick Greek accent.

I thought about re-raising but called instead. Everyone else folded.

"Heads up," the dealer announced, and laid out a flop: ace, seven, four, all hearts. I had top set, a great hand, but without any hearts. I had to worry about my opponent drawing to a flush. The Greek's eyes seemed to twinkle, and he tapped the felt firmly to check the action over. I read the firmness of his tap as a subconscious display of strength. He liked that flop.

I thought about the range of hands he should have, and put him on pocket pairs with one heart or two suited broadway cards. If they were suited in hearts, he'd already made a flush.

"What are you thinking so long about?" the Greek demanded. "Bet or don't bet!"

I looked up at him for a few seconds before checking back.

The dealer put out the jack of spades for the turn card. The old Greek saw it, and immediately grabbed two black chips and set them firmly in front of him, glaring some more.

"Two hundred," the dealer announced. I still had the Greek on the same range. There was a 23% chance of the board pairing on the river, making me unbeatable.

Otherwise there seemed a good chance I was behind a made flush.

"What is taking so long?" the Greek asked, spreading his arms wide and shaking his head. "You got jet lag? Airport lose your luggage? Forget to pack your balls?"

I tossed in two blacks to make the call.

"*Argo! Eisai poly argo!*" he yelled at me. *Slow! You're too slow!*

The dealer pulled in the chips, burned another card, and laid out the river, a deuce of hearts.

"All in," the Greek said. No change to his demeanor. Same searing glare.

My set of aces was now losing to any hand containing any heart. I took a last peak at my cards before flipping them into the muck.

"Ha!" The Greek tossed in his cards face up for all to see. They were the queen and ten of diamonds. A stone-cold bluff. He'd had nothing but queen high the whole time. "Star spangled idiot! Now go think about that!"

CHAPTER 12 The Girl Parade

The Old Greek smiled evilly at me, like a taskmaster dealing a lesson with his whip. I thumped the table twice, the universal symbol for "nice hand." No one else at the table reacted at all. As far as they were concerned, I'd made a bad read and it cost me. That's poker. On to the next hand.

It bothered me that my read of my opponent had been so far off. This was no time to be off my game, so to speak. When the big blind came around to me, I racked up my chips and left. I looked around the room once more while walking to the cashier. Still no Soner. I pocketed the orange and black chips and cashed the rest.

<<Heading back to the room soon>> I texted Sondra.

As I walked back across the poker hall, I noticed a large group of people, maybe three dozen or so, walking through the lounge toward the buffet. As I got closer, I saw that almost all of them were women. By the time I ascended the stairs to the lounge, I saw that the women were all young, probably in their twenties, and very attractive. A parade of beautiful girls, all casually dressed, entering from the direction of the hotel.

I moved straight to the buffet for a late-night snack, and to investigate. There are plenty of female poker players, including some world-class players who'd be competing here. But women are very underrepresented in poker as a whole, making a large moving group of them an odd sight.

I passed on the pizza this time and got in line for the beef carver, just because it was the longest line. I tried to appear tired and bored as I looked around and listened. Several of the women were in line with me, talking to each other. I didn't understand the language, but it sounded like the samples of Czech I'd heard before. Local girls?

They filled their trays and sat together at tables. Beyond them, Veronique still loomed, still sitting alone at a bare table. She seemed to be watching them as well. It was then I noticed the motion patterns of the girls. The flow of their movements seemed to avoid Veronique, bending like a school of fish keeping its distance from a shark. I quickly lost count of the number of them who walked near Veronique, but then changed course slightly away from her, and without a single one of them looking at her.

It dawned on me, finally, that the women were the female half of Soner's entourage. It made me wonder where their men were, and whether they were also mostly Czechian. Anton had promised to give us their roster in the morning. Until then, I was in the dark. Still no sign of Soner.

The carver served me a few slices and I sat at a table. I tried to eat slowly and looked up from my phone intermittently. In contrast, most of the women ate voraciously. One of them slumped back in her chair, closed her eyes, and sighed deeply. Considerable tension released from her face and shoulders in one quick shudder.

Halfway through her plate, her body was expressing a palpable sense of relief. I got the distinct impression she hadn't eaten all day.

Suddenly, several of the women picked up their smartphones and looked at them simultaneously. A few seconds later, several others did the same. I glanced quickly down at my phone to see the time: 2:22am. Had they all just received a mass text?

I finished my roast beef and got up. I grabbed a cookie off a dessert tray and started back toward the hotel, biting into it as I took one last, quick look around. Veronique seemed to be watching me as I walked back toward the hotel.

When I got back to the room, I gave the agreed code knocks—one, then three, then two—before opening the door. Sondra was lying on the couch, propped up by several pillows. Most of her tech was on the table beside it. Her right hand held the Sig Sauer, finger on trigger. She set it back down on the table after the door closed behind me.

"Make any new friends?"

"I didn't see Soner or al-Karchi at all. And…I wouldn't call her a friend, but I'm pretty sure I saw Veronique tonight."

"In full garb?"

"Nothing showing but her eyes. And they were watching everybody, especially the parade of girls that marched into the lounge just after 2 o'clock."

Sondra sat up at attention at hearing this. For the first time, I could see her true physique. She'd been napping in a sports bra and yoga shorts, and her arms and leg muscles rippled as she moved. She had the body of a power lifter, yet still curvy and feminine. She wouldn't be out of place standing atop Olympus.

"Somewhere around two dozen young ladies, all of them pretty good looking, in my opinion," I said. "They all came in at once, and…well…they looked famished. Like they hadn't eaten all day. And I think they were Czechian, most or all of them. Local maybe. But I'm not sure, I don't speak Czech."

"You could have used the translation app on your phone," Sondra pointed out.

"I would have had to scramble quickly and use earbuds to keep anyone else from hearing it. I didn't feel confident I could do it inconspicuously. I'll be ready next time."

Sondra shrugged. "Well, you're probably guessing right. I speak a little Czech. Probably one of the reasons I got tapped for this. Maybe I can get close to them next time." She grabbed a *trdelnik* out of a now half-empty bag. "And your interest in these girls is….?"

"I'm positive they're the female half of Soner's crew."

"Explain."

"They avoided Veronique. I watched them carefully, and I'm certain they were deliberately avoiding eye contact with her. Never a single glance in her direction."

Sondra winced and shook her head. "That doesn't mean anything. You're jumping to conclusions."

"No, it's just math. Let's think it through for a moment. Suppose you're sitting at a table, not doing anything to draw attention, just sitting there. Now a random person walks by. What do you think the chances are of them looking at you?"

Sondra shrugged. "I don't know. Maybe, maybe not. Probably not, I guess."

"Alright," I continued. "Let's say there's only one chance in three a random passerby looks at you for a moment. Now…suppose twenty people walk by. What are the odds that not a single one of them looks at you?"

"Just tell me."

"Less than one in three thousand."

Sondra leaned back and closed her eyes for a moment, in thought. She opened them and stared into mine, and I felt the need to look away. She grabbed her bag of *trdelniks*, pulled one out, and tossed it to me.

"OK, I'll buy that. But where have they been all day? Where are the men? And where the hell is Soner?"

"Some of the men might have been playing poker out there. I wouldn't know. Hopefully Anton can clear that up tomorrow."

"He'll meet us at noon tomorrow. Breakfast."

I nodded and walked over to the dresser, unloading my pockets. In the mirror, I saw Sondra hunched over the table, elbows on knees. A tiny tattoo of a crucifix decorated the back of her neck, just below the hairline, high enough that it would be completely hidden beneath a more feminine hairstyle. She looked tired, but that didn't stop her muscles from flexing and rippling with every breath. I was tired from the long day as well and stifled a yawn.

"Let's get some shut-eye," she said. "Turn off the lights when you're done with whatever it is you're doing."

"I'm going to have a quick shower before bed," I said. "Um, I don't mean to be awkward, but…which side of the bed do you want?"

Sondra laughed and turned in her seat to look at me.

"I like it right here, on the couch. Facing the door, with a gun by my hand. Bed's all yours, Casanova."

CHAPTER 13   One Lump or Two

We slept in past 10:00am. We were both tired from travel, and besides, it seemed unlikely there would be much to see downstairs this morning. Maybe a few cash games still running from the night before. Most of the serious players would emerge in the afternoon or evening. The first major tournament was scheduled to start at 1:00pm, a Hold'Em tournament with a 1,500 Euro entry fee and unlimited rebuys on the first day. Probably half the field would start at one o'clock, while the other runners would "late redge," skipping some of the early levels by entering later in the day.

I made myself poker-presentable in a fresh dress shirt with the sleeves rolled up, jeans, sneakers, and earbuds with a cord running down to my smartphone. While Sondra cleaned up and dressed, I took the opportunity to check email and look in on Dante's teaching preps. It was still early Sunday morning back in Pittsburgh. Knowing Dante, he'd write his lesson plans in his apartment later today between morning mass at St. Paul's and the Steelers game. I was sure he'd do fine.

And Marina would be in bed, enjoying her morning off. I imagined her face half-buried in her pillow, beautiful and still. Then I imagined it was one of my pillows, in my bed, by my side. My fingertips gently brushing one side of her face, not waking her, but bringing a peaceful smile to her face as she lay sleeping. And that would be my day. My whole day made perfect in a single smile.

Sondra emerged abruptly from the bathroom, breaking me away from my daydream. She wore a loose, flowing blouse tucked into a calf-length skirt with her physique well-hidden. I was getting used to how different she looked wearing her shoulder-length blonde wig. She regathered her gear into the duffel bag and locked it in the room safe. She called the lobby and insisted upon no maid service. It turned out Anton had already made that arrangement.

"Anton should have made his first report a few hours ago," Sondra told me, as we left the room. To dodge any potential interception, covcom protocols required him to travel at least twenty kilometers from the casino to call in to the Prague office. Pertinent details would then be forwarded to Control, wherever he was, on an encrypted channel. Normally, 4:00am would be a typical time for such an excursion, a time of low activity. But this being poker culture, 8:00am or 9:00am would be more appropriate.

We walked together around the perimeter hallways and back through the main hall, just to have another look around. The noise and lights were less overwhelming the second time. We made small talk as we passed gaming tables. Sondra slipped into her persona with the ease of an improv actor, pointing out the machines she thought would be lucky, and making catty comments about another woman's shoes.

A large crowd of onlookers were enjoying morning coffees and watching the tech crew set up the TV table. It was an impressive operation. They were testing out various camera angles, checking that the RFID cards could be read at each table position, and making sure the visual graphics looked right on screen.

We walked past and reached the crowded buffet. Sondra took my hand, and we walked as a couple, weaving through the crowd. The room was mostly men, bunched in small clusters, chattering in different languages from table to table. Lots of jeans and cargo pants, hoodies and thin sweaters, and well-kept hair. Men who look good dressing bad.

We grabbed a plate of fresh figs and pastries, and a coffee each, and found one of the few open tables. The crowd grew steadily as tournament time approached. Sondra took the chair positioned to look toward the entrance. She watched the incomers. Watched for Anton.

I took a packet of sugar from the condiment tray, ripped it open, and stood it up leaning against the side of my plate.

"What is that?" Sondra asked.

"What is what?"

"The sugar. You did that at Ramstein, too. Think I didn't notice? What's up with that?"

"Oh, that. It's just a superstition."

"You don't seem like the superstitious type."

"It's a long story," I said.

"Fine," Sondra said, rolling her eyes and with a bit of a scowl. "Keep your little secrets." She drowned her momentary disappointment with a long pull from her coffee. Her attention turned back to the people bustling around us. I looked down at the sugar packet and drifted back to a memory from The Farm…

*　*　*

Silent Stu's was a speakeasy in the basement of a family restaurant in Oley, Pennsylvania, not too far from The Farm. If you knew it was there, you knew not to mess with its clientele. A few local cops hung around some nights to make sure the CIA recruits didn't get too far out of line, or at least didn't let it spill into town if they did.

Three ice cubes rattled in my empty glass as I set it down. Marco was on the other side of the room shooting pool, cigarette smoke circling his head as he lined up the next shot. He'd left three empty beer bottles and the smoldering remnants of two cigarettes in an ashtray to keep me company.

I'd been social enough so far. The music wasn't loud in my corner booth. Most of the noise came from the central bar. Battle and his loud musclebound buddies were there, screaming at the Hershey Bears hockey game and getting more drunk and raucous with every goal. No one was paying me any mind.

My thoughts drifted to a research problem I'd been exploring at Drexel before leaving for my six months of training. I scribbled a few graphs on my cocktail napkin with a felt tip pen, watching the ink run in a few places near the ring from my drink. The noise and clatter of the room faded for a few minutes. I fell into the drawing, envisioning numbers inside the graph, finding one pattern, then another. A fleeting hint to the solution of a greater problem began to emerge.

People moving around me. Something set down on my table. Where am I? Did someone just talk to me?

I looked up and saw a bar tab on a plastic tray, a steaming cup of black coffee on a saucer, and a waitress walking away. Had I just disappeared into my head again? Did anyone see? I didn't stim or rock in my seat, did I? Is my expression blank? I looked around the bar quickly. No one seemed to be paying attention to me. I breathed a sigh of relief and dropped a twenty into the tray. I calculated that I was overdue to make small talk with someone, like everyone else was doing.

Women's laughter several tables away caught my attention. Donna sat on the edge of a large booth, one leg in and one leg out, leaning against another recruit. A waitress was serving them a giant plate of chicken wings and a fresh bucket of light beers, and arrived a moment too late to hear the punchline of some joke. Donna's creamy mocha skin glowed in the lamplight. She looked over and caught my eyes upon her. She smiled, nodded hello, and turned back to her friends.

I looked toward the bar and saw Battle bent over the dregs of a draught beer, looking back over his shoulder and glaring my way. We'd had our share of differences lately. His story was that he'd been regular Army for the last five years, and before that he'd earned black belts in numerous martial arts and won a lot of tournaments. He'd been putting me on the floor fairly consistently in hand-to-hand training. In recent days, he'd been looking for every opportunity to be extra hard on me. This probably had something to do with the candidate performance ratings posted a week before, and me being ahead of him in most other classes.

I looked away as quickly as I could. I opened a packet of sugar and poured it into my coffee.

"What the fuck is that!? Coffee!?"

I looked up to see Battle swaggering over. The swollen-muscle alphas behind him were watching with interest, holding back laughs. I gestured toward the empty seat across from me.

"Is that an invitation, schoolboy?" he said, trying to be loud enough for everyone to hear. "You pencil-pushing geek. No, I don't want to join you, Mop. Did you know we all call you Mop? It's because of how much fun we have polishing the floor with your face every day in the meat locker!"

I flashed a fake smile and opened another packet of sugar. This one I stood carefully upright, leaning against the saucer.

"Got nothing to say, Mop?" Battle stepped up to the table. He noticed the sketched shapes on my napkin, and quickly snatched it up, taking a few steps back and attempting to read it. "This is how you party, Mop? Are you an artist? What is this shit?"

I shook my head, aware that most of the room was now looking. I acted as though I was ignoring him and pulled the spoon out of my napkin-wrapped silverware to stir the coffee. I made sure it was obvious I was still gripping the rest of the silverware in a knife-like grip.

Battle crumpled the napkin in his fist and stuffed down the front of his pants.

"What do you think, Mop? Do you like how I'm appreciating your art?" He made gyrating sexual motions with his hips, playing for the crowd.

"Battle?" I interrupted. "Just curious. Ever been in a fight that didn't have a referee?"

His gyrations stopped instantly. The room grew silent except for the hockey game and some syrupy country ballad from the jukebox.

"I've been in fights all my life, Battle," I continued, making air quotes when I said his name. "And none of them were fair, and none of them ended with someone tapping out. But that ain't you, is it? You're nothing but a gym bunny. Phony tough. Why don't you go flex in a mirror and kiss your biceps."

"You want to throw down for real, Mop?"

"I've been wondering something, Battle. Your friends over there are all ex-Seals and ex-Rangers, right? But you've never seen any action at all, have you? Remind me…where was your nice comfy desk stationed, again?"

I slid halfway out of the booth as he rapidly approached. I raised the silverware napkin in my left hand,

and he easily clinched that wrist and turned it outward, loosening the silver from my grip.

"That your big threat, schoolboy?"

"That was the distraction."

My right wrist, gripping the bottom of the open sugar packet, flicked outward, sending a spray of sugar particles into the air and directly into Battle's face. He maintained his clinch on my left wrist, but I stepped into and under it, taking a leveraged position under his right arm.

And then I just kept punching. Targeting the liver.

At first Battle flailed a bit, trying to clear his vision. After a few painful liver punches landed, and had him wincing and doubling over slightly, he released his clinch to try to back off and distance himself. But I clinched back, advancing and staying with him, turning with him and staying under his right arm, and just punching, punching, punching. A dozen punches later, at the first retching sound of Battle trying to hold back bile-filled vomit, I finally stood upright and put everything I had into a haymaker.

Battle stumbled backward in a wobbly-legged daze and grabbed the bar rail to keep himself on his feet. It had happened so fast, some of his friends hadn't stood up from their barstools yet. One of them stepped between me and Battle, but didn't advance. They all stared at me with puzzled expressions, half-angry and half-afraid, like a pack of grizzly bears unsure what to make of some crazy mountain man. I looked right through them with my chest puffed out, standing my ground, and they kept back.

"Hey, Sean," said Donna, hustling over from her booth. "I think now might be a good time for that drink you owe me." She pushed me lightly back with a hand on my chest while looking back at Battle's crew, waving them away. In some part of my fight-enraged mind, I was dimly aware she was probably saving me from the beating of my life.

Donna guided me back to my table. I was obviously the topic of conversation at every other table. I sat in my seat and looked down at my right hand with its reddened knuckles and wondered how swollen they would be tomorrow. I wanted to crack them. I wanted to stim in some way, or just run off to somewhere quiet. I opened another packet of sugar and stood it up against the side of the saucer.

Donna gently caressed my forearm, and I nearly jumped out of my shoes.

"Walk me to my car?" she said. "Let's get the hell out of here. This will all blow over."

I looked up and into her eyes. Her fingernails continued to graze my forearm. My eyes lowered to her full lips, and I wondered what kissing them would be like. They parted slightly as I looked.

"Take me back to your room, Sean," she said. "Doesn't that sound a lot better than staying here?"

CHAPTER 14 The Drop

The snapping of Sondra's fingers in front of my face brought me back to reality. Sondra took another sip of coffee, eyes never leaving mine. I resisted the urge to look away. I had to be social and continue a conversation to put the person I was with at ease. I scrolled through my mental rolodex of techniques for masking autism with small talk.

"You've been here a few times before," I said.

"Between jobs, a few times. Never had much to do with the crowds here. I'm not the gambling type. Never saw a crowd this big here. Reckon it'll get even bigger as the week goes on."

"What else is there to do here?"

"Rest," Sondra said. "Recoup. Spa's nice. Quiet town outside, nice for just walking around. Peaceful country." She seemed wistful recollecting her experiences, and sank back into her chair, sipping coffee. Her posture was serene and demure – legs crossed, elbows in. She looked past me, and a glint of recognition crossed her face, a faint grin emerging. She shifted to a more forward-leaning, assertive posture, almost masculine, but the serene smile remained.

"Anton's coming up behind you. He might touch your shoulder."

Before I could respond, Anton had closed the distance. His hand clamped lightly on my left shoulder, like a friendly greeting, but I tensed up anyway. A wave of anger and adrenaline shot through me, and I blinked hard and fought to control myself.

Anton's light grip slightly repositioned my shirt so as to make my left breast pocket bulge open a little, and I immediately recognized the move. At the right moment, we would drop something in, discreetly. A standard passing maneuver. He wasn't just some asset. He knew a bit of tradecraft himself.

"The lovely couple! I hope your evening was enjoyable. Can I get you anything?"

"I love it here," Sondra said making a quick gesture with her arms. I felt something very light fall into my pocket as she made her distracting gesture. "Everything looks amazing. Hey, how good is the omelet chef?" Her grin widened to a smile, and her pupils were slowly dilating.

"World class, my dear," he said. He patted my shoulder a few times before walking on.

I watched him walk away, and made a mental note to be careful not to touch my pocket until we got back to the room.

"Thanks for the warning," I said, after a swig of coffee. "How did you know?"

"I saw him coming."

"That's not what I meant."

"I know," she said. "I know. It's OK. How are you handling the noise and lights so far?"

I stared at the croissant in front of me and tried not to be furious at it. Was I that obvious? Or had she simply read about my autism in her redpack? I wasn't sure which would bother me more. She reached forward and set her hand flat on the table, an inch away from mine. I finally looked up.

"So, what's Anton's story?" I said.

"Not here," she said.

We finished our breakfast and got up. Sondra suggested with a nod that we walk outside, and I followed. A brisk wind billowed our clothes as we stepped out into the sunlight. We walked across a small employee parking lot, and soon reached a grassy area overlooking an old forest. Colorful leaves fell from the wind-rocked trees, and misty hills stood on guard in the distance. We walked around the perimeter and enjoyed the fresh air on our way back to our room.

"Anton's been an asset of ours for years. He's got a family in Holysov. Wife and two teenage daughters. We pay him pretty well, and word is we'll be putting his daughters through Ivy League schools in a few years. We take care of guys like him."

"You've met the whole family?"

"What are you implying?"

"You and Anton seem rather close."

Sondra grabbed my shoulder and spun me around to face her. Her flash of anger quickly cooled, but the visible pulse in her neck made the intensity of her feelings unmistakable.

"I can see why you might have your concerns, but it's not like that. I'll clue you in, but this is just between you and me, got it?"

I nodded and we continued walking.

"I was in trouble a while back, don't ask me the details. People after me, way more than I could handle. Anton hid me in his home. For weeks. So yes, I've met them. They're wonderful, and they risked their lives for me. So that's the last I better hear about them. Understand?"

"I'm sorry," I said. "I didn't know."

We were silent the rest of the way back. I looked out at the swaying trees, and watched a murder of crows take off in unison before disappearing into the woods. I contemplated the seeming randomness of their flight patterns and wondered about the differential equations that might model their migrations. This brief diversion didn't make me feel any better about Sondra seeing right through me, or about how far off my emotional reads had been in the last twenty-four hours. I felt like one of the falling leaves, blown about by the October wind.

Once we got back to the room, I checked my shirt pocket and found a flash drive in it. I showed it to Sondra before switching my laptop to the hidden drive and plugging it in. A menu of files popped up. I clicked open a spreadsheet and a list of names appeared in alphabetical order.

"He's thorough," I said. "Looks like a roster of all the men who showed up with two trunks. No women's names here."

"Only takes one ID to make a hotel reservation."

"Always the guy, apparently. Thirty-two of them, by Anton's count. And it looks like he's managed to include scans of their passports."

"I told you he's good," she said.

"I'm going to need some time to go through all this."

"Perfect. I'll leave you to it."

I looked up at Sondra as she headed toward the door.

"Where are you going?" I asked.

"I'm going to walk around a while and see if I can spot any of the principals, or a lot of local girls, or anything else unusual. I might play some slots to blend in. And I'm really looking forward to blowing some of my poker boyfriend's money."

"Tip the waitstaff," I said.

I was already completely immersed in the data before the door closed behind her. The first thing that jumped out was that every one of the thirty-two men was from Turkey or Albania. As I looked through their passports, I recognized the Turkish player who had sat to my left the night before. He probably hadn't been the only two-trunker in the room. If some of the men were out and about, why did the women only show up after two in the morning?

I spent some time loading their names, pictures, and room assignments into the ghost drive on my phone. I tried to commit their faces to memory. I went back and read through the folder on Soner. I wondered how he'd recruited so many men so quickly. None of the men seemed to be in the background of any of the candid photos of Soner.

It was only when the code-knock sounded on the door, and Sondra walked in, that I realized two hours had passed.

"See anything?" I asked.

"Still no sightings of Kadri Soner. Sheikh al-Karchi is in the high limit room right now, playing baccarat at a thousand Euros a hand. He's got two personal guards with him, the same two every time Anton says. One of the guards watched me walk around the room the whole time, but the other and al-Karchi paid me no mind."

I couldn't help but chuckle at that. "See, one chance in three."

"Ok, smartass. I've got a puzzle for you, then. I went to the spa after that, for a nice chair massage and a mani-pedi. I was there for an hour, and not one young lady speaking Czech came in the whole time. What are the odds thirty-two poker girlfriends get dragged to a place where they have nothing to do all day, and not one of them even pokes their nose into the spa? I don't think I saw any of them in the lounge either, or anywhere else."

"Agreed," I said, and tossed her the last *trdelnik*. "They aren't ornaments. They're here for a purpose."

"See that, kid? I can do a little math myself," Sondra said. "Now it's my turn to study. Go do your thing. Eyes sharp."

CHAPTER 15 The Whipsaw

I returned to the gaming floor to find the opening tournament well underway. There seemed to be a different atmosphere hanging over the casino. It took me a few minutes to realize why. It was the sounds. The steady tone of the slot machines was still present, but the volume seemed as if it had been turned down, perhaps from having fewer players.

A whispering crowd of railbirds stood around the perimeter of the TV table. Behind the table, the giant screen displayed tournament information in large white lettering floating over a colorful and undulating background. Eight players were receiving cards from the dealer, and there was one vacant chair. It belonged to a famous pro player who had just late-redged moments ago and agreed to be interviewed for the livestream before sitting down. He stood on a small stage off to the side, a hostess holding a microphone up to him.

Beyond the interview stage, the lounge was also more crowded than earlier. Casino employees bustled about, preparing some of the overload tables for play in anticipation of more late-redgers. Many latecomers were already queued up at the registration kiosk.

There was an air of seriousness in the poker hall. The ocean of banter you'd expect in a cash game room was now at low tide. Instead, the clickety-clack of idle hands shuffling poker chips comprised most of the noise from the tournament tables, with much less table conversation. As I walked slowly through the room, I looked for familiar Turkish and Albanian faces, spotting a few here and there. The chip shuffling was like shaking of rattlesnake tails as I crossed a desert plain. Watch where you step, amateur.

Toward the back, I spotted a table with several familiar faces. Two cards per player, and not very big stacks. Looked like 1-3 Hold'Em. I flipped through the ghost drive images as I weaved toward the cashier. At least three of Soner's crew, maybe more, were playing at the same table, and it had two empty seats. Bullseye.

I quickened my pace a bit toward the cash games kiosk. The attendant looked up and smiled, brushing back silky, black hair.

"I'd like some low stakes Hold'Em," I told her. "And, if possible…"

I leaned in closer and lowered my voice a bit.

"Could I play at that table there, third from the back? I see a couple empty chairs."

Her sunny expression drooped as she looked in that direction. The corners of her eyes slanted down a bit, and one of her lips quivered for a moment. She looked back down at her clipboard and swallowed hard. By the time she looked back up at me, I felt a little angry, and wondered what hurtful thing one of them had said to her.

"I'm not supposed to do that," she said. "We have a system for filling the tables, and the next new player is supposed to go…"

"I know," I said. "This is kind of embarrassing, but…those guys over there, that came in all together? One of them said some terrible things to my girlfriend the other day. Had her in tears. And I just really want to clean his clock.”

She blurted out a quick chuckle and covered her face with her hands. The light instantly came back to her eyes. She shook her head, smiling, and scribbled something on her clipboard.

“Go ahead, I’ll take care of it.” She thumped the kiosk twice.

I carried my chips to the target table and sat down. I told the dealer I’d wait for my big blind to come around before playing. That gave me time to connect my earbuds to my phone, and flip through the images, looking for matches. To the rest of the table, I looked like a typical cash player flipping through music tracks as I settled in for a long grind. In reality, I was quickly able to confirm that the four seats to my right were all Albanian players on Anton’s list.

<<Gonna play some cash. Four suckers on my right>> I texted Sondra.

<<Anyone I’d know?>>

<<Maybe from that trip to the Adriatic>>

<<Gotcha>>

As the big blind made its way to me, I tapped the voice translation app and toggled the selection to “Albanian.” I set the phone down in my cupholder, and peeked at my first cards, folding them quickly. Seconds later, a voice began speaking into my left ear, loosely translating any Albanian nearby. The player three seats to my left, Ledeon Gjokaj, was complaining to his companions that the coffee was too weak for his taste.

I didn’t play well for the next hour, perhaps because I was paying more attention to their conversations than my cards. The translator didn’t catch every word and was mistranslating on occasion. I hypothesized that this was because they often spoke in slang and talked around things.

Gjokaj mentioned "walking the dogs" a few times to Armend Tomaj, the player on my immediate right, before I realized he might be describing the women they'd brought, using coarse language. We already suspected the women were here for a purpose. This made it sound like the men were somehow in charge of them.

What stood out more than their conversations was their fixation on their phones. It's not unusual to see poker players on their phones between hands, reading social media or watching videos. But the four Albanians were watching their phones together. Their fingers rarely moved, and when one of them started scrolling, usually so did the others. Many of their eye and head motions seemed synchronized. They were all watching the same thing, but as far as I could tell, they weren't talking about it at all.

I picked up my phone and mimicked typing. At an opportune moment, I fumbled with it and pretended to almost drop it, leaning hard to my right and bumping Tomaj. I caught a half-second glimpse of his phone's screen before he flinched away. He shot me a look of annoyance as I straightened up and apologized. I folded the next hand and then mimicked finishing a long text.

The glimpse of his screen showed me a poker table, but with only two seats and two cards showing at each seat. Heads up Hold'Em. He was on an online poker site, but the site didn't look familiar to me, and I'd been on quite a few of them. If they were all watching the same screen, they couldn't all be playing.

"What site are you playing?" I asked Tomaj. "Good action?"

"Fuck off," he blurted, turning his phone screen away from me. The other Albanians looked up at him, and me, and back to him.

"Sorry, man," I said, turning away from him. "Just being friendly."

I folded another hand and started playing with my chips. I watched the Albanians out of the corner of my eye as they reacted. My translator couldn't pick up what they were angrily hissing at Tomaj, but it was clear they were angry at him, not me. Whatever they were doing, or watching, was not meant for anyone else's eyes. There was no way I'd get another peek without being completely obvious. I decided to text Sondra about it.

<<Did you remember your prescription glasses?>> I texted to Sondra.

<<Sure did>>

<<Friend on my right wants to show you something cool. On his phone.>>

<<Be right down. Join me for lunch?>>

I peeked at my next cards as they were dealt to me. Pocket tens. Tomaj set out his big blind, and as first to act, I raised to fifteen. It folded around to Gjokaj in the cutoff. He stared down at the table and said something that my app translated as "missile." He looked up at me and set out three red chips to call. His colleagues on the button and small blind folded, looking at me as they did.

"Raise," Tomaj said, glancing sideways at me briefly before cutting out a min-raise to 30. I thought for a few seconds, and then slid out another 15 to call.

"Make it sixty," said Gjokaj, sliding out his chips.

"Hundred," answered Tomaj.

I immediately realized what was going on. I was being whipsawed. By repeatedly raising, they could prevent me from closing the action with a call. My only choice was to bail out now, or just shove it all in pre-flop and play for stacks. Missile? That's what Gjokaj said to Tomaj as a signal. Missile?

Rockets. Pocket rockets, another name for aces. Gjokaj was way ahead. I folded my pair of tens face down. Gjokaj saw this and smiled, and shoved all in. His conspirator Tomaj instantly folded.

"Hey," Tomaj said, nudging me with his elbow. "I'll show you, because we're friends." He flipped over a three of spades and a seven of hearts, and his three companions had a good laugh.

"Deal me out a few hands," I told the dealer. More laughs.

I got up and walked around, pretending to be agitated, but I was secretly pleased. They now pictured me as a weak player. Unthreatening. Someone to be pushed around, then forgotten. It played.

Walking around, I saw at least a dozen more of Soner's crew. Nearly all were playing low-stakes cash rather than the tournament. In the distance, Veronique had appeared, perched in the same spot as before, silently looking out upon the action.

I sat back down and folded the next two hands pre-flop. I was keeping an eye on Gjokaj in particular, who once again seemed fixated on his phone. The player to his left nudged him, and then nudged him harder until he looked up. The dealer was in the middle of taking a new deck of cards from the shuffler when he also looked up. He promptly fumbled the deck into a messy pile.

I turned to see Sondra approaching the table, hips swaying in a long, tight, black dress. She was wearing her camera-glasses and was putting her phone inside her handbag. She literally stopped action at some of the tables, just by walking past. So much for not attracting attention.

"How's it going, babe?" she said, slinking up between me and Tomaj.

"Not so great," I sighed, and nodded toward Tomaj. "This guy here just took me to school."

She turned toward Tomaj and leaned in close to him. He instinctively turned his phone screen down, to hide it, but looked up at her.

"I hope you leave him enough to take me to dinner," she said, her voice now husky and deep. She gave him a wink as her handbag brushed gently against his hand and phone.

She turned back to me, saying "I'll be in the lounge, lover. Don't make me wait too long."

The entire table watched as she slinked away. One by one, they all turned to look directly at me, amused expressions on their faces. I looked back and forth at the other players. I grinned sheepishly and threw my hands up with a shrug.

"Rack, please," I said to the dealer.

      Sondra stood leaning against a pillar, sipping an espresso, waiting for me. As soon as I made it to the lounge, she beckoned me to follow her. I took a quick look around as I crossed the room. Veronique was perched in her usual spot, a steaming cup of tea in front of her. She seemed to be looking our way. Two large Arab men in tan suits stood close behind her.

      "Let's find a more secluded spot," she said. An unconscious movement of her eyes told me she was nervous about being overheard and had also noticed Veronique. We found our way to a small table in a far corner. I held Sondra's chair as she sat down. She pulled her phone out of her purse and started flipping through it.

      "Veronique giving you the old hairy eyeball?" I asked.

      "Not her so much, but did you see those two big creeps behind her? They're the ones that worry me."

      "Did you catch a good look at Tomaj's phone?"

      "No, he turned it over too fast. But I think I got a good synch-up." Sondra scrolled a little bit more, and then nodded in confirmation. "Yep. His history and contents are uploading as we speak. Gonna take a few minutes. Why don't you get us a big platter of sushi in the meantime?"

"Good plan."

I walked back toward the food tables, thinking about what information Sondra might have obtained. Bringing her phone into proximity of Tomaj's had been enough to transfer a viral program designed to bury itself in Tomaj's operating system. It would be invisible during any routine audit of his software and was slowly transferring his data to a folder in her phone's ghost drive.

I filled the plate, artfully arranging a variety of sushi and maki. I held out my phone near the plate and positioned myself to make it look like I was taking a picture of it. Veronique and her companions were in front of me. I looked up for a moment to see if they were looking my way. They weren't, so I quickly rotated the phone up to snap a picture of them in between two pictures of the plate.

I brought the plate back with two sets of chopsticks and the standard accompaniments of soy sauce and wasabi. Sondra was fixated on her phone and seemed pleased with her results. I set the plate down and checked out the pictures I'd taken. The picture of Veronique and her guards was a little dark and blurry due to the brightness of the poker hall behind them. But more importantly, none of them had been looking at the camera. I'd gotten away clean.

I posted a picture of the sushi on a social media site while waiting for Sondra to start talking. After a few minutes, she nodded some more and looked up. I showed her the Veronique pic as she eagerly scooped up an eel roll with her chopsticks. A tilt of her head showed me she wasn't sure she approved of my taking the chance, but she shrugged it off.

"We'll clean that up later and show it to Anton," Sondra said. "He's seen al-Karchi's bodyguards, too. They were wearing matching blue suits, not tan suits like these guys. I don't know if we can rely on their fashion choices for information, but I'm pretty sure these are different guys."

"I've seen the tan suit guys before, the first time I walked in here. But there were three of them that time. These two big goons, and there was a smaller guy, too."

"The opposition keeps growing. We need to keep track of them all."

"How does she drink her tea?" I asked, nodding toward the steaming cup on Veronique's table. "Is it just ornamental? Or did she pull her face covering down at some point?"

"Could belong to one of the guys, I guess," Sondra said with a shrug. "I haven't noticed her drinking any."

I sampled the fresh sea urchin while Sondra kept reading Tomaj's data. I took a longer look at the picture, focusing on the men. Their posture seemed wrong for their part. A bodyguard would typically be a little stiff and tense, with an alert and mindful sense of his surroundings. The men in the picture seemed too relaxed and at ease.

I was about to ask Sondra about her progress when a small entourage entered the room. When I saw who it was, I gently kicked Sondra under the table to get her to look up.

Kadri Soner had finally appeared.

Three of his fellow Turkish players walked in with him, and the group barely broke stride as they crossed the lounge and headed straight for the poker hall. Soner was dressed in a light suit coat with patches on the elbows, and his shoes were freshly shined. He looked just like he did in his photographs—focused, wary, and hurried.

Soner pushed wire-rimmed glasses back on his nose as he looked sideways at the tan-suit guards. One of them gave some sort of hand signal to the other before following Soner and his friends down the staircase into the poker hall. As they descended out of our view, I turned to Sondra to find her already looking at me.

"Before you get right on that," she said, "you might want to know what I found." She slid her phone over to me, and it displayed an image of a head's up poker hand similar to what I'd glimpsed before. The URL at the top of the screen showed the site to be "pokergeyser.eu," apparently a new poker site that I'd never heard of.

"Over eighty percent of his time since one o'clock, he's either been looking at screens like this, or a screen with a long list of poker-sounding things," she said. "You'd have to tell me what it is." She swiped backward and showed me an image of the list.

"It's a sit-and-go registration page," I explained. "You'd go to a page like this to enter a quick online game, rather than a long tournament or a cash game. Looks like this particular page is all head's up games. One-on-one poker, winner takes all. How's Tomaj been running today?"

"I'm not sure. I don't think he's actually been playing," she said. "He's never on the same screen for very long. But I don't know. You're the expert. You'll have to take a look later. I'll load everything onto the laptop first chance."

I thumped the table twice, and she looked at me quizzically. I explained that it meant "nice hand," or general approval otherwise. I grabbed a last piece of sea urchin sushi and popped it in my mouth as I got up and made for the poker hall.

I descended the steps slowly, looking for Soner, and it didn't take long to spot him. He had shed his three companions, but the largest tan guard was right behind him. He stopped at a table in the middle of the room and shook hands with several of the players. He turned a little toward me for one of them, and I could see an almost beatific expression on his face. He stood like a confident benefactor as he greeted them, and then moved on.

Soner reached his assigned tournament seat and set down his 50,000 in starting chips. He was late-redging, and the blinds were already 600-1200, so he'd be starting with just over 40 big blinds. He still had enough bigs to make some moves, but he'd find himself short-stacked soon if his first few moves didn't pan out.

I moved around the perimeter of the room, looking for tables near Soner that had empty seats. I spotted a cash game with an empty seat facing his table. I would be at his left flank, which would be perfect for watching him without him noticing me.

I walked to the table and sat down. The dealer asked where my chips were. I saw that the table was 5-5 Pot Limit Omaha, so I pulled out an orange chip and tossed it in front of him. I asked him to break it down to smaller denominations for me, but then deal me out for a while.

Two tables over, Soner folded his first hand while still talking to the tan guard. I guessed that they would be speaking Arabic, and so dialed that language up on my phone app. However, I was too far away to pick them up. Instead, all I heard was someone at my own table expressing annoyance with me for slowing down his game.

Soner folded his second hand as the tan guard walked off. I expected the guard to go back to Veronique, but instead he walked over to the side of the poker hall and stood against the wall, like a sentry. He reminded me of the MPs who'd escorted us around Ramstein. I wondered what sort of training he'd had in his past. Bodyguards of the very rich are frequently ex-police or ex-military.

Soner already looked bored and was flipping through his phone by the time he folded hand number three. I couldn't see what he was looking at and wondered if he too was logged into "Poker Geyser," or whatever Tomaj's site was called. His eye and finger movements seemed to be the same as the Albanians at my previous table. His fixation on his phone also mirrored theirs. When the fourth hand was dealt, he didn't seem to notice. The dealer had to tap the felt in front of him to get him to look up, and when he saw the cards in front of him, he just tossed them into the muck without even looking at them.

Out of the corner of my eye, I noticed a lanky man in a turtleneck sweater walking around with a rack of chips, scanning the nearby tables with a confused look on his face. I realized that the cash games attendant had been told of the open seat at my table, and she had sent him over to fill it. He looked befuddled and turned to walk back to her kiosk. I knew my time there was limited.

Soner finally played in his fifth hand. He was in the "under the gun" position, first to act pre-flop, and after peeking at his cards, he limped in with 1200. The action folded around to a young Canadian internet pro on the button, who raised to 3500. A somber-looking Chinese player in the small blind hesitantly called. The big blind on Soner's right rattled a hard candy around his teeth for a minute as he looked carefully at his competitors. He then slid out a raise, a three-bet squeeze to 13000.

I thought about the range Soner would limp with, and how those hands would react to that much pre-flop action. Unless he had pocket kings or aces, it seemed like he had an obvious fold.

"All-in," Soner announced, shoving the rest of his 50,000 into the middle.

The remaining players all folded quickly, except the big blind, who'd made the squeeze with only another 30,000 or so behind. He rattled his hard candy some more as he huffed and scratched his head. Beyond him, near the front of the hall, I could see the lanky player walking slowly back toward us, stopping to look at the table numbers as he did. I hoped he would arrive after Soner's big hand played out. I grabbed an empty rack from the floor near my feet and held it in my lap.

"Alright, I call," sighed the big blind. He tossed out a chip and flipped over pocket kings. Soner wasted no time showing his hand as well. An ace and a nine, unsuited. Several players at the table had raised eyebrows, surprised by Soner's weak hand. They looked at each other and whispered, shaking their heads. Those same players all grimaced or rolled their eyes when the flop came out ace-jack-three, putting Soner in the lead with a higher pair.

I quickly racked my chips and got up, apologizing to the dealer for "accidentally sitting at the wrong table." I walked off toward the cashier without looking back at my table or Soner's. I didn't need to see the turn or river. The final outcome of the hand was unimportant. I'd seen what I needed to see. I walked back to the lounge and stopped at the top of the stairs to have a last look back. Soner was still at the table, and the chair to his right was empty. His hand had held up, and his stack had nearly doubled.

I stepped into the lounge and found Sondra still there, still rifling through Tomaj's data. She acknowledged my presence by sliding the last remnants of the sushi platter toward me.

"Discover anything interesting?" I asked.

"Other than his fascination with the Poker Geyser site, just one thing. This is definitely not his phone."

"Huh?"

"No browsing history before a few days ago. Hardly any contact info, as in phone numbers or addresses. No pictures except a few selfies with female employees in this casino. None of them look happy about it. Creep."

"No pocket litter," I said. "They were bought new phones before they came here. And now that I think about it, the Albanians at my table seemed to have the same style phone. I bet they all do, then. All thirty-two of them."

"The girls too?" Sondra wondered aloud.

"Safe bet. We're starting to get a better picture of where some of al-Karchi's money went. New cellphones and room and board for that many people for nearly a month, in Prague, and then here. I estimate that's about two hundred thousand dollars already, and we still don't know what's in the trunks."

"OK, well…how about Soner?" Sondra said. "Learn anything about him?"

"Yes," I said. "He sucks at poker."

"Funny."

"No, I mean it, seriously. He's either awful, or doesn't give a damn, or both. In ten minutes of play, I saw him fold a hand without looking at it, and the next hand he went all in with junk, facing multiple aggressions."

Sondra shook her head. "Try to remember I'm not a poker player."

"OK, in simple terms…he used a strategy where he might get lucky about a quarter of the time and end up with a giant stack, which is what happened. But the other three quarters of the time he'd bust right out of the tournament the first hand he played. Soner was being deliberately reckless…and he just got lucky."

"How does knowing that help us?"

"It tells us one thing for certain," I said. "He's not here to play poker. It's subterfuge. Camouflage. He wants to make it look like he's here for the EPC, but he's really here for something bigger."

"Kind of like you," Sondra pointed out.

I was about to protest being compared with him when, as if speaking the name of the devil could summon him, Soner climbed up the stairs. He walked through the lounge and grabbed a kebab off one of the buffet tables, his tan guard following him about twenty feet behind. I figured he was grabbing a quick snack between hands, but to my surprise, he walked out of the back of the lounge toward the hotel. From my chair, I looked into the poker hall and squinted to make out the tournament clock. There was still twenty minutes to go before the break.

I got up as though to stretch, and casually walked over to the stairs. I looked out over the poker hall and spotted Soner's seat. Even from a distance, I could see that there were still stacks of chips on the table in front of it. He hadn't busted out.

Soner had simply gotten up in the middle of a 1500-Euro buy-in tournament, because he had something better to do. I was dying to know what.

"I know what you're thinking," Sondra said as I returned to our table. "And you better sit your ass down right now. You can't follow him into the hotel. Too damn obvious. Nowhere to hide."

CHAPTER 17   The Afterglow

    Soner and his bodyguard were heading back to the hotel and taking my answers with them. But Sondra was right—going after them would be foolish. The only way I could follow them right now was online.

    Creating a new Poker Geyser account was surprisingly easy. Suspiciously easy. I had no trouble using phony identity information linked to a bogus email account. The security on the site was so lax, it was as though it was meant to be. In only five minutes, I had an account with username "MS79912," under the false name Michael Saint of El Paso, Texas.

    Control had used one of the company's Bitcoin wallets to send me my mission bankroll. Some quick paperwork at the cashier transferred dollars back to it, and I used that to fund the Poker Geyser account. In a matter of minutes, I was already playing in a five dollar sit-and-go on the website.

    I looked up and noticed Sondra in the distance, walking through the lounge on her way somewhere. She had finished uploading Tomaj's phone contents to the computer and was now bouncing around the rest of the casino, keeping up appearances. Play a little here, play a little there, and watch out for anything unusual.

<<Wow, the high limit tables start at 100 a hand>> Sondra texted.

<<Bump into any friends?>>

<<Different friends than in your photo>>

Sondra was verifying that al-Karchi's bodyguards were not the tan guards. It seemed that these two guards always stuck close to the sheikh, while a different detachment was assigned to Veronique and Soner. I wondered whether anyone was guarding the hotel rooms. There was still one tan guard unaccounted for—the short one I'd seen on the first day. Where was he right now, and what was he up to?

I bought into a low-stakes cash game and played uneventful live poker while playing even less eventful poker on my phone. I was more interested in learning about the site than the actual play. I made note of a few quirks of the Poker Geyser site, with plans to discuss them with Sondra later.

Soner eventually returned to the hall with little fanfare. He would have seemed like any other player in the room, if not for being visited every fifteen minutes or so by one of the two-trunkers. Whatever those players were up to, Soner required constant updates.

Before I knew it, midnight had come and gone, and a mumbled voice over the public address system announced that tournament play would soon conclude for the day. Most of the tables in the hall were now raucous with cash games, many of them very high stakes. The cocktail waitresses carried full trays and scurried to keep up with demand. It was nearly an hour later when Sondra texted.

<<How about a late-night snack?>>

<<Be right there>> I answered.

I cashed in my chips and went to the lounge. Sondra was already there, at the same table as earlier, this time with a large platter of dim sum and two sets of chopsticks. A margherita glass, half-emptied, sat on the table before her. As I sat across from her, I noticed her jaw was clinched and tense. She wore an earbud that was connected to her phone, and I realized she was using her translator.

She looked up and made a subtle eye movement and head bob, telling me to look over her left shoulder. Soner was at the table behind her, finishing up a meal with four of his crew. One of the burly tan guards was sitting silently among them. I nodded back at her in acknowledgement. She had a look of concentration. She was probably struggling due to her distance from the target combined with the loud clamor of the room.

I sampled a few steamed dumplings while paying unfocused attention to Soner's table. I'd seen at least half of his crew at the tables today, and it was a safe bet there were more who had escaped my notice. But I was certain I hadn't seen any of the girls who'd traveled with them. Either they'd left already, or they'd been sequestered somewhere all day.

Sondra took out her earbud and shook her head.

"I'm not picking up much," she said, shrugging. "They're very pleased with themselves. Something just ended, like five or ten minutes ago, and it went well for them."

I checked my watch and saw it was 1:15am.

"Think it might be something to do with the girls?" I asked. "Where've they been all day?"

"Locked away like nuns in a convent," Sondra said. "Not how you'd treat wives or girlfriends."

Not how you'd treat a girlfriend. How the hell would I know? My thoughts drifted back to Pittsburgh. To Marina. The way she could bounce across a café like a feather in the wind and wrap herself around my heart and make me feel instantly light. She'd be wiping down tables at The Buzz about now, waiting for the last few students to finish up. It wouldn't be too late to give her a call. If I had any idea what to say.

A few of Soner's girls walked by our table, talking. The first we'd seen of them all day. Locked away and controlled, but now free again, at least for a little while.

"You were right," Sondra said. "That's Czech. One of them just said something about getting some fresh air after she eats."

"I don't think they're girlfriends," I said. "I think they're employees, and their roommates are in charge of them, somehow."

"Trafficking?"

"I don't get that impression. They don't look abused or frightened. They all got a group text last night at 2:22am, which might have been some sort of instructions. They're doing some sort of work all day. Something they need to be isolated for."

At that moment, Soner stood up abruptly. He looked at something behind me, coming from the direction of the hotel. As Soner's table quickly dispersed, Sondra leaned back in her chair, and I could see she was also looking behind me. I casually leaned and turned my head slightly to see what had gotten everyone's attention.

The girl parade had returned, at least twenty of them, walking in together. Most of the girls were talking to each other with a tone of excitement in their voices. They seemed much more energetic than the night before, but just as famished. They made a bee line for the buffet. Some of them gave quick waves and smiles in Soner's direction as they passed him.

Veronique and the other large tan guard walked in behind the girls. Wordlessly, the crowd of girls seemed to part for Veronique as she walked through them. She went straight to the beverage station and made herself a cup of hot tea. She and her guard then disappeared into the high-limit room, where al-Karchi would still presumably be playing.

"What's Anton think?" I asked. "Have you seen him?"

Sondra answered by lifting her margherita class up an inch and making an eye movement indicating I should look down. Under the glass, upon the napkin, was another flash drive. She set the glass back down quickly after a sip through a straw.

"He was here just before you. Told me he's been attending to al-Karchi on and off all day, but he's seen nothing unusual. He reported our progress to the Prague office this morning. Same plan for tomorrow morning. He's trying to find out about the girls, but he hasn't gotten anywhere. At least not yet."

"Invisible," I mused. "No names given at check-in. No ID's shown. They don't buy anything. They barely come out of their rooms. And when they do, they're supervised."

"Sounds a lot like trafficking to me," Sondra said.

"I have a different hypothesis," I said. "I think they're tech support."

Sondra raised an eyebrow and smirked. "You think Soner picks up thirty-two sexy girls in a matter of weeks, locks them away in rooms in a posh casino, and has them doing…IT work? You're overlooking the obvious."

I laughed. "Seriously, though. Their roommates are in charge of them, and those men have been watching things online all day on the other side of the building. That only makes sense if the girls are doing something that can be watched online."

Sondra's smirk widened. "You're making my case for me."

"Tomaj's phone data showed he was watching online poker tables most of the afternoon."

Sondra's eyes danced a little, reflecting the thoughts racing through her mind. She was lightly biting her bottom lip as she contemplated. She excused herself and walked over to the dessert table, which had a group of Soner's girls around it. Clearly, she wanted to overhear more conversation while she mulled over what I'd said.

I ate an egg roll and casually surveyed the room. Soner had gone back to his tournament table to bag up his chips, since tournament play was ending for the day. This particular tournament was scheduled to continue three days later, at which time all surviving players would be given back their signed and sealed bag of chips. The buffet was becoming crowded with players who'd just bagged up.

Sondra returned and sat down, staring across the table with her chin on her hands.

"I'm really getting a certain vibe off these girls," she said. "Models, or maybe escorts, to put it nicely. But even still, you might be right. Human trafficking isn't al-Alrasid's modus operandi, as far as we know. Fundraising for future plans is, but not in that way."

"Lotta money in this place," I observed.

We finished eating while keeping an eye on the principals. The hall thinned out considerably, with only a couple dozen cash games going. Soner, Veronique, and the two big tan guards gravitated to an unused table in the far back corner of the poker hall. Three of his crew were there as well, apparently for a meeting. Their table was well isolated from the other action in the room, but even from a distance it was clear that they were jubilant and self-congratulatory.

"If that's where they're going to meet every night, I'll talk to Anton about bugging that table," Sondra said.

"Last night, the girls all got a group text," I said. "Maybe it comes at the same time. Or maybe it comes after this meeting we're seeing. I'd like to see what it says."

"Me too. Maybe I can get near them at the right time."

"Has to be incognito. Somewhere out of sight of their supervisors."

Sondra sat back in her chair, and her eyes shifted back and forth as she mentally walked through the premises, considering the options.

"If I were one of them," she said, "I'd find any excuse not to just go right back to my room. The pool, the gym, the spa, the bar. Out for a walk. Anything."

"Can't get close to them on a walk," I said. "Can't follow them into a mud bath or a massage room. Might be overseen by Veronique or the tan guards if you try anything here."

"The bar's already full of Soner's guys," she added. "What do you think? The gym or the pool?"

CHAPTER 18   Overload

       We placed our bets on the pool. It was just past two in the morning. Back in our hotel room, I changed into my swim trunks as quickly as I could and threw on a T-shirt and sandals. I emerged from the bathroom to find Sondra having gathered up her swimsuit and camera glasses in a tote bag. She slung it over one shoulder as I followed her out the door.

       We didn't know what to expect, but I was hoping for a large crowd around a quiet poolside, which would make it easy to blend in and find a position close to one of Soner's girls. But as we turned down the final hallway leading to the pool, a heavy thumping at about 120 beats per minute killed those hopes. It grew louder still as we separated and entered our respective dressing rooms.

       Sondra decided to change in the dressing room, in case she could get close to one of the girls there. I walked straight through the men's dressing room, and found it empty except for a hotel attendant. A heavy smell of chlorine assaulted my nose and made me cough involuntarily. Rows of lockers lined the walls in alternating white and royal blue. The thumping was now much louder, to the point where I would surely be able to identify the song if I was into that sort of music. The metal handles of the lockers buzzed as they vibrated with each thump.

"*Wirst du heute Abend schwimmen?*" the attendant said.

I looked confusedly at him, partly from feeling overwhelmed by the sensations, and partly from not expecting to hear German. Eventually I nodded that, yes, I would be swimming tonight. He directed me to have a quick rinse under a lukewarm shower before entering the pool area. I tipped him an American fiver for the towels he handed me and went inside.

The pounding dance music of the live DJ nearly knocked me over. A tall, swarthy young man in a black Sex Pistols T-shirt and ripped jeans stood spinning techno beats behind his mixing board, dancing and fist pumping, one pair of headphones on his ears, and another hanging off his belt. Behind him, an erratically spinning globe of lights shot bright beams in random directions, lighting the walls and beach chairs in splashes of loud colors.

The room would be dark as a dance club if not for the bright underwater lights in the pool. A light blue glow rose from the shimmering water of the pool, filling the room with a strange ambiance. An artificial waterfall poured down rocks in the far corner of the pool, sending light-refracting ripples across its length. The shadows of those ripples danced in mesmerizing patterns all along the ceiling. I needed a moment to take in the spectacle.

I walked slowly around the perimeter of the pool, looking for a good spot to settle. Hardly anyone was actually in the pool. Mostly, people sat at tables or laid back in beach chairs, talking in small groups and sipping mixed drinks. There were still plenty of empty chairs around the pool.

I passed up one empty chair after another, observing the pool goers. My teeth rattled from the music volume as I approached the speakers. The swirling lights turned my vision into a kaleidoscope as I passed by. I winced from the onslaught, and my chest began to feel tense and tight.

Most of the people by the poolside were women, a mix of old and young. None of them looked familiar, and hardly any of them looked like twenty-something local girls. Too old, or too much jewelry, or too conservative a swimsuit. It took nearly a full lap of the pool before I saw something promising.

Near a large hot tub, two lounge chairs were draped with two of the hotel's complementary robes, and two cellphones lay screen-up on a small table between them. The tub churned with high-powered jacuzzi jets but was empty except for two college-aged girls. A buxom blonde and a svelte brunette sat close together, leaning back, talking and laughing. I walked over to a lounge chair adjacent to theirs and sat down.

I took my shirt off and tried to face away from the lights. I felt my heart pounding out of synch with the music. I closed my eyes and tried to forget about the music and loud jacuzzi jets. I fought off an urge to just lie down and cover my ears.

I leaned over to slip off my sandals, choosing the direction of my lean to try to get a better view of their phones. Swirling globe lights fell upon them sporadically— red, yellow, yellow again. In fleeting glimpses, I pieced together their image in my mind. They were the same type as the rest of Soner's crew. The screens were off at the moment. I wished they would awaken suddenly and show the mystery text. I glanced at my own phone. Still a few more minutes until 2:22am. It couldn't come soon enough.

Perhaps I'd been noticed looking too long at their table, because one of the girls chose that moment to stand up. She waded to the near side and exited, splashing up a few stairs. She wore only dark green boy shorts and a smile. She gathered her brunette hair in a bunch and wrung out water which fell over small, milky-white breasts and a lithe body.

She smiled politely and said something which, I presume, meant "excuse me" in Czech, before grabbing up both cellphones. She returned to the tub and sat next to her friend again. She set the phones on top of a towel behind them.

The brunette whispered something to her blonde friend, who then looked at me and then looked away. My eyes stung from the chlorine and brightness, but there was no point in turning back. I walked over to the tub, descended the stairs, and lay back amidst the warm jets on the opposite side. The warmth couldn't soothe me the way it always did at home. The jets were blasting hard, their sound loud in my ears, adding to the tumult around me.

My hands began to shake involuntarily, nerves jangling, so I quickly sat on them. I tilted my head toward the ceiling and watched the rippling shadows and wild bright colors zipping across it like shooting stars. But really, I was observing the girls in the periphery, while trying to take deep breaths. I sat up and looked about the room for Sondra but couldn't see her anywhere.

"I love this place," I said to the girls, leaning forward and raising my voice enough to be heard over the pulsing techno and churning water. They looked at me, and then at each other. Strange shadows fell on their faces, lit from below by the underwater lights, with flashing rays of color behind them. The blonde smiled and crinkled her eyebrows, and she mouthed something to me that seemed to be one syllable. She couldn't hear me, and that was good. It gave me an excuse to move closer. I fought off a wave of dizziness and did so.

"I love it here, it's so great!" I said, wading over to them. Lights and chlorine. Too loud to think. They looked at each other again, this time making subtle eyebrow movements and head tilts. They knew each other well and were communicating something without words.

"What games do you play?" I shouted to them over the din. The music seemed to be getting even louder, and the bass drum was pounding, pounding, pounding. My heart was pounding. My lungs were tight. Girls laughing with each other, turning toward me. Try to focus.

"Are you big player?" the blonde said, sitting up. She bobbed in the water, clad the same as her friend except in red.

"Yeah, poker," I said, fighting through the pain. "Bigger the better! Came to the right place, eh? How about you two?"

"We like big players," the blonde answered. They looked at each other once more, and then moved as one. Each girl firmly took one of my arms and guided me backwards to my original place. They leaned in close enough for me to smell the tobacco on their breaths. Beams of green light bursting in my eyes. Chlorine and cigarettes. Jacuzzi jet pounding on my spine. Noise and noise and noise.

A set of fingernails slowly ran up the length of my right leg, and I went nonverbal. Body locked into place.

"Big player," the blonde continued. "Looking for good time?"

They leaned in even closer on either side. Arms around me, holding me. Hands roaming. The brunette playfully nibbling on my shoulder. The blonde's hand working its way slowly up my thigh.

Behind them, their phones suddenly lit up.

"Think…someone…texted you," I said. My whole body shook. Roaring in my head like a jet engine. The blonde winked at the brunette before splashing back across the tub. She boosted herself up and out, and flopped on her side, looking at her phone. A momentary reprieve. I fought to regain control of my body, but there was too much light, noise, and physical sensation. No focus. No escape.

The brunette took over for her friend, straddling me. She pressed her body in close. Her fingernails through my hair. Brain short-circuiting. Nerves exploding. Don't flail.

"Got five hundred?" she said. "Zina and friend make you feel good. Want good time?"

I tried to speak, but nothing came out. In the distance, I saw Sondra enter the pool area in a red one-piece. She spotted me immediately and started walking over, a look of amusement on her face. Her amusement faded quickly, however, and she began walking faster. She put her glasses in her bag and tossed it on a table as she arrived.

"Who's your new friend, Thom?" Sondra said, sliding quickly into the hot tub. The brunette turned and noticed Sondra, and it took her a few seconds to register that Sondra was with me. The brunette looked back and forth a few times between Sondra and her friend. When she finally got off of me, she slapped my face hard. She and her friend left the hot tub area quickly.

In the moment, I was only distantly aware of my own body sliding down into the water. Waves gurgled up over my face. My eyes stung and my body was rigid. An arm encircled my waist and lifted me back up. It was Sondra's. She leaned in over me, her eyes inches from mine.

"Are you OK? You don't look so good."

I tried to answer, but only short gasps came out.

"People are watching so I'm pretending to kiss you. Talk to me."

"Pool," I said. "Need...cold."

"Alright, take it slow. I got you."

Sondra took my arm in hers, steadying me as we ascended out of the tub. We sat down at the pool's edge before sliding in. The water was only four feet deep. We made our way to the corner, her hand never leaving my shoulder.

I took a deep breath and submerged. The pulsing music was muffled beneath the surface, reduced to bearable levels. I closed my eyes and relaxed, suspended. I heard my heart slow down to a calmer rate. Sondra's hand on my shoulder was my lifeline.

She gave my shoulder two quick squeezes. I held out a "thumbs up" signal and stayed below the surface a little longer. My thoughts were unscrambling, and my hands no longer shook. I finally came up for air. Sondra guided me back into the corner and leaned in close again.

"Pretending to kiss you again. How are you feeling?"

"I'm sorry," I said. "I'm all jangly."

"It's going to be OK, Thom."

"I need to get out of here," I said.

We got out, and I dried off as quickly as I could while Sondra went back to her changing room. We met outside where we'd split up beforehand. She was still in her swimsuit, dripping, and I realized that she'd forgone changing. She'd merely slipped on sandals and grabbed up her items, to make sure she got here ahead of me.

"I'm sorry," I said again as we started walking.

"Good news. I'm pretty sure I caught a glimpse of the text, off a different girl's phone in the dressing room. We can check my glasses when we get back to the room."

"Then it was worth it," I said, rubbing my temples. The straight hallway ahead twisted one way and then the other, and the ceiling lights were as bright as suns.

"I should probably just shut up, but I want to tell you something else." Sondra went quiet for a few moments, weighing her words. "I have…a little brother…and he's on the spectrum too. Maybe that's why Bill recruited me. Maybe it's just a coincidence. I don't know."

"That's how you know how to help me. What's he like?"

"Not like you. But not bad. Asperger's, they used to call it. He has a harder time than you. I'd love to tell you all about him, but…you know."

"Yeah," I said. "I get it."

By the time we got back to our room, I felt like myself again, only with a dull headache. I downed a bottle of water in one breath and cracked open a second.

Sondra emerged from the bathroom dressed for sleep, but instead brought her glasses over to the computer. She connected a thin wire from the glasses frame to a USB port and dozens of images began uploading. She sifted through them rapidly, finally arriving at the one she was looking for.

"Bingo," she said. "Check it out." The image on the screen showed a woman in a yellow bikini from the waist down, facing away from a changing bench behind her. On the bench was her cellphone, a block-shaped text message glowing on the screen.

"It's a bit blurry," I said, "but I think I can clean it up enough to read it. Especially if you have several other frames of it."

"In the morning," Sondra said. "Take it easy tonight. We'll get more news from Anton tomorrow, and then we see where this text leads us."

She didn't have to argue the point. I fell into an exhausted sleep the moment my head hit the pillow.

CHAPTER 19   Funeral

       I was fourteen years old, back in Kill Buck, in my dream that night. My big brother Matthew's casket was heavy in my hand. My father and I had the front corners, and four of his friends from the football team carried the rest of the weight.

       It was a slow procession. It started at our house, where we'd held the showing, and it was about to reach St. Michael's Cemetery, only two lots down the hill from our house. A statue of the archangel Michael stood before a rusty gate that leaned to the right and hung perpetually open in a state of disrepair. Michael's arm was aloft as if to brandish a sword, but vandals had broken the arm off at the wrist long ago.

       Six of my older relatives carried my mother's casket. They followed us closely, and behind them walked the rest of our family and at least fifty of Matt's high school friends. A sports reporter from the Olean Times-Herald was among them. Officer Lightfoot's patrol car flashed its blues, siren off, halting traffic for us. It was Lightfoot who had found them.

The crunch of the gravel road beneath hundreds of plodding feet was not enough to drown out the sounds of nature. A chilling wind swooped down from the peak of Eagle's Hill. The chirping of robins and the buzzing of summer insects filled my ears. It was late morning, mid-June, with the sun breaking through the clouds. I looked up and saw it piercing the ancient, swaying oaks and maples, and my tears finally began pouring in earnest.

"Easy, boy," my father said.

We reached the gravesite, and slowly set down Matt's casket. I pulled my suit coat more tightly around me. Even in June, mornings can be cold in the Appalachians. I turned to see my father looking back at my mother's casket being lain down. Officer Lightfoot had been following close behind, and now stepped forward.

"I'm so sorry, Steve," he said to my father, and saluted. My father saluted back, and the two ex-Marines stoically embraced.

After they released, my father turned to me and beckoned me to follow. The large crowd shuffled about, finding places to stand in a loose perimeter about the gravesites. I recognized many of Matt's friends. I recognized only a few of my relatives. I followed my father to a row of chairs and sat next to him.

Father Ken from the local Catholic church stood before us, waiting patiently for the crowd to stabilize. His white vestments were adorned with sashes of lavender and black. He spoke about God's plan. The value of sacrifice and the pain of loss. His words bounced off me and scattered into the surrounding forest.

I thought about all the times I'd fled to St. Michael's to escape the bullying. Some of those bullies were now mourning my brother. I computed a quick estimate of the attendance. The number of funeral attendees seemed to be very close to the number of gravestones in the centuries-old cemetery. I found comfort in the numbers for reasons I couldn't describe.

Closing my eyes, I envisioned the entire cemetery in my mind, just as I'd done many times as a kid, up late at night, mind racing, unable to sleep. If quizzed, I could probably recite every name, birth date, and death date from every stone in the grotto. Even the tiny little stones in the back section, for Catholic babies who died during birth or in their first year. This place of peace, my sanctuary, was now swallowing my mother and brother. Anguish crashed down upon me. My hands shook.

A low rumbling in the distance grew steadily louder, and before long a train passed us close by. Father Ken did his best to be heard over the clackety-clank of train cars rounding a hilly bend, but it was a futile effort. All we heard was the screech of metal on metal as freight cars curved around Eagle's Hill, and all we could see was Father Ken giving unheard condolence and scripture.

Mom's car had been found in the Allegheny River. They'd been returning from some sort of high school pre-graduation event. Mom had driven off the road. She was found still buckled into her seat with no signs of struggle, and with a very high blood alcohol content. Probably died in her sleep. Matt was unbuckled and heavily bruised on his upper body and arms. He had tried to escape the submerged car, but didn't make it. None of this information had been made public, of course. I'd overheard it a few nights before, eavesdropping Lightfoot and my father as they grieved in our basement, over a card table and a bottle of whiskey.

The train vanished into the distance shortly after Father Ken gave up on his sermon. My father looked relieved. We all stood. Grown-ups seemed to weave in undecipherable patterns around me. I stood stock still and watched my relatives lining up to talk to my father.

Someone hugged me tight, and I fought against them, pushing them away. It was a woman. I didn't look up to see her face. I just wanted to get away. Another hugger touched me, and I stepped quickly back and away. I fled to the other side of the cemetery, crying. I closed my eyes and smelled the soothing petrichor.

Hours seemed to pass, though they were probably minutes. I sat near one of my favorite graves and waited. The crowd eventually subsided, and my father walked over to me.

"Come on, T. J." he said. "Let's go home."

We walked together through the old boneyard and then back toward home. My father grabbed my arm and spun me to face him. I cringed involuntarily, expecting a blow, but it didn't come. He just looked me in the eyes, and my eyes met his, for the first time in years, and for the last time in years.

"T. J. Can you hear me?" he said. "It's going to be different now. Do you understand?"

I looked completely through him, while trying to count all the gravestones in my head.

"Teej, I don't know what to do," he said, his crying eyes meeting mine. "I don't know how to talk to you like Mom did. It's gotta be different now. I don't know how, but it's gotta be different. Tell me what's going on in your head, will you? Can you tell me? Can you hear me?"

I just looked away. I didn't want to, but I couldn't help it. I cried harder. He took me by the arm, and we walked in silence back toward home. A very short walk.

Several folding tables were set up in our yard. Crockpots and large of CorningWares food lay out upon them. Our family and friends held paper plates of food, standing with beers in hand, talking. The wake. I walked toward them. Dad's hand felt strange on my shoulder.

A woman who was a distant aunt, I think, walked up to my father and embraced him. She expressed her condolences to him. She glanced at me for a moment, but then quickly turned back to my father, expressing more condolences. He looked at me, and she looked at me, and an expression I'd learned to be sympathy fell across her face as she looked at my father.

In that moment, for the first time in my life, I became aware that my parent was being given condolences for the pain of having a child like me.

"Teej, why don't you go to your room? Why don't you play your dice games?"

I weaved quickly through the minefield of relatives and escaped to my room. I turned on the radio and listened to Top 40 music from a Buffalo station. It drowned out the muffled sounds of drunken solace taking place on the other side of my bedroom wall. I set up a chess board and played both sides against each other, again and again and again. At some point I finally looked up, and it was dark outside.

I stepped out of my room and walked toward the living room. The house was silent. I was hungry. I looked around, hoping to scrounge leftovers from the wake, and saw my father standing alone in the living room. He was fixated on a family picture of us taken at Darien Lake amusement park, seven years before.

It had been a happy day. Matt had convinced me to overcome my fear of the Viper roller coaster, and then we'd ridden it five times. We'd gotten stuck at the top of the Ferris wheel for a half-hour, but we'd gotten a free bird's-eye view of a Billy Joel concert because of it. Mom won a giant stuffed dog at the ring toss booth and lectured me and Matt about how we'd all have to share it. On the drive home, Matt and I had fallen asleep leaning on each other in the backseat in a mutual sugar crash.

My father stood like a statue for several minutes, unaware of my presence. Finally, he grabbed a bottle of whiskey and poured himself half a small glass. He raised it to his lips and drained it completely in two desperate swallows. He slapped it down on the table with a harshness that risked shattering the glass. Leaning over it, shoulders flexing. Tired and beaten. Manly and morose.

"Dad?"

He looked sideways at me, and looked back at the picture, and then looked at me again.

"Dad?"

"I like it when you call me that," he said.

"Dad? I don't know what to do either."

And we just held each other for I don't know how long.

I walked him to bed, and he passed out in his funeral clothes. I stood there for a few minutes, fourteen, uncertain about my future and everything else. The house was peaceful and silent. The clock read 11:30pm.

I left the house and walked back down to the cemetery. The full moon cast the only light, just enough for me to find my way. I didn't make it as far as my mother and brother's fresh graves. I stopped at the statue. I fell to my knees before it. I fell asleep holding onto its base, praying that St. Michael would watch over us.

"Who's Michael Saint?" Sondra asked, looking over my shoulder.

"The persona I created, to play anonymously on Poker Geyser," I answered. "Routed a thousand through the same e-wallet Control uses."

"Can they trace it back to you?"

"They could trace the money back to the dummy corporation we use as a front. Zero chance of them linking it to us."

Sondra nodded. She grabbed her toiletry bag and a change of clothes and disappeared into the bathroom for a quick shower.

I'd woken up early, letting Sondra snooze on the couch, gun in her lap, while I showered and shaved. She was still resting when I came out, and Anton hadn't visited yet, so I logged into my university email to check on Dante's progress. Dante's last email told me he felt prepared and ready to teach class today. The lecture notes he sent me looked good, and I wrote back to tell him I was grateful and hoped he had fun.

I then switched over to the ghost drive and logged into the Poker Geyser website to play a little and learn some more about it. The more I probed its depths, the more of its unusual features became apparent. Sondra had awoken to find me playing and writing down notes.

In another window, I simultaneously assembled the clearest frames of the mysterious 2:22am text. Sondra's recording was a two-second-long video clip. While most of the individual frames were blurry, the image processing software could sort things out through cross-comparison. In a matter of minutes, a conglomerate image displayed a phone whose text message was just barely legible.

The text was a sequence of nine numbers, each thirteen digits long. I didn't see an obvious meaning to them at first glance, and so I wrote them down on a piece of paper, and then typed them into a Note file on my phone. Finally, I typed the numbers into a spreadsheet program, just in case it might help with our analysis.

A few more minutes passed before one, then three, then two knocks thumped on our door. As I stood up to get the door, Sondra walked out of the bathroom in jeans and a T-shirt, vigorously drying her short brown hair with a towel. She stood by the table, picked up the Sig Sauer, and tossed the towel aside. She gave me a quick nod, telling me she was ready. I opened the door.

As expected, it was Anton. Impeccably groomed as always, he stood before me in his casino host uniform, a beaming smile lighting his way. He pushed a metal serving cart inside. It carried a small tray of pastries and two steaming carafes of coffee. I closed the door behind him.

"How is the lovely couple this morning?"

"Making some progress, we think," Sondra said, easing up the moment the door lock clicked. The three of us sat around a small table as Sondra recapped our discoveries and observations. She talked a lot about the girl parade, and how she was pretty sure all of them were from Czechia, probably the Prague area, and that most of them were probably models or escorts. I felt grateful when she skipped over the part where I had a meltdown in the pool.

She didn't mention I'd clarified the text message, of course, because I hadn't had the chance to tell her about it yet. When the perfect moment arose for me to insert that into the discussion, I held back. It was a gut feeling. It was like a quiet voice deep in my subconscious, warning me to keep it on the down low, at least until we knew what the message meant.

Sondra ended her briefing by mentioning the precise table where Soner had held a meeting after the tournament.

"I'll see what I can do about bugging that table for you," Anton said. He got up and walked to the computer, looking at the screen. He seemed to hesitate for a moment. He turned to me and gestured to it with his hand, asking if he could use it.

"Please do," I said.

He minimized every window I'd had open, and then typed a URL into the dark web browser. He selected a few options on what looked like a black screen, and then turned to face us again.

"If I manage to place the bug, this site will record everything. You can listen live and rewind and playback, just like the lobby cameras, except that it will be audio only."

"That'll work," Sondra said. "Good luck."

Anton gave his customary shallow bow, grinning, his eyes never leaving Sondra, and then he left.

I poured us coffees and polished off a croissant while Sondra finished her morning routine. I sat back in a chair, notepad in hand, staring at the numbers from the text. Lines and patterns slowly emerged as I gazed. I felt as though the numbers were swarming around me. They had color and texture, and in my head I could walk among them, like trees in a forest. Slowly, the trees started talking to me.

0019978130539
0039400131446
0078300132208
0156100132821
0311700133304
0622900133755
1245300134143
2490100134517
4879700134816

When Sondra emerged from the bathroom, she walked straight over to the computer and examined the screen. She leaned in, staring at the bold numbers.

"You didn't mention you'd cleaned up the text," she said.

"I just finished. I don't know what it means yet. But I'm beginning to notice some things.

"Is it a code?"

"I don't think so," I said. "Encrypted numbers generally don't have patterns. They just look random. Or semi-random, technically. But I see definite patterns here."

"Like all the zeros in the middle."

We spent the next several minutes making observations about the numbers. The thirteens that appeared in the eighth and ninth digits in every line. Double zeroes before that in every line but the first. The fact that the numbers are written in ascending order, which must be intentional since the odds of that happening by accident were less than one in three hundred thousand. The more patterns we noticed, the more I was certain that the numbers could be taken at face value.

"Makes sense the numbers aren't encrypted," I said. "Soner's probably the one sending them. He's a software engineer, working with other people on a project. He'd value clarity. Efficiency. He wants to communicate something without distortion or error, in as compact a way as possible."

"But what?" Sondra grumbled. "What numbers have thirteen digits?"

"Maybe each line is two numbers," I suggested. On my pad, I drew a vertical line between the double zeroes and the thirteens, splitting all the lines nearly in half. I held it up to show Sondra. "If you break it up like this, the numbers on the right are all going up too."

We puzzled on the grid for several more minutes. I started thinking about the rates of increase of the numbers. It seemed as though the numbers on the left were increasing exponentially, nearly doubling each time, while the numbers on the right were increasing more steadily, almost linearly.

I told Sondra this, and she looked perplexed. Not a mathematician. She had her hand on her chin, staring off into space, lost in deep thought, mumbling the word "thirteen" to herself over and over. A few minutes later, she straightened up quickly and turned to me, a flash of inspiration in her eye.

"What times did the tournament run yesterday?"

"It started at one o'clock," I said. "I think I remember it ended a little after one in the morning."

"It started at thirteen hundred hours," she said. "Military time. Most of Europe, too. That's the last six digits."

I took another quick look and noticed that not only were those six digits always increasing, but the second and fourth digits from the right never got higher than five. The last four digits were minutes and seconds. I felt sure she was right. The right side was a sequence of nine times, precise to the second, between one and two in the afternoon. There were five minutes, give or take, between each of the specific times. And since the times were given to the second, it was reasonable to assume that precision was important.

"So the first seven digits maybe say what happens at those times?" Sondra guessed aloud.

"They're almost doubling, but not quite. Give me a minute."

I flipped to a new sheet on the pad and started trying to find the exact pattern. The last two digits on the left side were always two zeroes, except for the first row. I found that perplexing, so I ignored the first row and focused on the rest. The pattern then became clear almost immediately.

"Double and subtract five," I announced. "Just look at the first five digits, and each time you double the number, then take away five. Except for the first row, that one's off by a bit. That one would have to be 199.5 for it to work."

"Okay. Well…what doubles every five minutes?"

My mind raced. Doubling every five minutes. In poker? Double ups? Doubling your stack when you go all in and win a showdown. Double, double, toil and trouble. I had no idea. My eyes fell upon the page of notes I'd made about the Poker Geyser site. I felt my eyes go wide as it finally dawned on me.

"The clue isn't the doubling, it's the minus five," I said. "One of the unusual features of this site is you can set up a heads-up match for any stakes you want, and the site rakes five percent up to a maximum of five dollars. If you play a match like that, you win double your buy-in, minus the rake."

"That makes sense," Sondra agreed. "These numbers might be instructions on setting up matches online. But don't matches like that take longer than a couple of minutes?"

"If both players are trying, they usually do. They can take hours if both players are talented, and the stacks are deep. But what if neither player is trying? What if they don't care who wins?"

Sondra's face scrunched in confusion, and I ignored it for the moment and leapt up toward the computer. I brought the Poker Geyser window back up and clicked open the option for creating tournaments. Sondra watched as I showed her how easily I could make one. I set it for a five dollar buy-in. I pointed at the screen to show her where my match sat waiting, with a "(1/2)" next to the "$5" listing.

"That means one out of two players is ready," I explained. The screen showed about twenty similar listings of varied buy-in amounts, all of them with "(1/2)" next to the listing. As we watched, a few new ones appeared, matches created by some unknown players. They were waiting for someone to accept their challenges. A few other lines disappeared, and I explained that those were challenges that had been accepted, and that heads-up match was underway on some hidden table. The fact that the table was hidden, I pointed out, was another one of the unusual features of the site.

As we watched, my listing switched momentarily to say "(2/2)," and then the listing disappeared. A second later, an online poker table with two seats popped up on my screen in a new window. Cards were then dealt to me and my opponent, whose username was "AJAXgoool69." A side panel specified that the winner of the contest would be credited with $9.50. I pointed out to Sondra that this was the sum of our buy-ins, less five percent. I then closed the window.

"Wait a minute," Sondra said. "Weren't you just in a match?"

"Yeah, and I just forfeited," I said. "The site will blind me out. It'll fold every hand until I'm out of chips.

Some lucky guy out there gets a little of my money for free."

"That's how online poker works, huh?" Sondra mused. "And you're good at this?"

"Not really," I said. "I do well at live poker, but online is much harder. High stakes online is full of some of the best players in the world. I program bots to play micro stakes, just to collect data so I can learn from great players. Sometimes I play middle stakes just to work on aspects of my game, but I avoid the big games online. I'm not in those guys' league."

"Is Soner in that league?"

I laughed. "Not from what I've seen. Besides, online poker is illegal in Turkey. I don't think they have legal gambling at all except for national lotteries."

We fell silent for a few minutes, thinking over what we'd deduced. We drank coffee and ate pastries. Sondra leaned back on the couch and chewed her lip. We were onto something, and she realized it. I caught her discreetly eyeing her gun. I knew she had different orders than me, and I wondered exactly what those were. As if aware of my thoughts, she looked up at that moment and continued the discussion.

"So, the numbers on the left are dollars?" she surmised.

"I think they're buy-in amounts. That's why all the double zeroes at the end. Those are the cents. The first five digits are the dollars."

"They buy in for that amount, at that precise time. And if they win, they take their winnings and buy in for the next amount at the next time?"

"Exactly," I said. "They lose five dollars in rake each time, but every win doubles their money. They start with about two hundred dollars, and if they win nine times, they finish with almost one hundred thousand."

"But how do they make sure the matches are over fast enough?"

"By agreeing to both go all in on the first hand, every time, no matter what. They're basically flipping a coin every time."

For a few moments, Sondra wondered aloud what kind of degenerate gamblers would play like that, before it finally dawned on her too. The players were all playing off the same bankroll. The sheikh's bankroll. It didn't matter who won, because the money was all coming from the same place and going to the same place.

"How many…"

"Five hundred twelve players," I interrupted, anticipating Sondra's questions. "They all buy in for about two hundred dollars, and an hour later, after five hundred eleven matches, and a total rake of about twenty-five hundred dollars, one of them has everything left. About ninety-nine thousand and change."

"Money laundering?"

I nodded at Sondra's suggestion, but as I thought about it, it didn't make sense. Sheikh al-Karchi hadn't been concerned with disguising his transfer of two million to Soner. All his businesses, as far as we could tell, were legitimate. Something wasn't adding up. I looked at Sondra, and the crinkle of her forehead made it clear she was having the same doubts.

"I don't know," I said. "I think we're still missing some pieces. I still don't understand why they'd go to all the trouble of setting something like this up. And why here? And for what purpose?"

Sondra stared at the computer screen, eyes dancing along with her thoughts. Then she looked at me. Her eyes looked through mine, but without their usual intensity. Her eyes weren't ablaze with the ferocity I'd come to except of her. I saw a fleeting glimpse of faith in them. I had finally impressed her. Yet I still had to look away, unable to match them.

"Suppose this goes on all day," she said. "One o'clock to one o'clock. Maybe that's what they were happy about at the end of the day yesterday."

"That would explain why we don't see the girls all day," I said. "They're working. Playing these coin-flip tournaments."

"How much money are we talking about?"

I thought about it for a moment. Twelve hours a day, for the next twenty-one days.

"About twenty-five million dollars," I said.

That got Sondra to her feet. She paced around the room, similarly to the way she did on the plane. She was a coiled jungle cat, stalking fresh prey. The pulse in her neck was visible across the room.

I didn't have to ask her what she was thinking. I was equally aware as her. Aware of history. About how many of the worst anti-American terrorist acts had been funded for less than a million dollars. What could al-Alrasid do with twenty-five million, free and clear, spendable on anything without being traced? I didn't want to find out.

"I'm going to need some time on that thing," she said, pointing to the computer. I stepped aside. She sat in front of the computer and closed out everything, and then opened the folder containing my redpack information. She was obviously formulating some sort of intelligence gathering plan, and I left her to her work.

I didn't need a computer to look up the day's tournament schedule. My phone was adequate for that purpose. It showed me that today's main event was the first day of a 2,222-Euro 8-handed PLO tournament, expected to draw many of the world's greatest players. It was a tournament I had no business entering, but if Soner was in it, I'd consider entering just to keep tabs on him.

I watched over Sondra's shoulder as she read the file on Soner, and then sorted through the scattered information Anton had provided about the thirty-two men Soner brought with him. She was probing for weakness.

"You said you thought the girls were tech support," she said. "Knowing what we know now, does that still make sense?"

"Definitely," I said. "Suppose they're in their rooms following the protocols from the text message, all day long. Probably doesn't take much expertise. Soner's a software engineer. He could hack a site and program bots as easily as I could. Just needs people with basic computer skills, willing to do what they're told for money."

"Must be a step up from their usual work," Sondra said, with a smirk.

"That's what's in the trunks. They need five hundred and twelve different computers to make it work. Thirty-two couples. They each brought sixteen laptop computers and accessories, programmed in advance to be ready to play these tournaments. All they need is to be monitored and fed the right buy-ins and times."

Sondra sat back and thought for a minute. She turned to me, a devious and focused expression on her face. The jungle cat was ready to pounce.

"If you're right, then every one of their rooms should have a trunk with sixteen computers in it. What do you think you could do, if…say…I got you two minutes alone with one of them?"

The rest of the morning, I was a surgeon at an operating table. My patient was the half million lines of code that ran the Poker Geyser software on my laptop. My attendants were Sondra, occasionally looking over my shoulder, and a pitcher of black coffee.

"What exactly are you doing?" Sondra asked.

"I want to be able to see Soner's coinflip matches when they happen. Then, we'll be sure."

"You can't just watch them?"

I shook my head and pointed to the window where players create and accept challenges. "This page is programmed to reload and update itself every fifteen seconds. Now, suppose all of Soner's girls set up matches with the same specifications, and the same buy-in amounts, all at the same precise second?"

"Their matches would be created, accepted, and started instantly," she said.

"They'd probably never even show up on this screen," I said. "No one would know."

"But aren't there records of every game played?"

"Sure," I said. "But who'd think to look for them? Maybe far into the future, if a reason cropped up for an investigation, they might be discovered."

"But all the money would be long gone by then. So long gone there'd be no tracing it. If you're right, this is bigger than we thought."

I paused for a moment and turned toward her. "Who's we, exactly?" I asked.

"We…have been aware of al-Karchi for some time. We…have authorized me to act against any confirmed terrorist activity. And it looks like you found some."

"I understand," I said. Control was behind my assignment to the mission, but this mission was a piece of something greater, probably initiated above Control's level. Twenty-five million potentially disappearing into the ether, making its way to al-Alrasid's coffers. If our theories were correct, they'd already cleared the first million, and then some.

"I'll leave you to it," she said. "I'll go walk about, play a few slots, and see what I see."

I watched as she stepped out the door, blonde wig swishing behind her. What thoughts swirled beneath it? The gun on the table, which she had not bothered to put back into the safe, told me she'd be returning soon. I guessed she'd be looking for Anton, to update him.

I walked over to the window and looked out over the rolling, forested hills. My deep breaths matched time with the swaying of the trees. I listened to the faint creaking of the window glass, buffeted by the crosswind. The parking lot was still, and the helipad was empty. Not a soul in sight. What a beautiful and unexpected place for counterterrorism.

I refocused on my coding. Thankfully, the security of the software was primitive. It was almost as though it were inviting hackers. Kadri Soner was surely one of them, and now it was my turn.

By the time Sondra returned forty minutes later, I was certain I could make the challenges page refresh almost continually and was making progress on a means of creating and revoking a challenge within a split second. I looked up to explain it to her and saw that the corners of her eyes were slightly drooped, and her lips pressed together.

"You look disappointed," I said. "Something happen?"

"No. Yeah. Well, I couldn't find Anton, that's all. Guess he's busy."

"See anything interesting?"

"The buffet was packed, and the poker hall is bustling. Must be something big starting up soon."

I looked at my phone and saw it was nearly one o'clock. The big PLO tournament was about to begin, and more importantly, Soner's girls would be starting their second day of work.

"If Soner holds to his pattern from yesterday, he'll enter the tournament today. It'll just be for show, though. He'll be more interested in reports from his capos, as they monitor the girls."

"You should try to get close to him," Sondra suggested, as though reading my mind. "We need to know what his guys are telling him."

It wasn't long before I'd thrown on a hoodie and we were on our way down. By the time Sondra and I made it to the lounge, it was just past one. Most of the tournament players had settled into their tables. There was a short queue of late-redgers at the registration kiosk. We made ourselves small plates of hors d'oeuvres, as an excuse to look around.

I didn't see Soner anywhere, or any of the tan guards, but Veronique was at her usual perch. It seemed odd to see her, alone at a bare table, after she'd been accompanied by tan guards the last few times. I was careful not to make eye contact with her, but I got the eerie sense that she was watching us, and Sondra in particular.

"Check your nine," Sondra whispered, advising me to look to my left. I subtly glanced over, moving only my eyes, and saw the smallest of the three tan guards walking into the lounge. He walked straight over to Veronique's table and sat across from her. The two slightly leaned in, and I got the impression she was speaking to him in soft tones, inaudible over the room's clatter.

"I'm going to see where he came from," she said, and took her plate with her toward the main hall.

I made myself a seventh cup of coffee for the day and sipped it while standing at the ledge, looking out on the tournament. As before, Soner's men were mostly avoiding the tournament, playing at cash tables or just lounging around at empty tables. I felt my phone vibrate.

<<Found your friend. Come play blackjack with us.>>

I ditched the coffee and walked into the main hall. I expected to find Sondra talking to Anton at a blackjack table. Instead, she was sitting at an empty table, slowly playing 5 Euros a hand while pecking into her phone. I sat down next to her, waving off the dealer to indicate I didn't want to be dealt cards.

"Anton around?"

"Haven't seen him," she said, and slid her phone to me across the felt. I looked down and saw she was watching the official Casino Rozvadov stream of the TV table.

I looked at her, puzzled, until it dawned on me. Soner was sitting at the TV table, talking to the two burly tan guards who stood behind him. Play hadn't begun at this table yet, unlike most of the other tables. A few seats were empty, and the tournament director was standing off to the side next to Goran Urusov, the owner. Veins throbbed near Goran's temples as he leaned in toward the director. I was too far away to hear him, but he was clearly speaking forcefully and angrily, pointing at someone else in the distance.

"Odds are they're speaking Czech," Sondra said. "Good luck."

I nodded and put in my earbuds. I switched my translation app to Czech as I walked over. I could now see which player he was pointing at, but it was no one I recognized. I slowed my approach, hoping to hear as much as possible before reaching him.

"…we have two big names here … three amateurs, no good … explain coward rules …" the app spoke into my right ear, in a much more pleasant voice than Goran's.

"Excuse me," I said, tapping him lightly on his shoulder. "I couldn't help but overhear. See that guy in seat four? He coolered and slow-rolled me twice yesterday. Put me at his table, and I promise you good action. I owe that jerk some pain."

Goran's eyes widened slightly for a moment before he regained his poker face. He glanced at the director and then back at me.

"I like your spirit, young man, but we don't do that. Please go to your randomly assigned chair."

"Sorry," I said, and walked off.

I headed straight for the registration kiosk. I swiped an entry form for the tournament and started filling in my information, including that the entry fee should be taken from my credit line at the casino. I folded it up and tucked it in a back pocket.

I looked toward the bar and saw three of Soner's Turkish players there, having beers and watching a soccer match. I switched my phone app to Turkish and started walking over, when the phone vibrated in my hand.

<<Think you made an impression!>>

I turned and saw Goran walking quickly toward me, tense and grimacing. A security guard walked several paces behind him, apparently having just tracked me down and pointed me out.

"You there! Come with me, please!"

CHAPTER 22   Shaken, Not Stirred

Goran's eyes were ablaze, and laser-focused on me. A few players at nearby tables turned to see the commotion. I didn't look around to see whether any of Soner's guys were watching, but it was a safe bet. Everybody knew who Goran was. He was always the center of attention wherever we went.

"Is something wrong, sir?" I said.

"You still want the TV table?"

"Um, yes. Yes, sir."

"I'll make it happen. Follow me."

Goran led me back to the TV table. I explained that I had planned to have a drink and then late-redge, and he nodded. I handed him my folded-up form.

"Two thousand, two hundred twenty-two Euros from your account," he read aloud, holding the form in one hand, and clamping down on my shoulder with the other hand. I tried not to recoil from the shock of the unexpected contact. "Very good, young man. I'll have this paperwork taken care of. You just sit down and play. And I'll have a martini service sent to your table, on the house. You're doing me a big favor."

"How's that, sir?"

"See that punk ass in the racing scarf, there?" He motioned toward the guy I saw him pointing at earlier. "He gets drawn for the TV table, and he won't play on it. Throws a biiiig temper tantrum. Stupid internet punk."

"Isn't it right there on the form, the casino has the rights to his image and can use it for media and marketing?"

"Yes! See, you can read, unlike that punk. He says he won't sit down, and we can just blind him out until we switch tables at the break. I can't have that on my livestream. Looks terrible."

He slapped down hard on my shoulder twice. I suspected he meant it warm-heartedly, like a proud father might do to his son, but he didn't know his own strength. He was clearly someone who valued courage and toughness. From my redpack reading, I knew integrity could be added to that list.

"Thank you for the opportunity," I said. "I'll try to give you a good show."

We arrived at the table, and the other eight players looked up from their chairs as Goran himself ushered me to Seat Two. Soner sat two seats to my left, at my ten o'clock. I wondered whether I would be close enough to hear him whispering to the numerous visitors I expected him to have.

Behind Soner, the thirty-foot long screen alternated between two different, bright presentations. One was a swirling pattern of undulating blue and gold, which I found difficult to look at. The other was a detailed information screen featuring the tournament clock, level and a number of chip stack statistics, the bright white numbers seeming to burst from their background. I'd seen these images on the casino's livestreams before, but now that I was being forced to look into them from twelve feet away, I felt overwhelmed. The visual discomfort made me more aware of the constant rattle of chip shuffling and the murmurs of the railbirds encircling us. I tried to put it all out of my mind. I felt myself starting to rock in my seat and focused on stopping myself.

As the dealer laid out my stack of starting chips, I dialed Arabic into my phone app.

"Oh, I'm sorry, no phones at this table," Goran said. He pointed to a nearby rack of plastic bins. I was directed to put all electronic devices in the bin assigned to my seat. The idea was to prevent anyone watching the livestream from signaling me about other players' cards. Even though the stream was running on a thirty-minute delay, similar shows had been hacked before in other card rooms, and Casino Rozvadov wasn't taking any chances.

I sighed with resignation as I put my phone in the bin. I saw Sondra still playing blackjack, still pecking on her phone. She tilted her head for a moment as she met my glance. I shrugged. I sat back down in my chair, which faced away from her.

"Welcome to the table," the dealer said as he pushed the latest pot to a player and collected the cards. I tapped the felt back at him and sorted my chips. The swirling barrage to my left amplified my feelings of being out of place. This tournament's buy-in was more than ten times bigger than I'd ever played before, and my opponents had a hundred times my experience. My one solace was the fact that winning wasn't important. My goal was to monitor Soner, nothing more. Despite my promise to Goran, I'd be playing super tight, more interested in lasting a long time than in winning.

The fact that PLO doesn't have antes would help me last longer. In this game, a player is dealt four cards each hand, but if he plays, he must use exactly two of them at showdown, no more, no less. The other difference is that the maximum bet or raise at any time is only the size of the pot. And if you think that means the game plays smaller than no limit Hold'Em, you'd be sorely mistaken.

I watched Soner closely. He didn't have the same air of indifference as the day before. When he peeked at his hand, his eyes danced involuntarily, as though he were calculating. His throat twitched, suggesting subvocalization. He was talking to himself, thinking. I wondered if that meant his guard was down. With his operation going smoothly, he was less uptight and had the mental energy to actually play.

A few minutes in, I was dealt my first decent hand: a pair of kings and a pair of nines. I limped in under the gun, and play folded around to the button, a forty-something Las Vegas pro in a Golden Knights hockey jersey. He tossed in a pot-sized raise with the swagger of Billy Budd, and I felt myself wilting already. I was ridiculously out of my league, and positive half the table could smell it.

"How would you like your martini, sir?"

I slowly turned around as the blinds folded. An elderly man in a tuxedo stood behind me, awaiting my order. At his side was a linen-covered cart topped with stainless steel tumblers, assorted liquors, and other mixable items.

"Um … I don't know. How does Mr. Urusov like them? I'll have it how he likes it, please."

"Very good, sir." The loud shaking of liquors in tumblers directly behind my head distracted me and made me flinch. Action was on me. I slid in a few chips to call.

The flop came king of spades, six of hearts, seven of clubs. A fantastic flop for me, giving me top set, and if the board paired I would be almost unbeatable. It was also a "dry" board, unlikely to bring in a flush or straight draw.

"A squeeze of lemon, sir?"

I turned around again, paused a few seconds, and then shook my head.

"Hey! It's on you!" my opponent called.

"Sorry." I knocked once on the felt to indicate a check and then turned back to the man with the cart.

"Pot!" the Vegas pro said, indicating he was again making the maximum allowed raise.

"How many olives, sir?"

"Uh…just a moment," I told the waiter, and turned back to the table, trying my best to look irritated as I pushed in calling chips. Once I had, I turned back around. "Three, please."

Behind me, I heard the dealer slap down the turn. I looked past the cart to see Sondra, staring at me with a quizzical expression, chin resting on one hand. I winked at her. She just shook her head, expressionlessly.

I glanced back to see the turn card and picked up a few chips at random and splashed the pot. I received the martini while the dealer sorted it out, and my opponent began assembling calling chips. He was about to push them over the line, when he paused and stared at me. His expression was a mix of wariness and amusement.

"How's that martini?" he asked. "Not too dry, I hope."

"I wouldn't know," I said. "I've never had one before." Half the table laughed, including my opponent, who then folded a hand with pocket aces in it, face up. It occurred to me, as the table settled back down, that I might have "lost some value," in terms of not winning as many chips as I could have. But what I'd gained was better. Probably no one at the table considered me a serious player now. I was a fun and unthreatening tourist clown. I would inevitably be defeated and forgotten. It played.

For the next two hours, I only played four hands, following the basic tenet of "tight is right." Pocket aces and double-suited rundowns. Maybe one hand per two orbits. Little chance of reaching the money playing so tight, but a great strategy for treading water a long while.

I paid more attention to Soner than the cards. Not once in the first two hours did he go more than ten minutes without one of the tan guards walking up to him for a moment, or him getting up to speak briefly to one of his capos at the rail. I understood nothing of what little I heard, and my phone was twenty feet away, useless.

When the dealer announced it was the last hand before the first break, I sighed with relief. I looked down at garbage cards and mucked them, springing to my feet, eager to escape the assault on my senses for twenty minutes. But before I could head off to find Sondra, Goran walked up to the table. He was there to tell us that we wouldn't be changing tables after the break. He was satisfied with the action and would be showcasing us for another two rounds. Glancing back once more at the swirling maelstrom of the giant screen, I winced at the thought of having to deal with it for two more hours.

I saw Sondra at the rail and went over to her.

"How are you doing?" she asked.

"I'm okay. The bright lights are a little intense."

"No, I mean, have you gotten any more information about Soner or his operation?"

"No, I can't hear much," I said. "I think he's speaking Arabic to the tan guards, and Turkish to his players, but I don't understand it. I can tell you that he seems confident and on top of whatever's happening. He's just going about his routine, pretending to be here to play in the EPC events, and not playing too badly. He's actually pretty good when he's trying."

I looked around and saw Soner talking to one of the two burly tan guards. The other was waiting at the rail. None of Soner's girls were around, of course, but Veronique and the thin tan guard were walking in from the direction of the lounge area.

"You walked around a bit, the last few hours?" I asked.

"Of course."

"Did Veronique have tea in front of her?"

"Huh?"

"Did she have tea? Did she have a cup in front of her?"

"No," Sondra said, her eyes shifting up and to the left as she recalled her recent memories. "What does it matter?"

"I don't know," I said. "I'm just trying to see patterns. Sometimes I fixate on weird details. Her presence in a casino, just sitting and watching everything, is weird enough all by itself."

"Let's get out of here for ten minutes."

Sondra and I walked outside. A harsh wind greeted us, and I would have pulled my hood up if I hadn't been too overstimulated to notice. Sondra crossed her arms against the cold and walked with me, out past the valet parking and halfway to the highway.

"Any news from Anton?" I asked.

"Haven't seen him since this morning. I'm hoping to run some ideas by him before we make a move."

"Make a move…as in hacking one of their computers? Can he help with that?"

"Not directly," she said. "Ideas. Planning, maybe. But I'm the one who does it. He's sticking his neck out far enough as it is. We won't burn him, same as we won't burn you."

"I appreciate that."

"Just see that you don't burn yourself, kid," she said. "You're on the TV table. The chat on the livestream was pretty lively with people joking about that martini service. The opposition is aware you exist now. They better not figure out you're more than just a player."

"Gimme your phone," I told Sondra, as we walked back in. "I want to see the footage."

"Worried how you look on TV?"

"I'm looking for patterns. Probing Soner for weakness."

"Now you're talking."

I rewound the livestream footage for two hours as we walked. Entering the lounge, I sat at the first open table, studious. I was peripherally aware that Sondra had gone to get us lattes, but otherwise my surroundings faded away. Cards and numbers and suits. I fast forwarded through the footage, stopping only to watch the hands Soner played.

By the time she returned with our drinks, I had finished. I pushed her phone back to her.

"Well? What's the scoop, kid?"

"He only raised pre-flop once, when he had pocket aces, double suited. All the other hands he played, he had pocket queens, kings, or aces, not double suited, and he either limped or called. No raises unless he made a set or better."

"Reminder. I'm not a poker player."

"I think I have a good sense of what he plays and how he plays it. Maybe enough of a sense to use it against him. I don't know. Depends how the cards fall."

"Okay," she said, through clinched teeth. "Well, go do your thing. Eyes sharp."

I was deliberately late returning to the table and missed the first few hands. I had a lot to think about, and being casual about my return fit well with my table image anyway. Sondra was right in that I had to look like a poker player. If I hung at the same table with Soner for a day or more, never confronting him, he might be aware enough to notice it and wonder about me. I decided to look for a spot against him. Any excuse to get some chips in the middle against him. Just one big pot. Win or lose, it would serve as a plausible excuse for me to avoid him the rest of the tournament.

Unfortunately, he and I seemed to be "card dead" at all the wrong times. If I was in a hand, then he wasn't, and vice versa. Frustration propelled me to my feet, pacing to and from the rail several times. Each time was a temporary reprieve from the barrage of sound and swirling lights that continually blasted me like storm winds on a sailboat. I looked around for Sondra whenever I was up, but she was off somewhere else. There was no sign of Veronique or any of the tan guards either, though Soner was still being visited by his men every five to ten minutes.

Halfway through the session, I sat back down to an announcement that the blinds were going up again. My stack was slowly bleeding out. I wasn't in dire straits yet, but the next big hand needed to go my way, or I would be. But for another hour, my card dead woes continued. My stack was dangerously short by the time Goran walked up the table.

"Last hand before the one-hour dinner break," he said, and stepped back out of the camera view to watch. As the dealer shuffled, the tournament director walked around the table handing out sealable bags for our chips. We were being moved to a regular table after the break. I breathed a sigh of relief.

I was on the button and looked down at the king of hearts, jack of spades, jack of clubs, and three of clubs. The action folded to me, and I raised, expecting to steal the blinds. The small blind folded, but Soner peered at me through his glasses for a moment, and then called. Finally, a hand against him.

The dealer gathered up the pot, burned a card, and spread the flop. The cards made a light slapping noise on the table before the dealer spread them, but I wasn't looking at it. I focused on Soner, hoping to catch his reactions and microexpressions as he watched the flop. What I saw instead was him staring back at me. Trying to do the same. I felt instantly uncomfortable meeting his gaze, and broke it off, but still refused to look at the flop until he acted.

Soner looked, then slid out a half-pot bet before continuing to stare at me.

I finally looked at the flop. Three of diamonds, ace of clubs, jack of diamonds. I'd flopped a set of jacks, but on a dangerous board. I was way behind Soner if he had pocket aces, and another diamond on the board would make a diamond flush possible.

I cut out calling chips and splashed the pot with them. The dealer tried to suppress a look of annoyance as he collected the chips into a pile. He burned another card and laid out the turn. Again, I looked over to see Soner's reaction, only to find him looking back. He adjusted his glasses, never taking his eyes off me, the other features of his face set in stone. His eyes bore into mine, and again I had to look away.

This time I looked to see the flop card, the eight of diamonds, and then quickly looked back at him. He had raised his right hand to brush through his hair slowly, but really, he was hiding his eyes from me as he looked at the flop card. I could still see a slight flare of his nostrils as he looked. An almost imperceptible swelling of his nose. Erectile cartilage. He really, really liked that card.

He looked down at the felt and held stock still for the better part of a minute. A palpable tension settled upon the table like the calm before a storm. Normally, uninvolved players on the last hand before a break would get up, bag their chips, and rush to grab their phones out of the bins. They had all finished bagging, but not one had left the table. The Las Vegas pro from the martini hand, in particular, leaned in with great interest. The pot was already bigger than the shortest stack at the table.

Eventually, Soner looked up at me and tapped the felt with one finger, checking.

I knew he'd hit the nut flush. No doubt in my mind. But he'd made the mistake of giving me a free look at the river card. I checked back.

Burn card. River. Ace of spades. I'd made a full house, a "full boat," my set of jacks with the two aces on the board. But it was an "underboat." Soner had the ace of diamonds, so if any of his other three cards connected with the board, he would have a better full house. An "overboat."

Soner wasted no time sorting through his chips. He took a few from one stack, then another, seeming to calculate carefully as he did. Finally, he pushed an odd assortment of chips over the betting line.

"Can I get a count of that?" I asked the dealer, who nodded in confirmation.

I glanced at the Vegas pro, whose face scrunched with his head tilted to the side as he looked at Soner's bet. Through his perplexed expression, I half expected him to mutter "what the hell?" I looked back to Soner's stack to see how much he had behind. I counted his stacks twice—a nice, round 34,000.

"Bet is 14,350 to go," the dealer announced. It was close to but not exactly what I had left. This bet size didn't make sense, because he could have just said "pot" and accomplished the same thing, strategically.

It occurred to me that he wasn't counting a precise bet. He was precisely counting the chips he had left. He was making sure he had enough to last a while, bleeding through the blinds, just in case he lost. And if he thought he was beatable, then he couldn't have pocket aces. I decided to have faith in my livestream study, and assume his ace was accompanied by pocket kings or queens, and some dangler. And most danglers miss that board.

"Call," I said.

Soner looked at me quizzically. "What do you have?" he said. I'd never heard his voice before, and it surprised me how deep it was.

"You've been called," I said, invoking the standard rule that a called bet has to be the first to showdown his hand. Soner winced slightly at this. He glared at me for a few seconds, before flipping over his hand. Ace of diamonds, king of diamonds, king of clubs, four of hearts.

"Nut diamond flush," the dealer announced.

I flipped over my hand and pushed the two jacks slightly forward.

"Jacks over aces," the dealer announced. "Full house wins." The dealer shoved the massive pot in my direction with two hands, like a snowplow clearing a road. A few players slapped the table a few times, eyes lively and widened, and then made a bee line for the storage bins. I had to stay at the table for a minute to collect and bag my chips. I looked up for a moment to see Soner, still standing at the table, still staring at me, a silent rage burning. He thumped the table once, his polite gesture betrayed by vicious eyes. He turned and walked over to his tan guards, all three of them waiting at the rail.

I finished bagging and sealed it up, eager to get away from the table. Sondra stood waiting in the archway leading toward the lounge. But as I headed her way, a tall red-headed man in a polo shirt and jeans blocked me. The livestream techie. He pulled off his headset.

"Carly would like to interview you, please."

"Oh, I can't, I'm late for…"

"I have to insist, sir," the techie said, with the tournament director walking up behind him. I knew that I was contractually obligated to give a quick segue way interview if asked. It was on the waiver. It seemed I'd be unable to dodge it.

"Okay, just for a minute though. I'm late for something."

"That'll work," Carly said, walking up with a wireless microphone. I recognized her immediately from numerous poker livestreams, her high stakes play on television, and some of her modeling work in fashion ads.

"I've never done this before," I admitted.

"Just relax and be yourself. And try not to look at the camera."

"Okay, I'll just look at you," I said. She flinched uncomfortably, and then faked a smile to cover it. I tried to tune out the loud chatter of the railbirds. The bright lights and slot machine chiming of the main hall. A blinding white light from just behind the camera. The scent of Carly's perfume. I almost jumped as she gently grabbed my elbow.

"Just a few inches this way. A little more. There, perfect. Alright, here we go…."

The camera's red light came on. She introduced the two of us and gave my quick bio, memorized from an index card moments before. Amateur player from Pittsburgh. Thirty years old. Professor.

"So, Thomas, this is your first time at the EPC. How are you enjoying it?"

"It's fantastic. I feel constantly overwhelmed. The food is amazing. And everywhere I go, I seem to discover something new and exotic. And beautiful."

Carly nodded, giving another fake smile, and drifted back a few inches.

"That was some hand at the end of the last session. Would you like to talk about it for us?"

"No, thank you."

Carly stared at me with a look of disbelief for a long, awkward moment. She forced a quick chuckle to break the tension.

"I just don't want to give too much away," I said. "You're a high stakes player. You know what I'm talking about."

"Okay, well…tell me about the PLO scene back in Pittsburgh."

"Great bunch of guys," I said. "Have you ever been to Pittsburgh? Great town, you'd love it."

"Haven't been yet."

"The view of the city at night from the top of Mt. Washington. Breathtaking. Romantic. I'd love it if you came to visit me."

She turned away from me sharply and looked into the camera.

"Thomas Vale, running good in his first EPC. And that's all for now. We'll have a new table for you on the other side of the break."

The red light above the camera switched off. Carly tossed her microphone onto a podium and flashed me an angry look before skulking away, her techie in tow. I turned and walked in the other direction, to where Sondra was standing, hand over her mouth, trying not to laugh.

"I was trying to get away quickly," I explained. "I'm trying to maintain the image of someone who shouldn't be taken seriously."

"Congratulations," Sondra laughed. "I doubt you'll have to worry about being interviewed again." She gestured toward the hallway. "Come on, I want to go over some plans back in the room."

We walked back toward the hotel. A long quiet break would be just what the doctor ordered. As we turned a hallway corner, I glanced back for a moment, and saw the biggest of the tan guards following, ten yards behind us.

"Big tan company, six o'clock," I whispered.

"You wanted to make an impression. Now you pay for it. I can't help unless your life is in danger. Remember, you're just a player."

We reached the elevators, and I hit the up button. It opened immediately, empty, and we entered. Sondra hit our floor as the tan guard walked in. He was as tall as me, but had at least one hundred pounds on me, all of it muscle. He didn't turn to hit a floor button. He just stood in the middle of the elevator, looking at me, and waited for the doors to close. As soon as they did, he reached out with one hand and flipped up one side of my shirt collar.

"That's a nice shirt. Can I have it? Why don't you take it off and give it to me right now?"

"Get your own."

"I like this one," he said, and grabbed my shirt below the shoulders with both hands, using it to slam me back into the corner.

"Fuck off!" I yelled, punching him in the ribs as hard as I could. It barely moved him.

"Let him go!" Sondra yelled, cringing and shrunk in the other back corner.

A ding sounded that we'd reached our floor. As the doors opened, he pulled me in close, his bloodshot, crazed eyes inches from mine. He tossed me like a rag doll out of the elevator. Sondra took the opportunity to leap out of the elevator and throw herself on me, like a terrified girlfriend. He stood at the doors, holding them open, and looked down at us with fiery glare.

"I bet you think what you did to my friend was cool, right? You dump those chips back to him, or I'll be back for that shirt. And your bitch, too. You have no friends here. Remember that!"

And he let the doors shut. We got up and I straightened out my clothes. Neither Sondra nor I said a word until we were back in our room.

"You okay?" she said.

"Yeah."

"You did great. Now we know for sure those guys are enforcers. And also…they definitely have no idea you're intelligence."

"How do we know that?"

"Because that's not the sort of thing where they let you off with a warning."

CHAPTER 24   Before the Storm

"The best time for me to raid one of their rooms will be tonight at 1:20am," Sondra said, and I agreed. Based on the night before, Soner's girls should have made their exodus from their rooms by then, with most of their roommates still playing poker, or relaxing at the bar, or in a meeting with Soner himself at the far end of the poker hall.

Over the next thirty minutes, Sondra briefed me on her plan. The timing, my role in it, equipment, infil and exfil strategies, contingencies. Her experience and command presence reminded me of the instructors back at The Farm.

I set to work modifying a special flash drive, three of which had been included with my equipment. Inserted into a laptop port, it could download the entire contents of a laptop in a few minutes, but that wouldn't be fast enough for our purposes.

It took me the better part of an hour, but I managed to modify it to instead download a virus. The virus would cause the laptop to upload its contents to our ghost drive through the hotel internet. It would also discreetly turn on the laptop's microphone, transmitting audio continually to a dark web site, effectively turning the laptop into a bug. The program would run invisibly, not showing up on routine scans.

"Aren't you late for the restart," Sondra said.

"I had to make sure this was done in time," I said, handing her the flash drive. "Besides, they think I'm scared and intimidated. It plays for me to show up a little late."

"Are you actually going to dump chips to Soner?"

"Maybe. If he's struggling and I need to keep him in it. Or if I need to appear scared. Speaking of which, my distraught poker girlfriend…it's probably best if you don't show up downstairs at all."

"Suits me," she said. "I'll get us some room service. Stretch a little. And front load some sleep, 'cause it just might be a wild night. This part of the op right now…it's the hardest part sometimes."

"What do you mean?"

"The waiting."

On the walk back toward the gaming halls, I began to understand what she meant. The walk somehow seemed longer than before, and the lights brighter. I knew the difference was only in my mind. My stomach churned uneasily. It was the uncomfortable dread of being intensely focused, aimed arrow-straight at the solution to a problem, but unable to do anything yet. I yearned for the end of the day, and the relief of action.

We'd been moved to a new table during the break. When I arrived, about an hour late, I felt a momentary rush of panic at the sight of the tan guard standing behind Soner. It was the same one who had assaulted me in the elevator. I felt a chill in my palms, and unconsciously rubbed them together as I walked up to my seat.

Soner's eyes met mine, and his chest swelled for a moment with confidence. His strong gaze and half smirk made it clear he felt dominant. He owned me and wanted me to know it. I quickly quelled my own pride and anger and reminded myself—that's how we want him to feel.

I had lost a few orbits worth of blinds during my absence, but I managed to win a few hands here and there, hanging tough. I ended up dumping chips to Soner without even trying to, on a hand where he reraised from the blinds. By the time ten o'clock came around, and we got up for the last break of the day, it was clear that both Soner and I would likely survive to Day Two, which started tomorrow at 1pm.

I walked quickly through the lounge, passing all three tan guards, making sure not to look at them. I went straight back to the room, looking over my shoulder a few times, and taking the stairs rather than the elevator. The hallway was clear, and I gave the code knock before entering. Sondra beckoned me over with a wave. A large veggie pizza, still steaming, sat on the table before her.

"You just missed Anton," she said, through a mouthful of dinner. "Guess he's been busy with errands and a trip to Prague all day, but he's back now. Managed to plant a bug at that far table, too."

A small window in the corner of the computer screen displayed bars going up and down, indicating audio levels. We were recording ordinary cash play at the moment. But it wouldn't be difficult for Anton to pull a few strings and arrange for the table to be empty from midnight on. With a little luck, Soner might use it again, and we'd be listening.

"Did we get any hits on the Poker Geyser site today?" I asked.

"I didn't check. I'll leave that to you."

I snatched up the laptop and scrolled back through the screen recording, pausing near the time indices mentioned in the intercepted text message. The first several times revealed nothing. But finally, after several minutes of searching, I paused at a precise moment and turned the screen to show Sondra. For a split second, at precisely 1:45pm and seventeen seconds, a head's up challenge worth $24,901 had appeared on the screen. At normal speed, it appeared and disappeared so quickly, you could literally blink and miss it.

"That settles it," Sondra said. "No doubts now. They're moving over a million dollars a day through this site, for reasons we still don't know."

"Maybe after tonight we'll know."

"That's the plan, and the plan is a go."

I took off my hoodie and threw on a peach-colored sweater. It was a reversible sweater, which I could switch to dark blue by turning it inside out. I grabbed one last piece of pizza and headed for the door.

"Eyes sharp," she called after me. "You know what to do. Watch your six, kid."

I closed the door behind me, and just stood there for a moment. I took a long, deep breath. The walk back to the tournament seemed even longer than the last time. By the time I took my seat, I felt as wound up as a watch spring. I wished I could skip the last few rounds of the day and spend an hour in the gym instead, just to blow off some steam.

I spent most of the next two hours on my phone, just to distract myself. I read and responded to emails from Dante and a few of my students and checked social media. I played a few hands in between, and somehow managed to chip up and stay above the rising tide of the blind levels. But mostly I watched the clock, almost pleading with my eyes for it to speed up.

"This is the last hand of Round 10," the PA announcer said. "Last hand of the night. Officials will be around to help you bag your chips. Congratulations on making it to Day Two!"

I folded a garbage hand and bagged about fifteen big blinds worth of chips as fast as I could. I jumped the buffet line by grabbing a calzone and a napkin off of the Italian spread and found my way to a small table that overlooked the poker hall. The food was just an excuse to be there. What mattered was that I had a good vantage point.

Most of the poker hall cleared out as the tournament players bagged up. About two dozen cash game tables were still running. True to his word, Anton had managed to clear out all the tables at the far end of the room. Neither Soner nor any of his men seemed to be heading that way yet, but it was still early.

Across the lounge, I saw that Veronique had reappeared. I could barely see her past the broad shoulders of the two burly tan guards who were sitting across from her with their backs to me. I checked my phone for the time. Ten minutes until go. I had just begun to wonder when Sondra would text me, when it appeared.

<< Any interesting dinner company tonight? >>

As if by cue, the first signs of the nightly girl parade started walking in. Within minutes, at least two dozen of Soner's girls were at the buffet, lining up for their first meal of the day.

<< They look hungry tonight >> I texted back.

<< Pick from the menu. One, two, or three? >>

I flipped to the ghost drive on my phone. Sondra had created an image file depicting three of Soner's capos whose rooms she was considering raiding. I turned toward the poker hall and looked for them. It took a minute, but I found all three of them playing together at the same cash table in the middle of the room.

I watched for a minute as one of them raked in a large pot, turning one way and another, laughing with his friends. It was Tomaj, the Albanian who had whipsawed me two days before. He had a huge stack, and it was about to get bigger. He swigged a mixed drink while one of his neighbors slapped him on the back with affection. He wasn't going anywhere soon. I glanced at the file on my phone and saw he was the second option.

<< #2 looks delicious >> I texted.

<< How many waiters do you see? >>

Sondra was asking about the tan guards. The two I'd seen, plus Veronique, had gotten up and were walking toward the back of the poker hall. Soner's nightly meeting was about to begin. Soner was walking toward the bugged table from the direction of the bar, a bottle of local beer in hand. A few of his capos seemed to be heading that way as well.

<< Two so far >> I texted. I'd only seen the two big tan guards, but I hadn't seen the smaller one yet. Until we knew where he was, we couldn't be sure it was safe to make our move.

I took a big bite of calzone and watched as Soner arrived at the bugged table. As the tan guards and Veronique arrived, Soner beckoned them with one hand. Instead of sitting down, they all followed Soner, who guided them to sit two tables over from where they had before. I cursed under my breath at the sight of it. Anton's bug would be useless.

I glanced back at the table where Veronique had been and saw a waitress wiping down the table after clearing a full cup of tea. The tea. Something about it. Why is a woman who can't lower her facial coverings making herself tea sometimes, and not other times? What's the pattern?

My head fell into my hands. I massaged my temples with my thumbs and tried to think back on all the times I'd seen Veronique. The first time was when the Russian guys insulted me, my first time in the lounge. Two big tan-suited Arab guys with her, the burly tan guards. Where was the third?

My body shook for a moment as it finally hit me. I grabbed the phone.

<< Three waiters! Time for dinner! >>

There was no Veronique.

Whenever she had no tea, all three of the tan guards could be seen. But whenever she had tea, only the two big guards could be seen. Because their smaller counterpart was dressed as Veronique. And there he was, dressed as a woman, next to Soner and the other tan guards and a couple of Soner's players, having an end-of-the-day meeting two tables over from yesterday's meeting.

I looked back down at my phone, knowing Sondra's next text would be a status report. She was on her way to Room 249, Tomaj's room. I glanced over at Tomaj's table and saw him happily settled in, having the time of his life. Oblivious. All the major principals were in the far end of the poker hall. I felt a wave of confidence and assurance pass through me. I took another big bite of calzone, eagerly awaiting the text message that would indicate everything on Sondra's end had gone smoothly.

Only that's not the message I received, two minutes later.

<< Get here quick! Need you! >>

CHAPTER 25 Tomaj's Room

Senses instantly heightened, I scanned the lounge quickly as I rose. Nothing out of the ordinary. I moved quickly through the casino halls. Upon reaching the hotel, my gait hastened into a quick trot. I took the stairs three at a time, barely noticing the flickering light of the exit sign and the heavy stench of cigarettes.

My mind raced as my body sped down the hall past blue walls, gold wall sconces, and ivory painted doors. Sondra wouldn't call me to Tomaj's room unless something had gone wrong. What if she'd been caught, and someone else was texting on her phone? I'd be walking into a trap, alone and unarmed.

I slowed down and took several fast, deep breaths to frontload oxygen as I approached Room 249. With no one else in the hallway to see, I quickly switched my reversible sweater from peach to dark blue. I pulled a pair of rubber surgical gloves out of my back pocket and put them on before reaching the door.

The door was open just the slightest crack. I couldn't see what was inside yet. From the opposite pocket, I pulled out a thin black ski mask. I took one last deep breath, checking once more that the hall was still empty. I put on the mask and grabbed the door handle. Chills ran through my body for a moment, and a sudden sweat came over me, as though I were breaking a fever. My pulse thundered in my ears.

I went in.

I took several steps inside the threshold before I saw anything. The door swung shut behind me as my eyes adjusted to dimmer light. Sondra stood by the bed in a matching ski mask, dressed head to toe in black. She was wearing her black waist pack, which was a cross between a cummerbund and a utility belt. Her phone was in her left hand. The Sig Sauer was in her right. It was pointed at another woman who was lying face down on the bed, naked and dripping, with a large towel wrapped several times tightly around her head. The woman was shivering and audibly sobbing. It was obviously one of Soner's girls, the unfortunate roommate of Tomaj. Apparently, the young woman had decided to take a shower before coming out to eat, and Sondra had walked in on her as she emerged from it.

"Pozhalusta, ne obizhai menya," the girl whimpered. Russian. *Please don't hurt me.*

"Tiha! Ne dvigaisya!" Sondra answered, pressing the tip of the gun into the girl's side. *Quiet! Don't move!* Sondra's voice was surprisingly deep and masculine, her Russian flawless to my ears, no accent whatsoever. If I hadn't been looking right at her, I would have sworn I'd heard an angry Russian man talking.

Rather than aborting the raid, Sondra had decided to incapacitate the girl and continue. It was then I noticed the other problem. There were no computers lying out. That's why Sondra had texted me. She couldn't turn the room upside down while holding a hostage at gunpoint.

I didn't need to be told what to do. Quietly as I could, I dropped to all fours and looked under the bed. Nothing. The dresser drawers. Nothing. I looked at Sondra and noticed her making head bobs, trying to direct me toward the closet. I opened the closet door and saw the two large trunks.

I carefully slid a trunk out into the room and looked up at Sondra. Her eyes were wide and intense. She set her phone on bed and used her left hand to signal me. One finger pointing sideways, and then a fist. Naval flight deck semaphore for the number "sixty." She wanted us to be done and gone in one minute, preferably less. I nodded and flipped open the trunk lid.

I dug through a pile of cords and extracted a laptop. I looked up in time to see Sondra tossing me the flash drive I'd rigged. I caught it and plugged it in. The red light on its end started flashing. My viral program was uploading.

Sondra was busy working a snake cam out of her waist pack. I watched for the light on the flash drive to stop blinking and pulled it out and pocketed it the moment it did. I put the computer back underneath the cords, closed the trunk, and quietly slid it back into the closet.

Sondra handed me the snake cam as I passed her. We'd planted the program. The remaining goal was to escape unseen.

"Gdye tvoi parren pryachet svoi denugi?" Sondra demanded, again in a very deep voice. *Where does your boyfriend hide his money?* She pressed the gun more firmly into the girl's side for emphasis. The girl was visibly shaking, making the beads of water on her back shimmer in the lamp light. She didn't answer, only sobbing. Her fingers gripped the soaked bed sheets with white knuckles. Her life was flashing before her eyes.

Sondra slid open the bedside table drawer and found a small pile of casino chips. She grabbed at them left-handed, bunches at a time, and stuffed them into her waist pack. I didn't know what Sondra had planned for the girl, but the fact that the girl was still alive bode well for her. Her life probably depended on whether Sondra and I got away clean.

I slipped the lens end of the snake cam under the door, to take a discreet look down the hallway. Its long, thin, fiber-optic tube ran from the lens to a small screen, upon which I could see two figures approaching. I pulled the cam back smoothly and held my palm up to Sondra, and then two fingers. I stood up to look through the door's eyehole.

Two of Soner's crew stopped in front of our door. Sondra leaned over the girl and hissed something in the girl's ear that I couldn't discern. The girl stopped sobbing and fell deathly quiet, still trembling. I watched through the eyehole as Soner's men said something to each other in Turkish. Then one of them continued down the hall, while the other fumbled for a keycard, and then entered the room across the hall.

I slowly knelt back down as Sondra watched, tensed and flexed. I looked down the hall both ways through the snake cam, and beckoned Sondra over when the coast was finally clear.

"Ne dvigaisya, pahka ne poschitayesh sto," Sondra said, again with her deep voice, but with less menace than before. *Don't move until you've counted to a hundred.* Sondra grabbed her phone off the bed and tapped the girl lightly on the ankle bone with the tip of her gun, a last reminder that she'd better behave. Sondra slid the gun into a holster strapped to her back.

I opened the door and stepped out into the hall, and then one step to the side. Still clear. I quickly removed my ski mask and gloves and stuffed them hastily into a sweater pocket as Sondra emerged behind me. She left the door cracked an inch as she pulled off her mask and gloves. As she stuffed them and the snake cam back in her waist pack,

I saw her eyes glance across the hall. I could tell she was looking at the eyehole of the door across the way. I looked and saw a faint light within it. The room's occupants weren't watching through it, so no problems there.

She pulled the door closed, and we double timed it toward the elevators. But a ding from the elevators stopped us in our tracks, and she grabbed my arm firmly. We did an about-face and began walking at a normal pace the other way.

"Far end, stairs," she said, in a directed whisper. "Quick change on the landing."

"Understood," I said.

We walked at a normal pace, stride for stride, well ahead of the men getting off the elevator. I couldn't help but shudder a bit as we passed Room 249, where the girl we had terrified was surely still counting and praying for her life.

We reached the stairs, and Sondra pushed the stairway door open without turning, always keeping her face directly away from the people behind us. I did the same as I followed her. We moved quickly down to the landing between the first and second floors. The wall in front of us was all windows, and in the late-night hours, acted as a mirror.

We watched ourselves in this mirror as we made our quick change. I reversed my sweater back to peach, regaining the appearance I had taken for the last few hours of the tournament. Sondra pulled off her reversible black jacket and turned it inside out, putting it back on as a maroon jacket. She pulled her blonde wig out of her waist pack, and quickly positioned it to look natural.

We hurried to the bottom of the stairs and exited the hotel. We stood outside, in the cold wind, our breaths making white clouds as we huffed and puffed. No one was watching or following. We stood there in the October wind for a minute, cooling down and catching our breaths and letting our heart rates come back down to normal. We looked quite different from how we'd looked in Tomaj's room. We seemed to be in the clear.

We walked calmly along a lit sidewalk toward the back entrance. We reentered the hotel hand-in-hand, as though we were returning from a romantic moonlight walk. Then straight back to our room, passing no one in the halls.

A wave of relief fell over me as the door shut behind us. I immediately started emptying all my pockets.

Sondra pulled off her wig and threw it at the floor like she was trying to teach it a lesson. She tore off her reversible jacket, and unhitched her holster harness, slinging it with a loud clunk onto the table.

"Fuck!" she said.

Her head was in hands as she sat on the couch, slumping forward. Her tank top was soaked with sweat, and her muscles glistened as they heaved with each breath.

Her extensive plan had considered the possibility of walking in on one of Soner's girls, and the plan had been simple in that contingency. Abort. But in the heat of the moment, she'd refused to do so. I didn't know why. Perhaps she didn't either.

Sondra slammed a fist down on the table, and then stood facing away from me, raking fingers through her short, brown hair. She turned around slowly, and I couldn't tell if was sweat or tears she wiped from her face.

"I'm sorry," she said, finally. "I hope I didn't just compromise you."

"Now, they know," I said. "But how much do they know?"

Sondra looked at me for a moment, teeth bared and gritting, before looking back down at the table. She closed her eyes and regulated her breathing, calming herself. I picked her wig up off the floor and hung it over a chair as she paced around the room, hands behind her head, breathing deeply. She stopped at the window and stared out into the blackness for a few minutes. But she wasn't looking outward at anything. She was looking inward.

"You're right," she said, finally turning around. "Let's talk it through." And then she looked at herself in a mirror and chuckled. "After I towel off and change. I look like I fell in the pool."

While she took care of that, I logged into the dark web site that was recording from the laptop in Tomaj's room. Unsurprisingly, it was muffled, since the laptop was in a closed trunk. More importantly, the download folder was filling up at a steady pace. My ghost drive had nearly ten terabytes of storage, so the program we'd implanted would be able to download the entire contents of Tomaj's laptop, and two dozen more just like it if needed. I began sorting through the information but paused when Sondra came back into the room.

"I don't hear anything from Tomaj's room yet," I said.

"The girl is our big problem. How will she react?"

"I never saw her face. She seemed absolutely terrified. Terror responses can be hard to predict. Fight, flight, or freeze. I think we can rule out fight."

"Actually, you have seen her face," Sondra corrected. "She was the blonde girl from the hot tub." I flinched for a moment in surprise. It was just a coincidence, of course, as we'd had no knowledge of which girls were paired with which players.

"Is it weird I feel sorry for her?"

Sondra shook her head and looked me squarely in the eyes. "People get hurt in this business. She just learned that the hard way, and you learned the easy way. You gotta play this game aggressively, 'cause it's always better to be the one doing the hurting."

"What do you think, then? Will she try to run, or will she freeze up and try to hide that we were there?"

"I'm hoping for freeze, but I'd bet on flight. But the more I think about it, the more I think we got away clean. If they catch her and force her to talk, I don't think they'll be able to figure out who we are based on what she'd tell them."

Sondra went on talking about what happened before she'd summoned me to the room. She'd used her magnetic key to break in and walked into the room at the same moment the girl walked out of the bathroom in a towel. In the few seconds it took Sondra take control, the girl would have only seen a black-clad figure in a ski mask with a gun. Judging my Sondra's build and the voice she'd used, the girl would probably think she was a Russian man.

I added that I hadn't noticed any cameras in the room. But even if there had been, they would have never gotten a look at our faces, and our clothing looked different everywhere else we'd been the entire evening. We left no evidence we'd been there, and on top of that, the girl might not have even realized there'd been a second intruder in the room.

"I'm only worried about the hallway," Sondra said. "Casino security cameras would show our quick change in the stairwell, and our coming and going from Tomaj's room. Doubt anyone was watching us closely in real time, but if the casino is in league with Soner, they could roll the footage back, and we'd be nailed."

I shook my head. "From everything I've read about Goran, he'd never be in league with Soner. I hear nothing but stories of integrity and love for the game. He'd never align himself with cheaters or thieves."

"No way to be certain. And anyway, he's not the only guy who sees the security footage. We can't make assumptions like that. We need to be on guard from here on, against everyone. And I mean that exactly how it sounds. Everyone."

I nodded. We'd probably gotten away clean. But the opposition was now aware of us, even if they didn't know exactly who we were. Their complacent confidence was about to evaporate, to be replaced with caution and countermeasures. The game had changed.

"If it matters, I think you made the right call not to abort," I said. "But why did you take some of Tomaj's chips?"

"Couldn't gamble on the girl keeping quiet," she said. "Had to make it look like the break in was about something other than the computers. Robbing the room seemed the most obvious thing."

A quick beep from my laptop alerted me that the download had finished. The audio bars were moving on the dark web site, so I slid the volume bar to maximum. We heard multiple people talking in the room, though it was still too muffled to make anything out or identify voices.

I started looking through folders from the downloaded laptop, and it didn't take long to strike gold. Right there on the desktop was a folder containing a spreadsheet of names, credit card numbers, security pins and zip codes. One of the columns had X's next to some of the numbers, and multiples of two hundred next to others.

"I think we just figured out the point of these heads-up tournaments," I said, showing Sondra the spreadsheet. "It's not their own money they're laundering. They're stealing it from American credit cards, two hundred dollars at a time."

"Where'd they get the numbers?" Sondra asked. "Hey, Isn't al-Karchi a big shareholder in a credit card company?"

"Yes, but I doubt that's how they got the numbers. All of al-Karchi's businesses are legit. He'd have no reason to jeopardize himself by stealing corporate data. More likely, Soner bought the info off some hacker on the dark web. Probably paid five figures or more to get it. But consider the return on investment."

"Aren't there security protocols on the cards? To prevent foreign purchases, or alert the owners?"

"Sure," I said. "A lot of these numbers won't work at all. Some only once or twice. A few of them might work many times, until they hit their limit, or the owner cancels the card or has the card blocked or something. If Soner has enough card numbers, he can keep it going for a while."

"Won't the credit card companies eventually notice what's going on, and shut it down themselves?"

"That's a good point," I admitted. "Even if the credit card companies don't figure it out quickly, the Poker

Geyser site will. They track IP addresses. Right now, this is the only place in the world where five hundred people in the same building can log onto the same poker site at the same time, and it wouldn't raise any red flags. That's probably why Soner picked this place to do it. But the djinni's out of the bottle now. This might be the sort of thing that can only work once. Maybe Soner and al-Karchi both realize it. Or maybe one of them realizes it and is misleading the other. Hard to say."

Now that we knew for sure what was going on, the ramifications were clear. Even after deducting the expenses, and Soner and al-Karchi taking healthy cuts for themselves, al-Alrasid would be getting eight figures, neatly routed to them anywhere in the world through the Poker Geyser site, in the form of untraceable crypto-currency.

Reporting on them was no longer a sufficient outcome. They had to be stopped.

We wondered about the endgame. What was the take-down plan for Soner and his crew once their operation was completed? I suggested that the sensible thing for them to do would be to delete all their online accounts, and then completely dispose of all their equipment. Sondra pointed out that the same could be said of most of their personnel.

"I still say there's a reason they're using call girls," she said. "Easier to dispose of them. Or worse."

I was about to respond when she raised her hand suddenly, a hushing emblem. The sound from the laptop had suddenly gotten louder and clearer. We both stepped nearer to the computer and listened to the sound of things moving around. Something being set on a table. A quiet beep and the clatter of fingers on a keyboard. Someone was typing on the very computer I'd hacked.

This continued for a few minutes, and Sondra looked over at me.

"Think he knows it's been hacked?"

"I don't know who 'he' is yet, but it's unlikely," I said. "He'd have to know just where to look and what to look for."

We then heard the sound of a door opening, and people walking in. Irregular footsteps and a gasp. Someone was being brought in forcefully, struggling. An angry man's voice, shouting in Arabic. Then Soner's voice, speaking in Russian.

"I can't understand them…"

"Shh!" Sondra commanded me.

The sound of a scared and distressed girl answering. A loud slap, and then another. Shouting in Albanian. Several more slaps, amidst the sound of the girl crying a repeating her answer.

During a pause, I offered Sondra the headphones since I couldn't understand anyway. I could see anger welling in her eyes as she took them. The last thing I heard before she plugged them in was more slapping and sobbing. Sondra took the laptop with her to the couch, and laid back with it on her lap, listening intently and grimacing. Her biceps were involuntarily clenching.

I gave her some distance for several minutes, until finally she pulled the headphones off one ear and looked up at me.

"It's Soner, Tomaj, one of the tan guards, and that girl. Soner's checking all the laptops in the room, but I haven't heard anything that suggests he found your program."

"The girl?"

"They're beating her. Tomaj, or the guard. Maybe both. Seems she tried to grab up her stuff and get away, but they caught her downstairs and dragged her back up. Tomaj's pissed off his chips are missing. They accused her of stealing, and she's been trying to explain what happened."

"What's she telling them?"

"The truth. They weren't believing her at first, but then they noticed the bed was wet. She told them a Russian man in a mask blindfolded her with her towel and held her at gunpoint, and she thinks someone else came in too but she's not sure. I think they're starting to believe her."

"They don't have cameras in the room, then," I concluded. "Or they wouldn't have to guess whether she's telling the truth."

Sondra kept listening, and I looked on as she opened the window that showed Anton's front and back lobby cameras. After a short search, she rewound to a point where we could see the girl enter the back lobby and walk up to the counter. She had a full plastic laundry bag in her hand, probably containing her personal affects and some clothes. There was no sound, but she seemed to be speaking briefly to the desk attendant, who then picked up a nearby phone.

"She's requesting a ride," I said. "Doesn't have a car here, of course."

The camera then showed one of the tan guards walking into the lobby. The girl froze like a deer in headlights at the sight of him. He closed the distance quickly and seized her firmly by one arm. The attendant looked startled, but then gently set the phone back down and watched them walk back into the hotel, the girl resisting futilely.

"What's going on back in Tomaj's room?" I asked.

"It's gone quiet for the moment. They might be talking in whispers. Soner is still going through all the computers. I'll keep listening."

I left her to that chore, and laid back on the bed, thinking. There wasn't much more I could do, except try to think of ways to take down their Poker Geyser operation. We would report everything to Anton, of course, and he would relay it to Prague. Maybe they would act, maybe they wouldn't. But I was in the best position to act. I rolled a lot of ideas through my mind for the next hour.

Around four o'clock, one knock, then three, then two fell on the door. Sondra sprung up and grabbed her gun, and peeked through the eyehole before letting Anton in. Like the previous day, he pushed in a cart with another pastry plate and two steaming pitchers of coffee.

While Sondra watched, headphones on one ear, I reported the evening's events to Anton. He looked worried at what he heard, and his eyes kept shifting toward Sondra.

"If there's any way you can find out about the girl, that would be helpful," Sondra said. "Name, address, anything."

"I'll try," Anton said, shaking his head slightly. "But I don't have much to go on. Do you think she will try to run again?"

"I hope so," Sondra said. "In Russian, which she understands, Soner and Tomaj are talking about how they'll have someone stay with her in the room from now on, for safety. Soner even floated the idea of giving her the other half of her money and driving her home."

"No way that happens," I said, and Sondra nodded gravely before continuing.

"In Arabic, Soner's talking about where they'll take her and how to get rid of her body."

We fell silent for a minute, before Anton cleared his throat. He reaffirmed that he would try to find out about her, before giving his customary bow and showing himself out.

"It's very clear they're afraid of al-Karchi finding out," I said. "My guess is the sheikh will pull the plug himself if there's any risk of him being exposed as part of it."

"Here's what's puzzling me," Sondra said. "Why is she still alive? I haven't heard a peep from her in about an hour, but I'm pretty sure she's still alive. If they're planning to get rid of her, why don't they just kill her now and smuggle her out in a trunk?"

"Appearances. They need her to be seen walking out. Can't let the other girls know, or they'd bolt too."

"Maybe. Or maybe they have one last use for her. And that's what I can't figure out."

"Thom! Wake up, now!"

I'd managed to sneak in an hour of sleep, but now sat bolt upright, rattled awake by Sondra's voice. She'd been listening to Tomaj's room for hours.

"What's happening?"

"I think she just made a run for it!"

I snapped my fingers and pointed toward the general direction of the back lobby. Sondra was way ahead of me. Before I could even speak, she had already turned the laptop toward me, showing me the front and back lobbies on Anton's live cameras.

Seconds later, the girl appeared in the rear lobby. She was wearing a long nightshirt, and her bare legs scrambled until she stopped in the middle of the lobby. There was no concierge there to help her. Her hair flailed violently around her head as she spun this way and that, looking at her options with terror-wide eyes. Finally, rather than running outside, she bolted down the hallway leading to the casino.

Ten seconds after that, Tomaj and a tan guard arrived in the lobby. They looked around for a moment, seemed to say something to each other, and then both ran outside.

"Clever girl," I said.

"Her friends aren't going to be in the casino at this hour," Sondra said. "Probably all in bed. She knows she can't trust Soner's other players. Where's she going, then. Security?"

"That'd be the smart play," I said. "But did you see her eyes? She's in a full-on panic. Watch the front lobby."

She'd tried to get a ride before, and she'd try again. But this time, she'd try on the other side. Sure enough, thirty seconds later, she burst into the front lobby from the direction of the main hall. She ran up to the attendant, hunched over and gasping for breath.

"It's Anton!" Sondra said, fist pumping. "Good man! Always in the right place!"

Sure enough, it was Anton, the attendant with his hand on the girl's shoulder, walking her calmly outside toward the valet parking.

"Think he can hide her for us?"

Sondra shook her head. "Not without blowing his cover. But he can send her home in one of those high roller limos. Surely there's one available at this hour. And that means…"

"…he'll get her address, and maybe her name," I finished.

Sondra handed me the computer and sprung up. She quickly put back on her black jeans and jacket, and then emptied her duffel bag onto the table. I watched as she strapped on her lower back holster. She double-checked that the clip in the Sig Sauer was full, and then sheathed it in the holster, and pulled the jacket back down for concealment. She put the other four clips in four different inside jacket pockets. The melee knives went into numerous small, hidden pockets which ran the length of her outer thighs on both sides. Her garrote went in her right, back pocket. A pair of surgical gloves went in the left.

"Anton's back," I said, and she came over to look. He stood alone in the center of the front lobby and looked directly at his own camera before texting on his phone.

<<Package being delivered first class>> he texted to Sondra.

<<Thanks>> she texted back.

"He didn't give you the address."

"Covcom protocol," Sondra said. "He and I should both be a dozen miles from here to be safe, and then he can send it to me. Gimme the keys."

I tossed them to her. She looked at the keys in her hand, and then looked down and away for a moment. There was a slight, almost imperceptible droop to the corners of her eyes and lips. Guilt. She stood frozen in the moment until I broke the silence.

"I know she'll be alright if you can get there first," I said. "Wherever she's going, it's almost certainly east. German border is a couple of miles west."

"Copy that. I'll drive east at a normal speed and adjust when Anton sends me the exact address. Maybe I can get way out ahead of everyone."

"There's a good chance Soner's crew knows where she's going. They have the advantage."

"I know," she said. "That's why I've got to fly. If I get to her first, maybe I can bring her in. Find out everything. Expose everything." And she paused for a moment, solemnly. "And get her some damned protection. She's suffered too much already."

"Watch your six, Sondra."

"Hole up here until I get back."

And with that, she strode purposefully out of the room. I couldn't help but watch for her on the back lobby cam. She marched through the empty lobby with a quick and strong gait, a focused soldier. She wasn't going after the girl just for the good of the mission. She felt responsible for what had happened to her and wanted to make it right somehow. I couldn't blame her.

I turned the deadbolt on the door and went back to the computer. One hour of sleep would have to be enough. I poured the first of many coffees on the day and made short work of a croissant. I logged onto the Poker Geyser site and started thinking about how to alter my coding. It struck me that the only way to stop them was to invade their tournament and throw a wrench into it. Sabotage.

I had to assume that today's match times would be different than yesterday's. Otherwise, what would be the point of the nightly 2:22am text? Since we hadn't intercepted last night's text, today's match times were still a mystery.

My previous code had made the challenge page continually reload, which exposed some of the times we had expected to see. It occurred to me that, if the code could spot one of the match times in one hour, I might be able to jump into the mix at the same moment during the next hour. My mind raced against time to formulate a coding strategy, and as soon as it came together, I set to work.

It was hard to focus. I was tired. Wired. Excited. Concerned for Sondra's safety. She'd been gone about half an hour. What was bothering me? Something about the lobby footage. Bothersome. I set my programming aside for a moment and switched back to the rear lobby footage.

I rewound the footage back to Sondra marching through the lobby. I watched it three times. Nothing unexpected there.

I rewound it back to the girl's appearance. Frantic. Her face like a silent scream of pulse-pounding, hysterical fear. Terrified for her very life. I felt a great swell of sympathy.

Then Tomaj and the guard appear. Looking around.
Exiting. But with placid faces. Very little expression. Not
at all angry or tense. Could I be reading them wrong? It
didn't make sense.

<<Think I'll check out some real estate in this
beautiful city>>

I looked down at Sondra's text and did some quick
math in my head. Based on the length of her travel time
and the local geography, I deduced she was almost
certainly in Pilsen. That must be where the girl lived, and
where Anton had directed her to go. I thought for a
moment about how to respond, within covcom protocols.

<<You know those three real estate agents we've
been seeing?>> I texted back.

<<Yeah…>>

<<We don't know where all of them are at such an
early hour>>

A pause.

<<That's true>>

<<I think maybe they might know there's an
interested buyer.>>

A longer pause.

<<Thought occurred to me. Thanks for the
negotiating tip>>

I felt confident my message had gotten through. I
watched the lobby footage of Tomaj and the guard a dozen
more times. It just stank to high heaven, and every viewing
of it made me more and more worried. Before I realized it,
I had nervously dug small cuts into several of my cuticles,
and I had to stand up from my chair and pace about the
room to settle my nerves.

I looked out the window to see the aurora of a new
dawn filling the eastern sky. The tall, beautiful trees were
still for once, not swaying in the wind as I'd seen them
doing every other time I'd looked. It was as though they
were waiting for something, anxiously.

I poured another coffee and got back to my programming. A half hour and two more coffees passed. I was nearly finished when a new text arrived, sent from Sondra's phone.

<<get here>>

I stared at my phone for a few seconds, not knowing what to do. This was not a contingency we had even discussed.

<<help bring clothes hair>>

I hit the green telephone icon to initiate a phone call to her. It rang for a moment, but then dropped. I tried calling her again, and the second time it dropped more quickly.

<<don't call>>

I could imagine a number of scenarios for why she would need me, and none of them were good. The worst scenario was, of course, that she was dead or captured, and her phone was being used to lure me into the same trap.

<<hurt come now plz track>>

Sondra had our rental car. I'd have to get a ride from a casino courtesy van or use one of the taxis waiting near the loading circle. I stared at her text on my phone and tried to think of any way I could know that it was really her. It finally dawned on me, and I could only hope she would remember.

<<My name starts with TH…what does yours start with?>>

A long pause.

<< f u >>

I password-locked the laptop. Into Sondra's duffel bag went her wig, a change of clothes, the first aid kit, and several bottles of water. I looked around for weapons, but Sondra had taken everything except a stainless steel balisong, which I pocketed. I ran out of the room and hurried downstairs toward the taxi stand.

"Pilsen!" I shouted to the taxi driver as I approached. Our breaths were white ghosts haunting the crisp morning air. He pulled the rear passenger side door open and held it for me as I got in. He glanced down at the duffel bag as I passed him, and his hand flinched, as though he were about to offer to put it in the trunk for me, but then thought better of it. He shut me inside and circled round to the driver's side.

"Where in Pilsen, sir?"

"Just drive."

The driver shrugged and pulled away from the lot and toward the highway.

I opened the geolocation app on my phone and started locating Sondra's position. The screen first displayed a map of Western Czechia, then slowly zoomed in on Pilsen, telling me I had guessed the right city. As it continued to zoom in, the names of buildings, businesses, and major streets slowly appeared. It tracked her to a university district, near a large cathedral.

"I've always wanted to see St. Bartholomew's," I told the driver.

"Ah yes! Very old and beautiful. Very good, sir."

The cabbie turned onto the highway and put the pedal down. I estimated it would be thirty-five minutes until we arrived. He rambled on about the cathedral, and then about all the stores and cafes and bars in the university area, but I wasn't listening. I zoomed in as far as the satellite map would allow.

A red pin on the map pinpointed Sondra northwest of the cathedral, on a slight downslope near the Mze River. The map showed a main north-south road passing over an east-west highway there, with an arcing offramp descending from one to the other. The red pin was located near the center of the enclosed triangle, a heavily wooded patch of land. There was a sidewalk and staircase nearby, but I surmised that the area was big enough, and wooded enough, that it would be easy for her to keep out of sight there.

<<On the way>> I texted, once I was sure we'd driven at least a dozen miles. No response.

I shielded my eyes from the stabbing sun as we weaved east along a winding highway. The green of the hills glistened from misty rain that had fallen the night before, and the Autumn colors were emerging. Small plumes of smoke rose from the morning fires of some of the small shacks we passed. Tranquil life was continuing as normal in the remote farmlands, but somewhere in the city ahead, my partner was in danger. Hiding? Struggling? Dying?

I had no idea where the highway was taking me. My fingers moved over the phone screen with a mind of their own, and without consciously realizing it, I dialed a telephone number. The ringing of the phone was a distant echo, but the click of Marina picking up on the other end snapped me back into awareness.

"Thom? Is that you?"

"Hey, Marina. Yes, it's me."

"What time is it?" she said, groggily. "Oh my God, Thom, it's so early."

"Oh, yeah. I guess I forgot about the time zones. How are you?"

"OK. I gotta get up for a morning shift in a few hours."

"Sorry. I just really wanted to … hear your voice."

"Are you drunk?"

"No, no, I just…I miss you."

A few moments of silence passed. The driver glanced back over his shoulder for a moment, raising an eyebrow and grinning.

"That's really sweet, Thom, but…"

"I know, I know. I'm sorry. Go back to sleep."

"Are you OK?"

"Yeah, of course. I'm sorry I woke you up. I'll be back soon. Goodnight, Marina."

"Take care of yourself." And with that, she hung up.

For the next several minutes, the early morning quiet seemed too quiet. I was torn between two continents, and that was one too many. My hands roughly rubbed both sides of my face as I tried to clear my head. Focus. Focus.

I spent the rest of the drive studying the neighborhood around Sondra's locale on my phone, trying to guess what might have happened, and where, and why. Sondra had presumably been given the girl's address, which was probably a nearby apartment, but that did little to narrow things down.

As we rolled through the Pilsen morning traffic, I saw apartments everywhere, mostly above storefronts. Not surprising for a university district. Old but well-kept buildings with stone and brick fronts, several stories tall, stood shoulder to shoulder along most of the streets. Somehow the daylight still poured down in between.

Flashing blue lights caught my eye as we finally reached the large open square where St. Bartholomew's took center stage. On the west side of the square, three police cars blocked off the area in front of a large, arch-shaped, set of wooden double doors. A small courtyard beyond the doors contained a garden area for the apartments in the building behind it. A small crowd lingered around the scene, keeping their distance. A van with a small satellite dish was idling nearby, a news van by the look of it.

"Drop me off on the south side of the cathedral," I told the cabbie, and he nodded.

I pulled out a hundred-dollar bill and asked whether he accepted American money. His eyes widened as he smiled. Everyone in the world takes American. I told him to keep the change, and he thanked me as I stepped out holding the duffel bag. He sped away without another word.

The pin marking Sondra's position still hadn't moved. I walked north across the square, taking discreet glances over at the crime scene, but there was little to see. Whatever investigation was taking place, it was inside the courtyard, out of view.

The back doors of the news van were open, and two men were talking behind it. One of them held out what looked like a VCR tape, and the other looked around nervously before taking it in exchange for several bills of paper currency. The tape quickly found its way into the hands of a third man, inside the van, who was wearing a headset.

I walked with my head down and kept a good distance from the police scene. Almost certainly it had something to do with Sondra. Was that the girl's apartment complex?

Old cobblestone passed swiftly under my feet. A block north of St. Bartholomew Square, I found our rental car parked on the west side of the street. Sondra must have parked there before approaching the girl's apartment on foot. I continued north on the opposite side, looking around to see if the car was being watched. As far as I could tell, there were only a few normal pedestrians around.

I zigzagged a few more blocks north and west, past an education building, and finally reached the wooded triangle. I walked down some stairs, looking to my right over the stair railing, trying to spot her. Halfway down, after making sure I was out of sight, I leapt the railing and kept low as I moved through the brush and into a grove of tall trees. The light was dimmer under the trees, and my steps crunched through a soft layer of newly fallen leaves.

It was Sondra's face I saw first, as the rest of her body was clad in black, blending well with the shadow of the large tree she was leaning against. She was laying back, almost flat, but supported from her shoulders up by a large root. Her eyes were nearly closed, only thin slivers of white showing. Her head drooped slightly sideways. The tree behind her head was stained dark red.

"Sondra!" I called out, running up to her.

Her eyes opened slightly, and her head turned my way. In a snap motion, her right arm flew up, taking dead aim at me. Only her hand was holding her phone, not her gun. She looked at the phone in her hand, and then slumped back against the tree, dropping the phone and coughing out a pained laugh.

"You got me," I said, kneeling beside her. "Jesus, you look awful! What happened?" I switched on my phone's flashlight app and held it before her eyes. They were droopy and unfocused, with dilated pupils. Her eyes were sluggish as they tried to follow the light.

"Should see…the other guy…."

"Hold still. I need to look at your head. I think the bleeding has stopped."

"Think…you have…concussion…."

"I'd say one of us does," I said, gently turning her head. The back of her head was matted with blood, clearly the result of a sharp blow to the back left quarter of her skull. There was swelling, and the cut would require several stitches, but the bleeding had slowed to an ooze. I gave her a bottle of water to drink, which she took with her right hand. I realized only then that her left arm and her legs hadn't moved at all since I'd found her.

"Can you move all your limbs?"

She nodded, and raised each limb slightly, one at a time. Her left wrist was swollen and had developed light purple bruising.

"I'm going to wrap that wrist too, but first things first," I told her, pouring some of the second water bottle over her head, trying to clean the area. I applied suture bandages to pinch the cut closed, and gently pressed down with many layers of gauze. I worked automatically, reacting in accordance with the basic first aid training I'd been given back at The Farm. She winced a few times, but didn't complain.

"The water helped," Sondra said, managing to sit up on her own. "Thank you." She finished the bottle and crumpled the plastic in her hand. I wrapped her left hand with a thick roll of bandage, wishing I had some ice to help reduce the swelling.

"You're going to need medical attention," I said. "I'll call Control, let him know we're heading to Prague…"

"No!"

Sondra leaned forward and started to get up, but her feet were unsteady, and she leaned on me as I helped her stand. Then she turned suddenly and leaned hard against the tree, vomiting.

"Sondra, you need to see a doctor."

"What I need is to finish the job."

"Alright, alright. Let's just get out of here, and we'll figure it out on the road."

I helped her put on her maroon jacket from the night before and fix her blonde wig gently over the gauze on her head. She felt to make sure her Sig Sauer was still in her back holster and adjusted her jacket to cover it. If anyone looked closely, they might notice blood stains on her black pants, and of course the wrap on her left wrist was visible, but there was nothing we could do about that.

Sondra took my bicep in her right hand and used me to steady herself as we slowly walked to the stairs, and then climbed them. My head was on a swivel as we walked the two blocks to the car. I was watching for cops, Soner's heavies, or anyone else who'd be looking for us, but none of the pedestrians seemed to pay us any attention. As we reached the car, I saw the faint glint of flashing blue lights reflecting off a store front window.

"Know anything about the police presence near St. Bart's?" I asked. She just nodded and passed me the keys.

I helped her into the passenger seat. I got the car rolling and hung a sharp left, steering the car back toward the wooded triangle and away from the police. I took the first highway onramp I saw and couldn't help but breathe a sigh of relief. Sondra reclined her seat and lay back, eyes closed but still awake. She covered her eyes with one hand, bothered by the morning's bright light.

"That's where it happened," she finally said. "Where the police are. The girl's place. Katrina something-or-other."

"What happened?"

"Got jumped from behind. Tan guard. Waiting just inside the gate."

"The one that threw me out of the elevator?"

"No. The other big one." She involuntarily pulled her sprained wrist closer to her chest as she thought about him. She had grappled with him, it seemed.

"What happened?"

"I killed him."

The hum and vibration of the engine. The grind of pavement beneath wheels, and the whistle of the strong crosswind streaming over the car, shaking it a bit. The silence of the next few seconds was alive with sound and feeling. I glanced over and saw Sondra laying prone and placid, vulnerable but Olympic. Her eyes were closed, but she turned her head away from me and tilted it downward. The same mannerisms of someone averting eye contact, except with closed eyes. A warrior with a conscience too heavy to carry.

I switched lanes, following the directions of the onboard satnav. As we approached the exit from our current highway onto a different one, the satnav spoke its directions aloud. I tried to silence it, but was too late, as Sondra opened her eyes. She recognized where its directions were leading us.

"Don't you fucking dare take me to Prague," she said, gritting her teeth. "Job's not over yet."

"Sondra, you need…."

"Pull over!"

I slowed the car gradually and then pulled over on the shoulder. I cleared the satnav and reset its destination to Casino Rozvadov. Finally, I looked at her. Her eyes were still dilated yet riveted on mine.

"You want me to admit I'm messed up?" she said. "Fine. I'm pretty messed up right now. My head is killing me, and I feel like I'm gonna puke again. But I'm going to be OK with a little rest. Now…you look me in the eye, and you tell me this mission isn't important, and we should just abandon it."

I could only just shake my head.

"Alright, then," Sondra continued. "We get back to Rozvadov, and we figure out the next steps."

"One condition," I said. "You call it in to Prague. Not through Anton, you do it yourself right now. If you can handle reporting in, I'll believe you're fit enough to continue."

Sondra agreed. I navigated the highways, speeding westward back toward the casino, while she reported in. She was a bit unfocused, and I had to help with a few details. She spoke in vague terms about being jumped by Soner's man, but didn't give the blow-by-blow. The fight had taken too long and attracted attention, forcing her to leave his body in public. She hadn't seen the girl, Katrina, nor made it up to her apartment. She didn't mention specific injuries, only that I had come out to help. By the time we'd gotten back within twenty kilometers of Rozvadov, and she hung up to keep covcom protocols, I was convinced she was still mentally fit, despite her head trauma.

It was late morning by the time we pulled into the general outdoor lot behind the hotel. I stayed close to Sondra as we walked toward the entrance. She seemed steadier now, but still winced from the bright sunlight. Two smiling greeters stood on either side of the door.

As the greeters acknowledged us, Sondra quickly crossed behind me to my right side. She leaned in close, head on my shoulders, and slid her bandaged hand up under my sweater. I gasped and shuddered at the unexpected sensation of her nails on me. The greeters glanced at each other, and one of them smirked. To them, we appeared to be a romantic young couple, eager to get back into bed.

We got through the lobby, and she decoupled.

"Sorry about that," she said, holding up her wrist. We stopped by the ice machine and filled up a bucket before heading back to our room.

I set the duffel bag on the table as the door shut behind us. Sondra tossed her wig next to it and lay back on the couch with the ice bucket. She started gingerly unwrapping her wrist, uttering a few curses under her breath as she did. As she iced her wrist, now deep purple on the palm side, I wrapped some ice in a hand towel and slid it beneath her head.

"Thanks," she said, looking down at her wrist. "This hand still works, kind of, but if I go out there, I don't know how I'm going to hide this."

"Don't go out there. I'm the one who has to go out there. It'll be suspicious if I don't show up to play Day Two. Soner and his crew, the ones who know about what happened this morning—they're about to go to DefCon One. Maybe if we're lucky they'll pull the plug, and our job will be over. Certainly, they're going to be looking for anything out of the ordinary. Anything that could tip them off about who's watching them."

"So, I can't go out there looking like I've been in a fight. Gotcha. Kinda obvious. Dammit, I feel like a useless lump!"

"I'd say you've done enough for one morning," I said, sitting down with the computer. "Besides, I've been coding something. And if it works, I'm going to need you to be right here, anyway."

The room phone rang just before twelve noon. It was the front desk providing the wake-up call I'd ordered. Not that I could have slept. It served as a one-hour warning before the tournament restarted.

"Still awake?" I asked over my shoulder, still at the computer, still programming.

"Yeah, yeah. You almost done?"

"Just finishing up."

Basic first aid training told me I had to keep Sondra awake for the next twelve hours or so. She'd been a good patient so far, sitting up on the couch and flipping through TV channels. I heard her land on what sounded like a local news channel, a deep anchorman's voice speaking soberly in Czech.

I restarted the Poker Geyser site on the computer, and watched as my phone screen exactly mirrored the computer screen. I'd be able to monitor the action on my phone in real time, and even take it over remotely if necessary.

As I sat admiring and testing out my handiwork, I began to notice the volume on the television growing louder. I turned around to see Sondra leaning forward, eyes wide.

"Thom, you'd better see this...."

I joined her on the couch, and watched the television slowly pan inward on the anchorman, who spoke with a calm intensity. The camera then cut to what looked like a black-and-white security camera. The image was blurry, seemingly because of poor lighting and the footage being zoomed without image enhancement. It seemed to show a large man in a light-colored suit standing with his back against a wall, a large, arched double door to his right.

"Is that...?"

"Yes," Sondra said. "There must have been a security camera on the far side of the courtyard."

I remembered the exchange of the videotape behind the news van this morning, and finally understood how this footage had gotten out so quickly. I didn't understand the anchorman's narration, but he went quiet as a crack of light poured in through the opening double door. A black clad figure could be seen pushing one of the doors inward and pausing for a few moments in the opening. Both figures in the image slowly drew guns with their right hands, and both then froze for a few more seconds.

"Letting my eyes adjust," Sondra said. "Dammit. I knew something smelled."

My entire body wrenched tensely as I watched the video of Sondra taking a step inside, and the tan guard's gun immediately slamming down on her head with sledgehammer force. It dropped her to her hands and knees, her gun clattering to the floor several feet away. The tan guard stood to her side with his gun pointed at her head. He seemed to be shouting at her, but the video had no sound. He continued shouting as she slowly sat backward to a kneeling position, hands empty in front of her.

In a sudden motion, so fast it barely registered on the grainy video, Sondra countered. Her left arm snapped back as her upper body twisted. She clinched his right wrist with her left hand, while simultaneously punching his near knee with her right fist. A bright muzzle flash showed his gun going off, the shot narrowly missing her head.

She rose quickly, a melee knife finding its way into her hand, but the tan guard clinched her wrist. They danced a violent tango for several seconds, the gun going off again. The man was twice her size, and managed to drive her backwards, hard against a wall. It looked like he kneed her in the stomach once, then twice. Her knife clattered to the ground.

As he leaned in close, Sondra landed a perfect headbutt, directly onto the bridge his nose. He involuntarily let go of her hand, and she grabbed his gun wrist with both hands as the gun went off again. She swung her right leg up over the tan guard's head, hooking it behind her knee. Finally, she brought her other leg up, locking his head in leg scissors. He stumbled and turned off balance for a moment, before falling forward.

I flinched as the video showed them slamming hard into the ground. Sondra landed on her back, still furiously trying to twist the gun out of his hand. The guard was driven face-first into the ground, legs kicking, trying to push his way out of the leg scissors with his free arm. The gun went off a fourth time. He wouldn't drop it.

With one hand, Sondra pulled a second melee knife from a different thigh pocket. Just as she was about to use it, the video cut away. The anchorman resumed speaking, this time with wider eyes and with a higher pitch to his voice.

"Holy shit," I finally said. Sondra was looking down at the blood beneath her fingernails which had eluded our clean-up attempt back in Pilsen.

"Nice of them not to show the bloody parts, at least," she said. "They cut the part where I slashed his arm to the bone until he finally dropped the gun."

"And then you shot him with it."

"Emptied the whole clip into his skull. I was out of my head. All adrenaline, no brains."

"Better him than you."

She slouched forward with her head in her hands. The purple in her wrist was still spreading, though the swelling seemed to be down a little. I didn't have to ask her what the newsman was saying. I didn't have to be a mind reader to know it wasn't her injuries that had her worried. It was her exposure.

"I don't think anyone could ever identify you from that," I said. "Too blurry and way too dark. And you didn't leave your gun or knives, right?"

She shook her head. No fingerprints. And obviously no one had noticed her and followed her after she left. Otherwise, I would have seen police officers tracking her.

Sondra stood up and rolled her shoulders. She looked away with knitted eyebrows as the television began showing the clip of her fight again. She peeled off her shirt as she walked over to the mini-bar. For the first time, I could see she had several additional abrasions on her back and left shoulder. The sports bra she'd been wearing underneath was stained with blood.

She pulled two tiny bottles of generic whiskey from the mini-bar and poured them into the same glass. Leaning over the counter, she slammed the drink in two desperate swallows, and slapped the glass back down on the counter so harshly I was surprised it didn't break. She leaned over the counter, shoulders flexing. Tired and beaten.

"I don't think it's a good idea for you to be drinking with a concussion."

"Probably not."

She stepped out of her pants walking toward the suitcase. She grabbed a fresh sports bra and pair of yoga shorts from her sack.

"I've gotta wash this shit off me and soak a while," she said. "I'll leave the door open a crack so you can hear if I fall."

She disappeared into the bathroom, and I heard the shower turn on as I turned back to the television. The news program was showing the fight for a third time, only this time the anchorman and some other voice were talking over it. I quickly switched on my translator app and set it for Czech. From what it told me, the newsmen were speculating that it was rival drug cartels or something to do with organized crime. They reported that an unidentified young woman had been found strangled in her apartment above. They referred to Sondra and the tan guard as the "small man and the big man," which reassured me they couldn't identify faces. The Prague office would surely work damage control, securing the original tape before anyone with image processing technology comparable to ours could get hold of it.

As the clip of the fight started playing for the fourth time, I grabbed the remote and switched the television off. My chest was tight, and I was short of breath. I'd never seen anything like it. I glanced backward at the bathroom door. A puff of steam emerged near the ceiling. I glanced at the mini-bar. At the locked and chained door to the room. At the clothes and weapons spread over the floor and table. I paced around the room a few times, finally stopping at the window. Nothing could calm me.

Without even realizing what I was doing, I walked over to the bathroom door and pushed it slightly open to look inside. Sondra stood motionless, leaning with one arm against the shower wall. The shower spray was pointed directly down on her head, the water running down the length of her body. The shower floor was slightly pink from the blood.

She wasn't moving at all. I wasn't sure whether to be worried. Her back was heaving slightly, so she was still breathing. I stared far longer than I should have. For at least two minutes, I watched water fall over her firm, muscular body, without her making a hint of motion. Her short, brown hair was no longer matted with blood, and she seemed to shine from the light reflecting off her wet skin.

I couldn't help but wonder about Sondra's past as I stared. At which Farm did she train? How many fights like that had she been in? Where does someone like her come from? With her drooping posture leaning heavily on the wall, she almost looked like she could be weeping. All that water her tears, pouring over strong shoulders, tiny breasts, and a lion's heart. A creature of beauty, power, and terror. Goddess.

I pulled the door back until it was once again open a sliver and stepped back.

"Sondra, you OK in there?"

"Fine!"

I heard movement from the shower, and another quick peek through the sliver showed Sondra vigorously scrubbing herself. I instantly wished I hadn't disturbed her meditation.

I stepped away from the door and looked around the room. I decided to throw all the clothes in a pile and put all of the weapons back in the duffel bag, just to get us reorganized, and to give myself a way of burning off nervous energy. I had just finished and set the duffel bag on the table when I heard knocks on the door. One knock, then three, then two.

I walked over to the door, the sound of the shower behind me. I wasn't sure I should answer the door without her being ready. I peeked through the spyhole, expecting to see Anton, but it wasn't him. Outside the door stood Goran, the owner of the casino, flanked on either side by security guards.

"Dr. Vale, I presume. It was nice to meet you yesterday. Today, I'm going to need a few more words with you." He spoke loudly through the door, knowing I could hear.

I turned and looked around the room. There was nothing lying around in plain sight that would suggest we were anything more than a poker player and a tourist. Not that I was going to let them in, anyway. I moved quickly to the table and drew Sondra's gun from the duffel bag.

One knock, then three, then two fell upon my door again.

"Dr. Vale. Respond, please."

In giving Anton's code knock, Goran was making it clear he wasn't here to talk about poker. We'd been observed. I walked back to the door with the gun in my right hand, held behind my back.

"Good morning," I said. "What's this all about?"

"I'd like to come in and talk, please."

"It's not a good time. Can we talk later?"

"Please don't be difficult. I have matters of security to discuss."

I stepped back from the door. My mind raced through every bit of information my redpack had mentioned about Goran Urusov. I thought about how much would be revealed should casino security review every video of Sondra and I since we'd arrived.

The door lock clicked, as if opened by a magnetic card, and the door swung open several inches before being caught by the chain. I stepped forward quickly and looked out, coming face to face with one of the security guards.

"Hey! That's rude," I said. "Can you hear the water? My girlfriend is in the shower. Come back later."

Goran stepped forward as the security officer stepped aside. He had a calm but stern expression, arms crossed in front, eyes boring into mine.

"Apologies. But Dr. Vale…I need some clarification. My Security Chief…he's noticed a few irregular behaviors in the hallways in the last twenty-four hours. You and your…partner…among them."

I looked him in the eye as he spoke, and he looked back with equal intensity. We were reading each other, as though sitting across from each other at a poker table. I couldn't know what tells he would read off of me, but I was getting nothing off of him.

"Can you explain why one of my most trusted employees has a special knock for your door?"

"My girlfriend is superstitious. He's a friend and he always does that, for luck."

"I see. Are the tenants in Room 249 your friends, too?"

"No, sir," I said, and I paused for a moment for emphasis, and to choose my words carefully. "It's very important to me that you understand they are not." Goran fell quiet for a few moments, carefully taking in my words, and eventually nodding slightly.

"I think I'm beginning to understand what sort of fellow you are, Dr. Vale. Can you at least tell me…does any of this have to do with all the Turkish players we brought in together?"

Undoubtedly, he picked up on the hint of a grin that slipped through my poker stoneface. He was reading me like a book. A few moments passed by with no sound except the shower water.

"Turks and Albanians, sir."

"Are they a threat? Is there evidence of this?"

I looked past Goran for a moment. I made clear eye movements, tracking the positions of his security guards, and I lowered my center of gravity subtly, as though preparing to fight. Goran stepped back for a moment, reading precisely what I intended him to read. That messing with someone like me has consequences.

"I don't believe they pose a threat to you, this casino, or this event."

"I see. Well, I don't know what you think you are doing here, Dr. Vale, but I can't have this sort of thing at Casino Rozvadov. I must demand you take your business elsewhere."

"I'm sorry you feel that way," I said.

"I notice you're still doing well in the PLO event," he continued. "You may finish that, and then I expect you to check out. And it had better be without incident."

"I will finish up today," I said.

"You just make sure you do," he said, turning away. I closed the door. I peeked through the spyhole and verified that Goran and his guards had left.

I turned around and was startled to see Sondra behind me, in fresh workout clothes, gingerly towel drying her hair. The shower water was still running. She had left it running to make it seem she was still showering. Nice move.

"I didn't hear much with the water running," she said. "But I take it that wasn't Anton."

"It was Goran, with two security guys. We're burned here."

CHAPTER 30   Two Souls

Sondra stared into a tall dressing mirror and adjusted her blonde wig. She leaned in close to inspect her dilated pupils and squinted briefly before turning away.

She adopted a balanced stance in an uncluttered part of the room. She began to slowly move through a kata. It was a pattern I didn't recognize, but reminiscent of karate or kenpo. She only managed about ten seconds before her balance wavered, and she had to grab the top of a chair to keep from falling.

"Alright, alright," she said, laying back down on the couch before I could do or say anything. "I'll stop trying. It's no good, I can't back you up right now."

I brought over every pillow I could find. I propped her up to an almost comical extent, until she finally demanded I stop.

"You know, it's kind of you to say it like that. You can't back me up. But I think it was pretty obvious from the start that I'm your back-up, not the other way around."

"Well, the tables have turned," Sondra said. "And for the record, there's no shame in being back-up. We're on the same team, we play our roles, we get the job done, and we get the hell away with our skins intact. Got that, kid? Check your pride at the door. There's winning and there's dying."

"You keep calling me 'kid'…it's a tell, you know."

Sondra looked at me quizzically, but then looked away. I was bustling about the room, and it was a strain for her eyes to follow me. She didn't want to show weakness. Couldn't bear the thought of being weak. I tried to imagine how she must feel, and what I would need if I felt that way. I handed her the laptop.

"There's one thing I need to make my plan work, and only you can do it," I said. "I can handle all the Poker Geyser stuff on here through my phone, while I'm at the live tournament table. But none of that matters if you don't come through for me."

"What do you mean?"

"The tournaments Soner's girls are playing. I don't know the precise start times of each round. My phone isn't fast enough to pick them up. But this computer is."

I went through it with her carefully. I'd programmed the tournament screen to refresh nearly continuously, and I showed her how she could sift through the screen recording, frame by frame, to try to pick up the precise times when the rounds would blink briefly on the page. If she could intercept even just one of those rounds, it might be enough for me to do some sabotage.

"I think I've got it," she said, after only a few minutes instruction.

"I'm going to get down there early. I need to transfer everything I've got left back to crypto, to make sure there's enough capital to make this work."

"Wait a minute. First, tell me what you meant by…calling you 'kid' is a tell?"

"You can't be that much older than me," I said.

"You're a newbie, and I'm a veteran. That's all it means."

It crossed my mind that it might not be the best idea to share my observations in this instance, but I couldn't help it. And if I was right about her, I knew she would understand.

"Your redpack contained information about my background, correct?"

She nodded.

"What did it tell you about me?"

Sondra closed her eyes and sank back into the pillows. She moved the icepack from her wrist to her forehead. It shielded her eyes from me.

"It told me everything I needed to know," she said.

"Any special instructions? Specific to working with me?"

"Thom, I don't want to get into this with you."

She seemed to slump even farther into the pillows. Her purple wrist twitched and flexed, as though it wanted to curl into a fist, but couldn't quite manage it. She let out a great sigh and set the icepack back down on the table.

"You really want to hear it? Okay. It told me all about your skills and experience, your medical history, and a little about your family background. And it advised me to monitor you closely, watching for you to have difficulties with your environment. And to abort the mission if you couldn't handle it."

"Why didn't you?"

"You mean at the pool? I don't know. I really don't. I guess…I just wasn't ready to give up on you."

"When you pulled me out of the hot tub, I could see deep concern in your eyes."

She stared at me. I had her rapt attention, and a quiver in her eyelids betrayed her emotion. If I hadn't been sure before, I was absolutely sure now. It was more than her not giving up on me. It had hurt her deeply to see me struggling with my senses.

"You reminded me of my mother," I said.

Her jaw tensed for a moment, and she involuntarily looked down at her bruised left hand.

"You told me you had a brother on the spectrum. The implication being that you knew how to help me because of that. Not really your brother though, right?"

Sondra's face untensed in an instant. The tension release of a secret revealed. Her eyes drifted off to the side, seeing memories instead of our room. Her chest swelled with love and pride, and a tear fell from her eye. Nearly a minute passed before either of us could find another word.

"My son," she finally said. "He's a savant. Music. Like you are with numbers…that's him on a piano." Her face seemed to glow warmly as she reflected on him. "For the life of me, I cannot get him to wear long pants. Or eat anything green." She laughed hard enough to squeeze out a second tear.

"How old is he?" I asked.

She looked at me, and the brightness in her eyes dimmed.

"You know…I must be really fucking dizzy to be talking about this. Back off, Thom. My life outside of work is strictly Eyes Only, got it?" I nodded as she got up and walked to the suitcase. "I hope I have something in here that can disguise my wrist a little. Then I'll move everything we have except the computer to the car, and have it parked in the valet lot in front of the casino. That's in full view of cameras. Should keep the flies away."

"I'll leave you to take care of that while I go transfer my funds," I said. "Where's Anton? He should help you, and you could get him up to speed."

"He's standing by downstairs. I'll call him up here after you leave. And if you pass him in the hall, don't say anything about my injuries. He'll only worry and try to convince us to abort."

"I think he's in love with you," I said.

Sondra looked at me suddenly, eyes widened, and a smirk formed on her lips. She shook her head, holding back a chuckle.

"It's not like that," she said. "What he and I have, it's just beyond friendship. Besides, he's married, with a wife and two daughters, and I…just…never mind."

I turned and walked to the door, but with the handle in my hand, I paused. Patterns and images were flashing through my mind, and they suddenly, finally came together.

Sondra's sturdy frame standing in the shower, smooth skin glistening under the cascading water. A nearly flat chest. Almost androgynous.

Slamming down a whiskey glass the same way my father did.

"I can see your gears are turning," Sondra said. "Your eyes are doing that weird wiggle thing."

I turned toward her and looked her up and down for a moment. She stopped sorting through her clothes and just looked back.

Her deep voice in Tomaj's room, which sounded exactly like an angry man's voice.

"Stop, Thom. Stop that right now."

Sondra's very short hair. Not regulation length for American military women, but easily within regulations for men.

"Of course…you can't stop, can you? You have to see every goddamned pattern, whether you want to or not."

Walking onto the plane at Andrews. The officers who pointed me toward the back of the plane were angry and irritated about something. I'd thought it had been my presence that bothered them.

"There's just no escaping you, is there?"

I wondered how many glares and putdowns Sondra had endured over the years. How many times some shortsighted regulation or bigoted superior officer had given her grief. Countless times, probably.

"I'm sorry," I said. "I only just realized…you're…"

"Is that going to be a problem?"

"Of course not," I said. "It has nothing to do with the mission. But I think my respect for you just tripled. I can't imagine how much boo-yah alpha male crap you must take on a regular basis. But you're still you."

"And who's that?" she said with a shrug. "It's complicated, Thom. You know, I think my favorite thing about my job is I'm someone different every time. They tell me at the start exactly who I'm going to be for the next week. I carry out the mission, and that's that. But when I'm off duty, I crash back into myself. And she's a different person every time too. I feel like I have to figure myself out all over again. Every time."

"Were you still male when you enlisted?"

"You don't get it," she said. "I was never male. Not really. If you must know, the clinical term is 'XX Intersex.'"

Sondra must have known I was confused simply from the look on my face, because she didn't hesitate long before continuing.

"When I was born, I looked like a boy. You know … downstairs. I was misgendered by the doctor and raised as a boy, but I wasn't one."

"You thought you were a boy your whole childhood?"

"Of course I did. That's what they told me I was. That's how my parents raised me. That's how I looked, and how I dressed. That's how I felt. Until I was twelve, and one day … well…it became clear I wasn't a boy. And then when I joined the Army, I got misgendered again because of what it said on my birth certificate. They still

officially consider me male, even after my operations.
When Bill recruited me, that was finally the end of that
bullshit.”

“I’m glad you found a place that felt right for you.”

“Feels right,” she corrected, looking at herself in a
mirror. “It’s just complicated. I still have all those
feelings. Boy feelings. Wanting to grow up and be just
like my Dad. Sometimes I look in the mirror and I see that
boy bringing home a big fish from the lake or carrying the
ball on a Pop Warner football team.”

I couldn’t help but smile for a moment, and she
gave me an awkward look.

“Sorry. It’s just that you reminded me of my big
brother,” I explained. “He was a quarterback.”

“My father wanted me to be a quarterback. He
hasn’t spoken to me since he kicked me out of his house.
You know why I joined the Army in the first place? It was
better than being a homeless teen.”

A shadow seemed to fall across her face. Was it a
trick of the light, or a lifetime of pain? Backlit by sun
through the window behind her, the blonde hair of her wig
glowed like a halo. I’d never before had someone stand
before me as strong or as vulnerable.

“Did you know I grew up on a Seneca Indian
reservation?” I asked. “Where I’m from, they would say
you have two souls. ‘Two-souled’ people make the best
medicine men, or so I’ve been told.”

“Yeah? Well…they had different things to say
about me where I grew up. I’m no medicine man, or
whatever. Honestly, I’m really not sure who I am.”

A sense of peace and clarity washed over me, and
made my head feel light.

“You’re a warrior, and you’re my friend,” I said.
“That’s who you are.”

CHAPTER 31   Hijack Position

For the last time, win or lose, I stepped out of the elevator and walked toward the gaming floor. The hallway lights seemed brighter. The blue motif of the walls seemed to undulate in my peripheral vision, like rolling waves. The ever-present black ceiling bulbs of the pan-tilt-zoom cameras looked down on me every thirty feet. I knew they'd have their eyes on me today.

A small group of players shuffled slowly in front of me, fellow survivors to Day Two. I crept up closer to the pack and used their numbers to blend in. I saw no sign of either of the tan guards, nor any of Soner's girls or players. I didn't know what to make of that. Had they all pulled out and gone home? Were they holed up in their rooms, under strict watch?

I broke from the pack and walked straight through the poker hall to the cashier. The usual cash games were going on in the back of the hall. Toward the front, the PLO players were settling into their tables. Our tournament was minutes away from restarting. At my table, there was no sign of Soner yet.

"Withdrawing my entire balance," I said, sliding the cashier my passport.

"Are you sure you want to put it all in play, sir?" she said.

"No, ma'am, just the opposite. Checking out soon." I set my phone on the counter, rotated so she could read the information in my crypto wallet. "Transfer everything back to here, in Bitcoin, please."

She smiled as she borrowed my phone for a moment. She adjusted her glasses as she read the long string of digits and diligently typed the information. I turned around as she typed and saw Soner enter the room with the two remaining tan guards. He walked up to our table and quickly debagged and stacked his chips. He then turned and marched back out the same way he came in, both tan guards in tow.

"All done, sir," the cashier said. "Transfer should be complete momentarily. I hope you enjoyed your stay with us."

"I'll know that soon," I said, taking back my phone. She raised an eyebrow as I turned and walked back to my table.

I dumped out my chips and stacked them. The dealer spread two decks across the felt for the players' inspection, but all I could focus on was the empty chair behind Soner's chips. I looked up toward the lounge to see Veronique, or whoever it was dressed as her. She was at the railing, looking down at our table. She instantly turned and walked away, and I had the uneasy feeling that she might have been watching me. I was about to text Sondra about it when she texted me first.

<<Our favorite porter will be collecting our luggage in 30 minutes. How tough is your table today?>>

<<One noteworthy absence>> I responded, as the cards began to fly.

<<I'll breeze through soon. Need some air>>

I folded my first hand, with plans to keep folding every subsequent hand, at least until Soner came back. If he came back at all. His brief appearance to debag his chips may have been to keep up appearances. It told me that his employer, Sheikh al-Karchi, probably didn't know anything had gone wrong. Or at least, if he did, then he hadn't heard it from Soner himself.

I folded again and again, clockwatching. I used the time to transfer my entire Bitcoin bankroll to the Poker Geyser site. And then I waited.

The button completed a full orbit before Sondra appeared in the lounge, leaning over the rail. She was wearing the same flowing zebra-striped blouse as when we'd left Ramstein. A smart choice, as its long sleeves could be pulled down to cover her bruised hand, with only her fingertips protruding. It also adequately concealed the back holster and Sig Sauer she was undoubtedly carrying. I told the dealer I'd be away for a few hands and made my way over to her.

"I blew most of Tomaj's chips on a couple hands of blackjack in the high roller room," Sondra said. "But it was worth it. Saw Veronique talking to al-Karchi in there. He looked pissed!"

"Did you hear her voice?"

"No, she was whispering. But he was plenty loud enough. I didn't catch everything, but I heard something in Arabic about 'Tell my man to summon the helicopter and make preparations,' or something like that. And then both of them, and those two guards who follow the sheikh everywhere…all four of them walk out together. Back to their room, I think."

"He's bailing," I said. "He doesn't want to be around when it all comes crashing down."

"Now, the best part. I walk out after them, casually, to try to see where they're going. I see them heading toward the hotel, and then one more guy joins them. The smaller tan guard."

Sondra grinned as she could see the realization in my eyes. The two big tan guards were personal hires of Soner, while the rest of the crew were al-Karchi's people. Now we knew that the smaller tan guard was also al-Karchi's man, there to monitor Soner and report back. We also knew he dressed as Veronique some of the time.

"I've got to get back to our room and start looking through the screen recording," she said, after a pause.

"How are you feeling?"

"Back off, I'm fine." And she walked back toward the hotel.

I returned to my table in time to set out my big blind but ended up folding rags again. Soner's chips sat untouched except for the dealer tossing in his blinds whenever they came around.

After a few more orbits, the player on my right busted out on a missed combo draw. Another player took his place, moved from a different table, just in time for the next round. He looked at least sixty years old, and his T-shirt and jeans looked at least forty. A glance at his greasy grey hair made me wonder whether he'd recognize a comb if he saw one.

And moments after that, Soner reappeared. The last remaining tan guard, the one who had thrown me out of the elevator, stood above us at the lounge rail. His usual fierce focus was gone. Instead, he slouched forward, hands on the rail, as though it were the only thing keeping him standing. His barrel chest heaved with burdened breaths. He was looking all around the room, beads of sweat on his brow, not seeming to know what he was looking for. I felt myself slide an inch lower in my chair and decided to keep my eyes on my phone and the cards.

Soner wasted no time getting into pots and took down two of them post-flop with aggressive betting. He leaned forward in his chair and pushed chips forward with smooth confidence. His operation was still running, and today's first hour had clearly gone well. Another hundred thousand dollars stolen and laundered. The death of one of his guards didn't seem to faze him.

Maybe he just had no choice. I ran the numbers through my head and calculated his crew should have cleared just under two-and-a-half million dollars so far. The sheikh had given him two million as an initial investment, and Soner had probably spent most of it setting up his operation. He owed payment to his guards, his players, and his girls. If he stopped now, he'd be a bankrupt failure with a terrorist group angry at him. Yet his face betrayed no nervousness, unlike the giant bodyguard behind him at the rail.

An emoji of praying hands appeared on my phone screen, followed by a message from Sondra.

<<You know how I find solace in reading the Bible sometimes?>>

<<Sure…>>

<<For the seventh time already, would you please read Genesis 43:12 and tell me what you think?>>

<<I understand. Let's be inspired together later.>>

I looked two seats to my left, where Soner was in another large pot. He was staring down his opponent confidently, neatly shuffling a stack of chips with his right hand. I almost felt sorry for him.

Sondra's text indicated that the seventh rounds today were happening at 43:12 on the hour. I flipped through my ghost drive to find the correct dollar amount for that level. I then switched to the Poker Geyser site and keyed in the information to create a head's up match for that amount.

"It's on you, sir."

I looked up to see the entire table awaiting my pre-flop action. I quickly looked at my cards and folded them.

The player to my right leaned over to try to peek at my phone screen, but I turned the screen down before we could see. He brushed back a filthy mop of shoulder-length grey hair and poked my shoulder with his finger. He reeked of tobacco and cloves.

"What's so damned important, you can't pay attention to this game? Not enough money at stake for you?"

"Just barely enough," I said, and smirked at him. He blinked twice, trembling with anger, and then turned back toward the table, mumbling something bitter about young internet players.

I finished creating the challenge for the online match. It was ready to go at the push of a single button. I checked the time and saw there were only two more minutes until that match.

The small blind reached my position, and I slid out chips from my meager, dwindling stack. I sat way back in my chair, closed my eyes, and took a long, deep breath. This was it. I put in my earbuds and switched the translator app to Arabic. When the action came around to me on the live table, I pretended to look at my cards for a moment before mucking them. On my phone, I clicked the button to create the $12,453 head's up challenge and held my breath.

Seconds later, as an ordinary PLO tournament hand played out on the live table in front of me, a No Limit Texas Hold'Em match for $24,901 popped onto my phone screen. I wondered for a moment which of Soner's unsuspecting girls was on the other side of it. Not that it mattered. A ten second clock ticked down to the start of the online match, and as soon as it started, my opponent would simply go all in, expecting me to do the same.

<<Good luck>> Sondra texted, letting me know that she was watching in our room, on the computer, as per the plan.

The website software randomly assigned the button to my opponent for the first hand. It dealt me the ace of hearts and the ten of clubs, and my opponent instantly went all in. Against any two random cards, my hand was likely to win, but I folded anyway. The point wasn't to win. The point was to let them know they'd been invaded, and to induce panic.

My chips slid into my online opponent's stack, and the software made a brief shuffling sound before dealing the next hand with me on the button. Jack of hearts and two of spades, a garbage hand. I let my fifteen second clock tick down in the online match while I folded another hand in the live game. I glanced over at Soner for an instant as I did, and then up at the tan guard. No reactions yet. I let my reserve clock run a bit before I clicked to just call the online hand.

My online opponent didn't instantly jam. Her clock ticked down, and her 90-second reserve clock started running. She didn't know what to do. Out of the corner of my eye, I saw Soner suddenly stand bolt upright, hand on his left ear. Up on the rail, the tan guard was also touching his ear, eyes wide and frantic.

The translator app picked up snippets of Soner talking, into some unseen microphone it seemed, as he got up from the table and walked hurriedly away. "Take over! Keep going! I'm coming!" The dealer called after him, explaining that there would be a break in just fifteen minutes, but Soner ignored him. Up on the rail, the tan guard had already bolted.

With no principals left to observe me, I took the opportunity to get up from the table. The dealer looked at me and shook his head but said nothing. I moved to an open area where there was no chance of anyone eavesdropping on my phone screen.

My online opponent went all in, and I folded the jack deuce. The third online hand was dealt, and my opponent jammed again. It was too soon for Soner to have gotten back to the hotel, so I knew I was probably still playing one of his girls ordered to just keep jamming. I looked down at the ace of hearts and the nine of diamonds, almost as good a hand as my first. I took another deep breath and hit the "call" button.

My opponent showed the two and three of Hearts. I was way ahead, about a three-to-two favorite. I tensed up as the flop came jack-six-four rainbow, meaning my opponent would win with a pair on any two or three, or a straight with any five. She had ten outs, twice. I breathed a sigh of relief as the turn brought an eight, and the river brought a jack. We'd both missed the board completely, and I'd won with ace high. I could feel my heart pounding inside my chest and sat down in a chair at a nearby empty table.

And then the fourth hand was dealt. It caught me by surprise, until I realized that, because I'd folded twice before the all-in, my opponent still had a few chips. But I was so far ahead in the match that I could just jam with any two cards, and winning the match would be almost inevitable. I jammed with an offsuit nine-ten, expecting my opponent to instantly call, but she didn't. Her timer ticked down, and then her reserve clock started ticking down. Soner had reached her.

[[Is that you Soner? Peekaboo, Turkeyboy!]] I typed into the online chatbox.

The reserve clock continued to tick. My hands were trembling. I looked around the poker hall to make sure no one was watching me.

[[Who is this ?!]] typed my opponent.

I slowly walked back to my table, typing one last message into the text box, but not sending it yet. The reserve clock ticked all the way down, and my opponent's hand folded automatically. He was stalling. I scanned the room one more time and saw nothing out of the ordinary.

I jammed hand number five, and again my opponent let the full time expire, auto-folding. On hand six, just after I jammed, I looked up to see the big tan guard bustling through the lounge. He was stopping at tables and looking. Searching for anyone on their phone, playing on Poker Geyser. Hunting for me.

[[Who are you ????]] my opponent chatted again.

Hand six auto-folded to me, and the blinds went up. For the seventh hand, my opponent was down to one last chip, and the website automatically put them all-in. I quickly hit enter and sent my chat message.

[[TELL THE GIRL NEXT TO YOU WHY YOU KILLED KATRINA !!!!!]]

I set my phone down in my lap as four real cards were being dealt in front of me again. I took a few moments to peek at them and folded them. I had better things to do. The tan guard was still making his way across the lounge. By the time I glanced back at my phone, the cards I'd been dealt had held up against my opponents' and I'd won the match.

[[You're dead]] my opponent typed into the chat.

I flipped to the challenge screen and saw that a head's up challenge with a $24,901 entry fee was sitting open. In the confusion, Soner had forgotten to halt the next round of his tournament. I quickly clicked to join it, and seconds later I was in the next match, playing for nearly fifty thousand dollars. I typed one last message into the chatbox.

[[LOL GG PUNK! DOUBLE OR NOTHING ???]]

I closed that window and saw I'd been dealt and ace and five of hearts for the first hand of the next match. The tan guard was descending the stairs down to the poker hall, and I saw him look directly at our table as he came down. I tried to steady myself and calm down my breathing. I was playing a head's up match for fifty grand, against men who'd kill me if they discovered me.

I quickly moved all in with my suited ace and slid the phone discreetly below the table as I watched. I was expecting my online opponent to stall, but instead she called immediately and showed a pocket pair: the four of clubs and the four of diamonds. A classic "coin-flip," almost fifty-fifty.

With the tan guard moments away, I swiped the screen to switch from the ghost drive back to a normal phone setting, and texted Sondra.

<<Why don't you join me for an early lunch?>>

Just after I hit the "send" button, a meaty hand clamped on my wrist and wrenched my arm back. The tan guard controlled my wrist with one hand and swiped around on my phone with the other. The whole table stopped its action to watch.

"What the hell?!" I said.

"What are you doing on here?"

"Let go of me!" I yelled. "Security!"

The dealer stood up and waved down a casino security officer. The tan guard wrestled the phone from me and surfed through it as fast as he could for about ten seconds. At that point, the security officer was approaching, and the tan guard gave up. He threw the phone on the ground at my feet with a grunt and stomped off in the other direction.

I put the phone back in my pocket as the players at nearby tables all wondered aloud what that was all about. I just shrugged repeatedly as they asked, and pretended my wrist was sore. The security officer stopped to check on me, putting his hand on my shoulder. He looked up at the tan guard lumbering up the stairs and swallowed hard. He then spent the next minutes asking me over and over if I was okay and whether my phone still worked. I couldn't blame him. I wouldn't want to confront that guy alone either.

"Last hand of the round" was announced over the loudspeaker. My paltry stack of chips had diminished to the point where I'd have only a few big blinds left after the break. As I got up, I saw Goran in the corner talking to the tournament director. I kept my head down and my thumbs in my jeans pockets as I walked in the other direction, following the break crowd toward the lounge.

Sondra was there, leaning against a pillar, arms crossed but smiling.

"Good game, punk," she laughed. "I wish I could have seen his face."

"I just hope they don't kill anyone on their way out," I said.

CHAPTER 32   Before It's Over

Sondra and I walked slowly through the gaming hall as I told her about my encounter with the tan guard. The dazzling lights and loud slot machines that had overwhelmed me on the first night—they had faded into the background. Dulled. Distant. It was as though I was hearing them from underwater. Only my conversation with Sondra existed.

It suddenly occurred to me that I still didn't know whether I'd won the second online match.

"Oh, you won," she said. "You turned a flush and it held against two pair. And then I logged out and shut it all down. Computer's in the trunk with everything else."

"Perfect. Great work."

Sondra's blouse kept slipping off one shoulder as she self-consciously pulled the sleeve down over her wrist. She looked back over that shoulder as we walked, but I saw no danger in her eyes.

"I'm not sure it was such a good idea to needle Soner like that in the textbox," she said. "I mean, driving him into a rage works toward making him self-destruct, but…now he knows his enemies are fluent in English.”

“That’s more than half the players here, and almost all of the staff,” I said. “But I take your point. Nothing but caution from here on in. I’m just glad it’s almost over.”

“Kid, if you learn one thing on this mission, learn this: the most dangerous thing in this business is thinking a job is over, when it isn’t.”

We walked through the front lobby and stepped outside into a harsh wind and fast-moving clouds above. The sun wasn’t quite low in the west yet, though it pierced the clouds brightly and made us turn our heads. We walked past two tournament players having a smoke, and then across a small lot to valet parking. Sondra fished the keys out of her handbag and popped the trunk. The computer, my suitcase, and her dingy green sack were there, and she seemed satisfied they hadn’t been tampered with. She closed the trunk and tossed me the keys.

“Why do we have the keys if the car’s in the valet lot?”

“Anton arranged it,” Sondra explained. “More cameras here and no foot traffic.”

“Friends in high places,” I said. “How much trouble do you think he’s in with Goran?”

Sondra shrugged and turned her head away from the sun again. She leaned back against the car, slouching a bit, and rubbed her temples with her good hand.

“Goran’s no dummy,” she said. “Anton handles every high roller who comes through here. Goran will keep him, only maybe on a shorter leash. We may have to cut him off as an asset, though, or at least not use him for a while. I don’t know. Not my paygrade.”

Sondra suddenly tensed and stood up, looking past me, squinting into the distance to the southwest. At first, I had no idea what had gotten her attention, but slowly I began to hear the distant drone of an engine and thumping of helicopter blades. It was flying in low, not yet visible past a distant tree line.

"al-Karchi ordered a helicopter a little over two hours ago," I said. "From that direction…."

"Switzerland," Sondra said. "Zurich, maybe."

We watched for a few minutes as a white helicopter appeared on the horizon, approaching quickly. It slowed as it neared the casino and seemed to hover exactly over it for a moment, but that was an illusion. We watched as it gently descended and disappeared behind the casino, no doubt onto the helipad just east of the rear parking lot.

"Looks like the evacuation will take place on the other side," Sondra surmised.

"We should watch it together. But first, I've got just enough time to grab a snack before I bust out of my first major tournament."

We walked back in the front entrance together, but then parted with a mutual nod. Sondra went back to the hotel to find a good vantage to watch the helicopter. I hurried back to the poker hall, grabbing half a sandwich along the way.

I looked around as I took my seat and saw no sign of Soner or any of the two-trunkers. Just the usual bustle of a tournament as it steadily approached the "money bubble," the moment when all players still in it would be guaranteed a prize. I would not be among them, having blinded away most of my stack in the last few hours. I smiled at the thought of the greasy-haired curmudgeon to my right enjoying my imminent bust-out.

<<Great view from the fitness room>> came Sondra's text.

The dealer at my table finished displaying the new decks and put one in the automatic card shuffler. We'd be restarting as soon as the deck was shuffled, and the missing players at the table settled into their seats during those thirty seconds. I could feel the weight of the stares from

those players as they eyed my short stack. They knew I'd
either bust soon or hit a big hand to get back in it. They
were hoping for a bust, of course, every elimination putting
them one step closer to the money.

I looked up into the lounge and saw a glorious sight.
The girl parade was flowing into the buffet area, in the
middle of the afternoon.

<<I love a parade, don't you?>> I texted to Sondra.
<<Good sign!!!>> she responded.
<<My bestie still hasn't come back from break>>
<<Aww…try not to be sad>>
"Get off your fucking phone already, will you?"
said the player to my right. "For Chrissakes!"

I smiled at him as the first cards of the round flew.
I scooped my four cards together and peeled up the corners
to see pocket aces, double suited, with a king and a nine.
One of the best hands possible for a short stack shove.
When the player on my right raised, I went all in to call,
and we ended up head's up to the flop.

The flop came ace, ace, seven. I'd flopped quad
aces, a hand that was practically unbeatable. Another
seven on the turn cinched it for me.

"Showdown, gentlemen," said the dealer, setting
out a meaningless river. My opponent sat hesitantly,
staring at the board with a long face.

"You've been called," I said to him.

He looked at me through narrow eyes, jaw clinched.
He slowly turned over a hand with pocket queens and two
rags, which had missed the board completely.

"Dammit!" I said. I took one more peek at my
cards, sighed heavily, and tossed them facedown into the
muck. "You're too good, sir. Run deep for me." I
thumped the table twice, and he thumped back once with a
surprised look on his face as I got up and left. I took one
last glance at Soner's stack, which still sat there still
dwindling. I wondered whether it would be enough to

make it past the money bubble. I wondered whether he himself would survive to claim the prize money if it did.

I walked slowly up the stairs to the lounge, hanging my head and trying to look disappointed. But I couldn't help but smile when I saw Sondra bustling about the buffet area, bouncing like a honeybee from table to table. She was grabbing a tidbit here and a tidbit there, eavesdropping the conversations of Soner's girls.

I ordered us up two lattes from the coffee station while I watched Sondra do her thing. I stood against the wall and kept looking around. Still no Soner, or any of his players. I wondered what they might be up to and put together a good theory. Sondra confirmed the theory several minutes later as she joined me at a small table, setting down a giant plate of food.

"Just realized I haven't eaten all day," she said. "So, get your own."

"I'm good. How's your head?"

"Better. Nothing a few aspirin and a couple weeks of sleep won't fix."

"You earned it."

"Speaking of which," she continued between bites of ravioli, "those girls are done, as far as I can tell. They're being sent home, by someone they just refer to as the 'old witch.' "

"Veronique," I said. "Or whoever is posing as Veronique at the moment. That ties al-Karchi in. He's not just an investor. He played an active role in their operation."

Sondra nodded. "One of the girls said she was sad she wouldn't get to see Dubai, since the plan didn't work out."

"They were told they'd be going to the UAE after this? For more work? An afterparty?"

"I didn't catch that, but like I said before…there might be a reason they hired escort girls. When this is over, I'm sure we'll be making an effort to turn a few of these girls and get the details out of them."

This was big. Our assignment had been to merely gather intelligence. Only we had taken a detour, on Sondra's call, to shut down the al-Alrasid operation we'd uncovered. But it was the sum of all the information we'd be reporting back that was truly valuable. There would be many future missions and operations, carried out by more qualified operatives, using the intelligence we'd gathered.

Once Sondra finished eating, we walked together up to the fitness area. It was predictably empty during the afternoon. She led me to the windows and directed my gaze to the helicopter in the distance. A white pick-up truck was positioned halfway between the helicopter and the rear exit. Sondra indicated that it hadn't been there before. We watched it for several minutes. There appeared to be black trunks in its flatbed. Two men were carrying another heavy trunk toward it.

"They're taking down the operation," Sondra said. "Getting rid of the evidence."

"They think they are," I said. "They don't know my laptop completely downloaded one of theirs. They can do whatever they want with their equipment. We've got a copy of everything important."

"Those guys carrying the trunk…are they two of Soner's players?"

"I can't tell from here," I said. "Probably."

"We need a better view."

We watched as the men loaded the next trunk into the flatbed, and then went back inside. A minute later, they reemerged with another. I could only guess that this was part of al-Karchi's "arrangements for departure." A systematic dismantlement. And then he'd fly back to Switzerland, which was probably where he'd flown in from. But the truck was clearly local.

"Where do you think that truck is going?" Sondra asked.

"I estimate they'd need five or six trips to carry all the trunks. Or maybe only three if they're loading more computers per trunk than when they came in here. Judging by how much the guys carrying them are straining, that might be the case."

"This must have been built into their plan from the start," Sondra said. "Otherwise, it couldn't have been organized so quickly. The destruction site can't be very far."

Sondra reached behind her and pulled up her blouse to reveal the Sig Sauer tucked neatly in her back holster. She thumbed the safety off before adjusting her leggings and pulling her top back down.

"I'll watch them from here until you can move the car to a good vantage point," she said. "We're gonna see this through to the end. It's not over until they're all gone."

I nodded and left. Something told me to use the stairs on my way out to the car. Maybe it was the elevator encounter with the tan guard, who was still at large. Images of that gigantic man flooded my mind and sent shivers down my spine. More images flashed in my mind as I descended. Katrina, the blonde girl at the pool, now dead in her apartment. Soner staring me down across the poker table. Veronique watching me.

By the time I got to the car, I needed to catch my breath. I took off my hoodie sweater and unbuttoned the top two buttons of my dress shirt. The cold wind helped. The ever-swaying line of trees helped. The quiet helped most of all. It was even quieter inside the car. Before long, I had driven the car to the back lot and parked it between two other cars.

<<All set>> I texted.

<<About time. Be right there. You didn't miss much>>

The truck's flatbed was almost fully loaded. The two men carried out what ended up being the last trunk of the load. After loading it, they flipped up and locked the tailgate, got in, and drove away. I checked my phone to mark their time of departure. They had just gone out of sight when Sondra came walking up to the car.

"Truck just left," I informed her. "Yes, those were two of Soner's men. And I haven't seen any of the principals yet."

She got in and shut the passenger door behind her. She kicked off her two-inch heels and seemed to breathe a small sigh of relief. Her head fell back on the headrest, and she winced almost imperceptibly. She let out a long, slow exhale. Her eyes were sunken and slightly darkened.

"I'd love to hear more about your son," I said.

A thin smile crossed her lips, and her body seemed to relax for a moment. She opened her eyes and turned her head toward me, serenely.

"You're a good man, Thom," she said. "But fuck off."

We didn't talk much over the next half hour. We saw a few small groups of Soner's girls leaving together in casino shuttles, each of them carrying either a hotel laundry service bag or a bulging backpack. They weren't turning their heads or bodies frequently. They weren't huddling together. None of them were pressing their arms closely against their body. It was hard to tell due to the distance, but their body language didn't seem to show any signs of fear or hesitancy. They seemed entirely unfazed.

"They don't know," Sondra concluded. "They don't know their boss had one of them strangled to death. They got paid and they got dismissed early. They're thinking they lucked out. They have no idea how lucky they really are."

When the white pickup truck returned, it's flatbed empty, I checked my phone for the time. It was nearly five o'clock. The cars in the lot were casting long shadows, but the streetlamps had not switched on yet. I heard the high-pitched whine of an engine starting up.

"Thirty-two minutes round trip, minus unloading time," I said. "I'd guess their destruction site is ten minutes or less away."

Sondra's left elbow gently nudged me. She wanted to make sure I could see what she was seeing. The rotors of the helicopter were slowly rotating.

"I wish I had a good rifle scope to watch through," she said.

Sheikh al-Karchi was first to emerge from the back exit, his two constant bodyguards flanking him and matching stride, their faces chiseled from stone.

Trailing twenty feet behind, Soner was walking alongside Veronique, who had a hand clamped firmly on Soner's forearm. His face was blank, and he looked pale. His gait was unsteady and wobbly-legged. At one point he looked at the helicopter and stumbled for a moment.

"There he is. I was beginning to wonder if Soner was stuffed in one of those trunks," Sondra said.

"He might as well be. If he isn't marching to his death, he sure as hell thinks he is."

We watched as they boarded the helicopter. The rotors began to pick up speed as the doors closed behind its occupants.

In a sudden, jarring moment, the rear driver-side window of our car shattered inward. Sondra and I both shrunk low in our seats for a moment, before turning to see what happened. Sondra's eyes went wide, as I suspect mine did too.

"Don't move, either of you!"

The large tan guard was leaning into the window, with a Glock G19 pointed at Sondra's head.

CHAPTER 33   Third Wheel

"Hands behind your head, both of you!"

The tan guard aimed his gun at the back of Sondra's head as we complied. He opened the rear driver-side door with his opposite hand and slid into the back seat. In my peripheral vision, I saw Sondra turning her head slightly, trying to watch him. In the rearview mirror, I watched him awkwardly scoot across. He grunted and struggled the whole time due to his size, the lack of room, and the difficulty of keeping his gun trained on Sondra at all times. His frantic, desperate eyes darted about wildly, absorbing everything around him. His suit was unbuttoned and open. His shirt was soaked with sweat. He eventually made it to the seat behind Sondra.

"Take off your seat belt," he told me. "Then we're going for a drive."

"Oh my God!" Sondra cried. "Just take our money. Take it and go!"

"Not about money, blondie. Why are you watching that helicopter?"

I slowly brought my right hand down and clicked open my belt lock. I turned my head a bit to look at him and saw him quickly pull the shoulder harness of his seat belt around his gun arm. He clicked his own seat belt shut, then noticed me looking and shifted his gun in my direction. His head tilted back slightly and his mouth fell open as he recognized me.

"Well, now. I told you I'd be back for that shirt. Face forward! Hands on the wheel!"

"Where are we going?" I asked.

"No questions! Just drive! Now!"

I started the car and put it in drive. As the car crept slowly out of its parking space, the tan guard reached forward and unclicked Sondra's seatbelt. She looked over at me with urgent eyes as the strap slipped off of her. She motioned with her eyes toward the passenger side mirror.

"Turn out of this lot, then head north. Past the highway. Just keep going north."

As I made a left turn out of the parking lot, I winced from having to look directly into the low sun. I subtly slipped my left hand to the door for a few seconds, just long enough to angle Sondra's side mirror as far inward as possible. Sondra shifted her position a few inches, trying to get a better view of our captor.

My mind scrambled through the images of the local terrain from my redpack. To the west, the German border was only three klicks away. To the north, mostly small country roads and farmland beyond the highway. Open fields and forest. A few abandoned historic landmarks. Not many people.

I heard the thumping beat of helicopter rotors. On our three o'clock high, also heading north, the white helicopter flew past us. If it was going to where the truck went, I knew it couldn't be far. Maybe another five minutes by car, ten at the most. It was now or never.

"Why aren't you on that helicopter?" I said. "Not invited?"

"Shut up and drive!"

"They'd kill you on sight, and you know it…just like they're gonna kill your boss. You think bringing us to them will get you off the hook? If I were you, I'd just leave. None of this was your fault. They'll forget about you."

The car fell silent for a minute. I could hear my pulse pounding in my ears, even over the tumult of the wind buffeting the broken window behind me. The highway was fast approaching. The tan guard shifted his gaze back and forth, between me and the road ahead. One side of his face was glowing from the bright sun, and the other was shrouded with shadow. It was as though two sides of him were weighing options, but in the end, there was one key factor in his decision that I couldn't have foreseen.

"It was you, wasn't it?" he demanded. "You're the one that killed my brother. Say it!"

Sondra's entire body tensed at hearing this. Her breathing was shallow, but the pulse in her neck was visibly pounding. I saw no cross-traffic as we approached the highway. I ran the stop sign and pushed down on the accelerator as we crossed to the other side.

"Was it you who strangled that whore, upstairs in her apartment?" I asked, accusingly. "What a tough guy. Think you can do that to me, tough guy?"

He snarled and turned his gun back toward Sondra, grabbing her left wrist with his free hand. Sondra let out a gasp of pain as he pulled her purple wrist back forcefully.

"First I'll strangle your woman and make you watch…wait a minute…what is this…?"

I pressed down on the gas some more, building up even more speed. More speed than was safe for a bumpy, dirt road. The tan guard paid no need. He had finally noticed that Sondra's wrist was injured. The motion of his pulling her hand away from her head also caused her wig to slip noticeably. He let go of her wrist and grabbed her wig, yanking it off cleanly. The crude, blood-stained bandage on her head lay bare before him. His eyes went wide with realization and rage.

"You! It was you, woman! Who the hell are you?!"

Sondra suddenly pulled the release lever on the side of the passenger seat. She pushed off the floor with her legs and threw herself and her seat back into the tan guard as hard as she could. His gun went off, shattering the other back window, piercing my ears with a deafening crack. The sun stabbing my left eye. The whole car shaking wildly.

I simultaneously slammed down on the brake pedal while pulling the parking brake. The car screeched to a halt on its front wheels, the back wheels lifting off the ground for a second, as momentum threw us all forward. Sondra was thrown hard against the glove compartment, trying to catch herself with her arms. I glanced off the steering wheel and struck the dashboard to its right and flopped to the right behind Sondra as the car's back wheels slammed back down. The tan guard stayed put, belted in place, his upper body wrenched forward with his gun arm down toward the floor. The car bounced hard on its shocks as it kept slowly rolling forward.

I shoved Sondra's seat back into the tan guard again as I scrambled to grab her Sig Sauer. The guard's gun went off a second time, this time shattering the passenger window. The grip of Sondra's gun was upside down in my left hand as I drew it from her right-handed back holster. My left pinky smoothly found its way to the trigger. The muscle memory of training I thought I'd long forgotten.

The tan guard screamed something in Arabic. The passenger seat was between him and me. I couldn't see him, but I didn't need to see him to know exactly where he was. He still had his seat belt on.

I aimed the barrel of Sondra's gun directly into the middle of her seatback and squeezed the trigger. My ears rang from the proximity of the gun to my head, but I just kept firing. Two, three, four, five shots in total before the sound became too much for me and I had to stop.

The car stopped suddenly with a jolt. It had rolled off the road and into a tree. The impact was jarring but not sufficient to set off the airbags. The engine was still running, and cold wind rattled through the car, in one shattered window and out another. Over those sounds, I heard gurgling and gasping.

Sondra and I both pushed ourselves up, and I switched the gun to my right hand. Sondra turned slowly, breathing as heavily as I was. Her left arm hung limply, and her face was ghostly pale. She peered back through the gap between her seat and the head rest. My view of the tan guard's blood-soaked chest and collapsing lungs was unobstructed. His gun arm lay limp at his side. His eyes stared forward, not focusing on anything. His mouth was painted bright red, teeth spattered with blood, he sprayed with each gasp.

"Who…are…you…."

I put the next bullet between his eyes.

"I'm sorry," I said, to no one who could hear me.

Time stopped as I watched him die. A last ugly spasm, and then stillness. His head fell to the right, his face now completely enshrouded in shadow. The flow of blood slowing, then stopping. The heart no longer pumping. Blood pooling next to him on the back seat, looking thick and dark in the setting sun. I wouldn't have imagined it would be so dark. My eyes lost their focus. Waves of nausea convulsed my stomach.

"We can't stay here," Sondra said, snapping me out of it. I handed the gun back to her, and she reholstered it with some effort, her left arm completely limp.

The car was still running, in drive, pushing against a tree. I backed the car off, and turned onto the road, again heading north.

"We've got to ditch this car," I said. "Can't go back toward the casino. You think Anton can make this car disappear?"

"No way. This is too big. Gotta call this one in."

I told Sondra I thought I remembered, from the redpack, an old, abandoned church further up the road. She pecked at her phone, trying to find it on a map. By the time she could do so, it had already appeared in the distance. It was a crumbling, stone church with no doors or glass in the windows any longer, but with a well-kept lawn and cemetery. A historical marker and information kiosk stood near the front gate.

"This will do," Sondra said. "Pull around back."

There was no pavement at the site, and no parking lot, but that was a good thing. I carefully drove through the grass around to the back of the building and parked the car as close as I could to the middle of the back wall. I shut the engine off once I was certain the car couldn't be seen from the road.

I scooted out the passenger door after Sondra, who then reached back through the shattered window and grabbed all the rental paperwork from the glove compartment. I popped the trunk, and Sondra leaned in to start going through the luggage, but then stepped back with a look of frustration, holding her left elbow in her right hand. She turned and sat down on the bumper, hanging her head.

"Is it broken?" I asked.

"I don't think so. But just trying to move it. Too much pain. I get dizzy and sick."

And then she shushed me. We both listened carefully and could hear the sound of a car approaching in the distance. I moved carefully to a position where I could look through one of the Norman windows on our side, through the small empty church, and spot the road through a window on the front side. As the car passed, I got just enough of a flash image of it to tell it was the white flatbed truck, full of trunks again.

"Their truck just went by. Didn't even slow down. They're not looking for us. They have no reason to even think about looking back here."

"We're not sticking around and taking that chance," Sondra said. "Border is right over there. We're marching."

With the sun nearly down on a cold Tuesday night, the chances seemed good that no local would stumble upon the car if we left it behind the church. The Prague office would send "cleaners" out over the next few hours to make it all go away. Sondra was right. The best strategy would be for us to extract any identifying information, weapons, and technology, and leave the rest for the cleaners.

I took the duffel bag of weapons and tech out of the trunk and stuffed the car rental paperwork in the laptop case. I fashioned a crude sling for Sondra's arm out of one of my dress shirts, and then helped her put her good arm through my thickest hoodie. She slipped on a pair of tennis shoes, and tucked the laces inside, too proud to let me tie them for her.

The sun glowed large and orange as it finally reached the horizon. We were about to head west through the woods when Sondra remembered she needed one last thing. She reached down through the passenger window and grabbed her blonde wig, which had fallen between the front seats. She stuffed it into my laptop case.

"She and I have been through a lot together," Sondra explained.

The sunset sky glowed red behind us as we clambered up Eagle's Hill. I was twelve years old, trying to keep up with my big brother. Matt reached the halfway point first and turned to watch me catch up. I had to look down to keep my balance. My scabby knees and dusty hands touched down on rocks, disappearing and reappearing in the undulations of my moving shadow.

"Hurry up, slowpoke," Matt called down.

He was still about twenty feet away along the ground, and about twelve feet higher in altitude. I had to stop to catch my breath, and I looked up at him. His left arm was in a cast and rested in a sling by his side. He'd still gotten there faster than me, surefooted as a goat, not even needing a hand for balance.

Matt was squatting by one of the small traps we'd set. It was a long wooden box open on one end with a pressure plate on the floor in the back. We'd put food on the plate, and then the weight of an animal would cause a wire cage door to snap shut over the opening. Our grandfather built several of them years ago. Matt and I had spread them all around the hill, and we checked them every few days.

"Get anything?" I asked.

"Yeah. Just a squirrel."

"I told you we should put them lower down. All squirrels up here."

"You just hate climbing."

As I clawed my way up the steep, stony path, Matt released the catch and opened the trap. A grey squirrel burst out quickly and scampered up a nearby tree. It was lucky. Mom only cooked rabbits.

We climbed the rest of the way together. In a few minutes we reached the clearing at the top of the hill. We sat down on a giant tree stump, facing west, as the last arc of the sun dipped below distant hills. The last rays of sunlight to fall on Kill Buck today were falling on us. I studied the hill which the sun was setting behind, and wondered how far away it was.

Over the tops of the trees below us we could see our backyard. Night had just fallen down in the valley, but our yard was lit by the glow of our father's halogen work lights. Dad was still chopping wood with his axe, as he had been most of the day. He had an impressive mound for one day's work, at least a full chord of firewood. Between his strokes, if we strained our ears, we could just make out the crackle and buzz of his AM radio blasting a Toronto Blue Jays game.

"Thank God school's finally out," Matt said.

"What's high school like?"

Matt hung his head and shook it back and forth. He glanced down at his cast for a moment, and then looked at me.

"You're supposed to be special and great at everything, but you have to be just like everybody else."

"That doesn't make sense."

"Welcome to high school."

Matt fumbled around in his sling for a moment and pulled out a steel flask. I recognized it immediately as the one Mom kept hidden behind her cookbooks. He unscrewed the top and threw his head back as he took a swig. He turned and offered the flask to me. I took it.

"Coach Dempsey's gonna skin me if my arm doesn't heal in time for August double-sessions. But it will. Least it's getting me outta chopping wood for the next month. Dad's already telling all his friends about how this is the year. 'Warriors all the way! Matty's goin' all the way!'"

I laughed at Matt's unflattering impression of Dad's voice. I looked at the flask, shrugged, and decided to throw my head back and take a swig like my brother did. The burning sensation made me cough and splutter, and I spat it out on the ground. Matt laughed and swatted me on the back as I gave him back the flask. He took a longer pull than his first.

"Maybe you should go out for another sport," he said. "Might get Dad off your back." But I only half heard him. I was imagining the sun in the sky, shining over the peak of the distant hill, casting the shadow of that hill on our backyard below. Then I imagined the sun slightly lower in the sky, casting the shadow of that hill on us where we sat. I began assembling the equations that would estimate the distance to that hill, based on the height of Eagle's Hill, the curvature of the Earth, and the speed of the Earth's rotation.

"I just like baseball," I said.

"Because of all the stats, right?" Matt said, after another long pull. "Numbers. Is that all you think about? Is that where you go when you play those dice and card games? You sit there for hours, just rolling dice and writing stuff down. You look kinda nuts. You know that, right?"

"I'm imagining sports. Playing out games in my head. I don't need all the other people."

Matt shrugged. He screwed the cap back on the flask. Down the hill, Dad was still chopping away, but it looked like he'd be finished soon.

"You amaze me, T.J. Your brain is like, I don't know, Einstein or something. Four years younger than me, but only two grades behind. You're gonna be anything you want to be."

"Think I can be a football star, like you?"

Matt was silent for a moment, but then a wicked grin slowly crossed his face.

"You'd make a good kicker, judging by what you did to Cory the other day. Serves him right for picking on you. That skinny jerk limped all the way home." Matt laughed heartily as he remembered. His laugh seemed to echo off the hills. "Good for you, Teej. Don't ever take shit from anyone."

"You up there, boys?!" came Dad's voice. "Get down here before it's pitch dark!"

We took a last look at the sky. Venus was shining brightly in the east, and some of the brighter stars were already visible. As we made our way down, there was more than enough light to see every tree. Not that we needed it. We'd both snuck out plenty of times just to stargaze at night. We could find our way blindfolded.

About halfway down, Matt stopped suddenly. At first, I thought something was wrong. Maybe he'd heard or seen a bear. But I noticed he was just staring down through an opening in the trees. He was staring at our father, who was splitting his last piece of wood for the evening.

"I'm going to be a General someday, Teej," he said. "You watch me. I'll show Dad and all his stupid war stories. I'll put him to shame."

He unscrewed the cap. He downed the rest of the flask in one long drink. He threw the flask overhand into the woods with enough force for it to ricochet off an unseen tree with an audible clang.

"I'm gonna play for Army. We're gonna win a national championship and I'm gonna win the Heisman. I'm gonna serve my country and rise through the ranks. I'm gonna have an office in the Pentagon. When people come to see me, the Heisman will be on a shelf behind my desk, next to all my medals. And when Dad comes to see me…my secretary will tell him I'm too busy to see him."

* * *

The wispy clouds before us were stained blood red as we plodded across a rolling plain. I struggled to keep pace with Sondra as we double-timed it toward the German border. I told myself it was because of the extra weight I was carrying, or the cold headwind we were walking into.

I calculated that we had approximately fifteen more minutes of useful light, and that it should be just barely enough. Looking back, the old church was no longer visible through the copse of trees enveloping it. Before us stood another row of trees. Just beyond that, the border.

There would be no fence to jump, no river to cross. No outward indication that we had left one country for another. Any manned patrol units or heat-detecting drones would have been called off. If all went according to plan, the next people we'd see would be an Army dispatch, ordered to collect us and bring us in.

We crossed the open plain, passed the thin stripe of trees, and walked across the wide fallow field of a farm. As the last hint of light disappeared and the sky above turned jet black, we came to a small dirt road. Germany.

We turned around once more and inspected the open field behind us. The light of a waxing quarter moon showed it to be empty. Sondra and I let out sighs of relief.

"I think I'm going to sleep for a month," she said.

About two miles in the distance, further into Germany, two headlights sprang to life. A few moments later they started moving toward us. A car with its high beams on.

"Would that be our ride?" I said.

"I certainly hope so," Sondra said, right hand sliding under the hoodie, finding her holster. "But just in case it's trouble, stand in front of me as they approach, so they can't see if I pull."

The headlights made slight swivels and bounced a bit, indicating the bumpiness of the road. They were the only lights in sight, except for a distant farmhouse, and a soft glow to the south which I guessed must be the border stop along the highway. Steadily, the sound of the engine and rolling tires grew louder.

"Something I need to say right now, Thom. When we get back, Bill's going to debrief you. Or if not him, then somebody."

"Of course."

"Listen. This is very important. The stuff you figured out about me. Not a word of that."

"Bill doesn't know you're trans?"

"No, he knows that. Lots of people know about that. It's in my military record. But officially, I haven't been active military for a long time now."

"Bill doesn't know you have a family," I realized. Her son, and whoever else was in her life. They had to be protected. If her identity was ever compromised, they would be endangered. And more than that, they could be used as leverage against her.

"Bill knows about my family, but nobody else does. And I need to keep it that way."

Even in the dim moonlight, Sondra's solemn tone and heavy eyes cast a spotlight on her dilemma. But it was no different than my own dilemma. We were trusting each other with our identities, I even more so than she.

"Like I said before…you're a warrior and you're my friend. That's all I know."

The oncoming car finally arrived, still bobbing and shaking on the bumpy back road. I could now identify it as a Feldjager van, the make commonly used by German military police. It slowed to a stop, but its motor kept running and the high beams stayed on. Sondra had already taken position a step behind me. I heard two doors open, passenger and driver. The passenger stepped out of the car but stayed behind the door. I couldn't see the driver.

"Code in, please," came the passenger's voice. Kentucky accent.

Sondra recited the alpha-numeric sequence we'd been given in our redpacks. The high beams immediately dimmed. The driver was now visible standing by his door, an American MP officer, gun drawn and trained on me. The passenger came forward, reholstering his sidearm. He wore unmarked camouflage fatigues but pulled a small penlight from his pocket as he identified himself as a medic. I stepped aside and he walked directly up to Sondra. He shined his light in her eye and made her follow it, then the same for her other eye. He took a quick look at the top of her head.

"Orders are for rapid extraction," he said. "Can y'all handle two more hours back to Ansbach?"

"Yes, sir," she said, eyes drooping. He directed us to the second-row seats in the van as the driver retook the wheel. He then slipped into the shotgun seat and turned to address Sondra again.

"Suture bandages have slipped a little," he observed. "That's gonna need some stitches, and some antibiotics. You're still symptomatic of concussion. What happened to your arm?"

"Fight. Car crash. Can't do much with it."

"Still have feeling and movement, though?" he asked, and she nodded as I helped her buckle in. "That's a good sign. We're gonna fix y'all up, ma'am."

Sondra sunk back into her seat, a wadded-up blanket making an improvised pillow against the window. By the time we'd reached the highway, and the driver put the pedal down, she was already out cold. I told the medic the details of her injuries, omitting any details about the mission itself. He nodded as he took in the information, looking back and forth between the two of us.

"And she marched out of there herself?" he said. "Damn."

"I need you to take good care of her," I said.

"Copy that."

The ride to Ansbach Army Base was smooth once we got to the highway. The ride seemed shorter than the ninety minutes it actually took. Watching Sondra sleep reminded me of when I met her, just three-and-a-half days earlier, lying back on the reclining chair in the plane. My mind replayed the images of her walking through the poker hall and turning heads. Her pulling me out of the water. Her fight on the video. Finding her in Pilsen.

And then the image of the tan guard in the back seat, spraying speckles of blood with each of his last gasps of breath.

I was dimly aware of the medic talking on a two-way radio as I turned and looked out the window at the night sky. The stars were bright above the line of trees which zipped past beneath them. I found Orion first, as always. The rest of the stars were hanging in the same places they always had, ever since I was a kid, stargazing on top of Eagle's Hill. There was too much ambient background light to see the Milky Way, so no white stain across the sky. Instead, the sky seemed stained red, and the speckles of light were speckles of blood, and I was once again staring into the eyes of the man I'd killed.

I closed my eyes and turned my head away from the window abruptly. I shook my head, futilely trying to dislodge the image.

"Are you OK, sir?" the medic asked.

"I'm just really tired."

"Almost there. Ten minutes."

The beige brick border walls of the base couldn't appear soon enough. We were waved through the blue front gates with only a momentary pause at the booth. We veered away from the civilian area and passed the mess and a physical plant. I saw a small runway and several helipads in the distance as our car slowed to a soft stop. On the sidewalk to our right, another medic was approaching on a wide sidewalk, pushing a wheelchair.

Sondra's eyes flickered open after I tapped her knee lightly. She sat up with a start, angry and confused. For a moment, she didn't seem to remember where she was.

"We drove you to Ansbach," said the medic. "Infirmary's that way. Bed with your name on it."

"Yeah," she said, unfastening her belt. "I remember. I got it." She looked around outside the van, and then opened her door and quickly stepped outside. The rest of us then scrambled quickly out of the van, and the medic gestured Sondra toward the wheelchair. She shot him a defiant look before walking straight past the wheelchair, toward the infirmary.

"I know the way," she grumbled.

The medic from our car hurried to catch up to Sondra and walked alongside her with the wheelchair attendee trailing behind them. The driver's hand on my shoulder kept me from following. Without a word, he made it clear he would be escorting me elsewhere. I stood there for a moment, watching Sondra walk away. Left arm in a sling and completely exhausted. But also strong, fierce, and refusing to show weakness of any kind. Sondra Sampson.

Halfway down the sidewalk, she turned for a moment and looked back.

"Hey, kid!" she called. "Thom with a T-H!"

"Yeah?"

"You really know how to show a girl a good time!"

She raised her good arm for a moment and gave me a salute. Then she turned and continued on, not looking back again.

CHAPTER 35   Debriefing

I woke up to the sound of firm knocking on a wooden door. From face down above the coarse, green blanket, I snapped onto my feet and into a fighting stance by the side of the twin bed. The room seemed unfamiliar, and was plain and drab like a hospital room, except without any machinery or medical devices. Guest quarters. The clock on the wall read six o'clock.

I looked into a square mirror hanging over a white sink. The bruise under my left cheekbone was more pronounced than the night before when the chief medic of the base had looked me over. Not quite a black eye. Obviously, it was a remnant of bouncing off the dashboard of the car, and it was accompanied by some left shoulder soreness. In the adrenaline of the moment, I hadn't felt the impact at all. I was feeling it now.

The knocking persisted. I finally remembered walking into the room the night before, closing the door behind me, and immediately faceplanting onto the bed. And now I was waking up to loud knocking, still fully clothed. My laptop case was on the floor where I'd set it down the night before. I turned the deadbolt and opened the door to see a soldier holding a clipboard.

"Oh-six-hundred, sir," he said, checking something off with a pencil. "I'm supposed to escort you to the mess for breakfast."

I nodded and grabbed my laptop bag. The soldier looked puzzledly at the bag, and then at me.

"This can't leave my side," I explained. "Do you know anything about the woman I came in with last night? Is she still in the infirmary?"

"I don't have that information, sir."

He led me outside into the dark, early morning. High-mounted floodlights lit the sidewalk before us. Out in the field, a team of technicians used those lights plus some portable lights to perform inspections on a camouflage-painted Chinook helicopter. Beyond them, out by the perimeter, a group of soldiers was counted through their morning PT.

"Slept in those clothes?" he asked, and I nodded. "I'll see what else I can requisition for you. You have a chopper for Ramstein at oh-seven-hundred. Find your way back?"

"That'll work," I said. "Thank you." He checked something off on his clipboard, and with a tip of his cap, he turned and left me at the main door of the mess hall.

I walked in and found my way to the chow line, laptop slung over my opposite shoulder, like a paperboy walking his route. Some of the soldiers turned and looked me over for a moment, but ultimately they all ignored me. I scanned the hall for Sondra but didn't see her.

I wolfed down a plate of potatoes and sausages and a black coffee, and then hurried back to the guest quarters. A sentry waved me into the building. When I got to my room, I found an olive drab battle dress uniform in my size, a small canvas sack, and a shaving kit. I welcomed the chance to clean up.

I remembered Sondra's wig, still stuffed into my laptop case. I took it out and looked at it for a moment. They'd been through a lot together, she said. I'd be turning in the laptop case at some point, probably Ramstein. I moved her wig to the sack, which would be my luggage for the flight home. A souvenir. Or perhaps I'd have a chance to return it someday.

A long hot shower soothed and numbed me, and the white noise drowned out my thoughts. I took long, deep breaths and felt my body relax for the first time in days. I lost track of time and spent too long in the water. I barely had time to shave and dress before the seven o'clock knocking came, exactly on time.

I opened the door wearing the BDU, laptop bag slung across my shoulder, and last night's clothes in the sack. The same soldier as earlier greeted me. He looked down for a moment at my white high-top sneakers, which looked ridiculous matched with the BDU. He politely cleared his throat to keep himself from laughing.

He escorted me back to the open area. The silhouette of a Boeing AH-64 Apache stood before us. Its top rotor was motionless and hanging with a slight droop, and the new orange dawn was breaking behind it. The pilot hopped down and came out to meet me as I approached. She pulled her headset off her ears, and it hung around her neck. She spoke very loudly, clearly accustomed to shouting over the roar of motors.

"Dr. Vale? Warrant Officer LaShauna Jackson. You're my only cargo today. Put your cans on. Gonna get loud P-D-Q."

She tossed me a matching headset.

"Long flight?"

"Oh, prolly seventy-five minutes or so, once this heap gets going," she said. "Helluva crosswind today. Better gotta iron stomach!"

It wasn't long before she had the Apache in the air. The flight wasn't rough at all and passed quickly. Views of beautiful German countryside rushed quickly beneath us as we rocketed west at over two hundred kilometers per hour. The lush green morphed into cityscape toward the end as we passed Heidelberg and Mannheim.

The morning was brightly sunlit by the time we touched down on the Ramstein tarmac. I stayed in the cabin as the rotors slowed down and watched as a black sedan with dark-tinted windows rolled up, stopping twenty yards from the chopper. I fist bumped the pilot and hopped out with my bags. The back door of the sedan opened as I approached, and a familiar face greeted me.

"Airlines lose your luggage?" Control laughed.

"It's been a wild week, Bill."

"Bill? You're ready to call me Bill now? Well…just might bring a tear to my eye, seeing you ready to leave the nest."

I slid into the backseat beside him. The driver took us on a short jaunt past the runways and several buildings. I was surprised when the driver took a right turn away from the center of the base. A minute later, the car pulled up to a baseball field.

"Not a lot of military bases have baseball fields," Bill said. "I thought this might be a fun way to welcome you back. Or maybe appeal to your sense of the surreal."

I looked out at the field, past the chain link fence dugouts, and saw a card table and two chairs set up at second base. Memories of my childhood flooded back. Being coached by my father. Feeling like I had to fit in with the team and be one of the boys. Wanting to be a good son. Wanting to be like my brother. Bill knew my psychological profile well. He wanted me to see him as a father figure. I didn't appreciate the ploy, but I respected his strategy. He wasn't called "Control" for nothing.

The car sat idling outside the fence as we walked together out to the middle of the field. A sealed, clear plastic pouch sat on the table. It contained my cellphone. I set the phone he'd issued me on the table as we sat down. Bill put it quickly in his coat pocket as I tore open the plastic around mine.

"Let's hear it," he said, putting on his sunglasses.

I started from the beginning. Our arrival and first meeting with Anton. Figuring out the intercepted text message. The raid on Tomaj's room. Sondra's fight in Pilsen. Hijacking the online tournament.

The man I killed to escape.

Bill had been leaning back before, nodding, making mental notes, and mostly just listening. I could tell he'd heard most of the story already. Wherever Sondra was, they'd already spoken. But he leaned in attentively as I talked about the tan guard. He didn't speak until I was finished.

"I'm going to set up a counselor for you to talk to," he said. "One of ours. I got someone right there in Pittsburgh."

I nodded and looked away into the distance. I tried to estimate the distance from the plate to the left field fence, but my mind felt too cloudy to concentrate. I rubbed my eyes. I wondered if they looked as dry and red as they felt. More than anything, I just wanted to lie down somewhere and not talk to anyone for a long time.

"Hey! Did you hear me?" Bill said. "You're going to talk to a counselor when you get home. Tell me you understand."

"I understand."

"Alright. Brass tacks, then. Your orders were to observe, assess, and report. How do you explain your involvement in Tomaj's room? You risked exposure."

"Snafu," I said. "Sondra was supposed to go alone. In and out in a minute. But that girl was still there. Katrina."

"Why didn't she abort?"

"I don't know," I said. "Her plan was to abort in that contingency, but in the moment, she made a different call. I don't know why. But the more I think about it, I think she was right. We needed the intel. And once she'd been seen…it was too late to go back."

"You could have just left."

"Could we? What were her orders, exactly?"

Bill sat back and crossed his arms. He stared silently at me for several seconds. My reflection looked back at me from the lenses of his sunglasses.

"That's need-to-know," he said.

"Well, she needed backup, and I backed her up."

"Alright," he said. "I can get behind that. But then you hacked into their tournament. How do you justify that? You could have let it run and reported everything you knew. We could have followed the money. Seen who it led us to."

"Wasn't leading anywhere," I said. "Except maybe some offshore account that'd be empty by the time you tracked it. They were going to steal twenty-five million for al-Alrasid and get away clean. Knowing how they did it after the fact wouldn't matter, because they probably can't ever do it again anyway."

I explained the money laundering scheme in detail. After going through the numbers and taking into account Soner's expenses and the sizable payments he'd probably promised his crew, as well as reasonable compensation for both Soner and al-Karchi, it was probably more like ten million for al-Alrasid. But that number was still enough to make an impression on Bill, whose posture of hard interrogation began to soften.

"In our judgment, we had to act immediately. Reporting wasn't good enough."

"Not your call," Bill said. "Nonetheless, I find myself in agreement. Don't beat yourself up too much, son. These things are never black and white. We just write them up that way. If this ever comes to the light of day, I'll back your play."

"That's what Sondra said about you," I said, raising his eyebrow in interest. "She said you're a shyster, but you've got our backs when we need you."

He laughed and leaned back in his chair, peeling off his sunglasses, and rubbing his eyes.

"Some week, eh?" he said, smiling. And in a matter of seconds, he wasn't my boss anymore. He was an old friend.

"How's Sondra?"

"She's alright," he said. "As you probably guessed, I spoke to her first. By commlink during her ambulance ride to Landstuhl. She's even more pissed at me than usual. I'm giving her time off until the end of the year, at the very least."

"Well earned."

"She was rather impressed with you, too. And if you hadn't guessed, she isn't the type to impress easily."

I couldn't find the words to respond. My chest swelled, and I felt light as a feather, as if the air in my lungs might be enough to float me away.

"How about Anton?" I asked.

"Don't worry about that," Bill said. "We were able clean everything up. You'll get all your stuff back as soon as it's been checked. Might take a few weeks. Procedures."

"Yeah, I know. I mean, what about Anton himself? Sondra was worried we'd pushed him too far, and Goran Urusov made him as one of our assets. What about him?"

"We're taking care of that."

Bill didn't divert his eyes for even an instant. A normal person's gaze would sporadically wander, but his was fixed on me. As though he were making a conscious effort not to give off information. A poker face. I didn't say a word. I let him see my eyes wander over his face, then his neck, then his face again. I let my face droop, sadly. Without a word, I let him know that I could see through his deception and was disappointed. He'd taught me too well. He'd taught me enough to beat him.

"He's gone missing," Bill said. "We're not sure what's happened to him."

"Jesus! Sondra's gonna go apeshit! You know how they feel about each other, right?"

Bill nodded, and just sat there. Infuriatingly. I stood up and flipped the table in one motion. Bill stood up with me.

"Don't just sit there like I'm some kind of asshole for giving a damn! You can't throw me into a pot of boiling water and tell me not to care!"

"Yes, I can," he said, calmly, eye-to-eye. "That's a pretty good description of what I do, actually. I play chess. With people. I move them around the board, and I try not to sacrifice them over nothing. But in the end, I make whatever moves win the game."

Maybe it was the surging adrenaline. Maybe it was the battle dress uniform I was wearing. Maybe it was the violence of the past week combined with the violence of my sudden disillusionment. Thoughts of tearing Bill limb from limb coursed through my mind. The only thing that calmed me was the sight of two red, glowing dots of light on my chest. Laser sightings from distant rifles.

"You did your job, Thom. And you did it well. Now you go home, and I'll do mine."

I took a deep breath and calmed myself. We walked slowly back to the sedan. Halfway there, the red lights disappeared from my chest. When I opened the back door, I saw that my small sack of clothes was still there, but the laptop case had already been taken away. I got in, but didn't close the door behind me, as Bill was holding it open.

"My driver will drive you to your jet," he said. "And there's something else you should hear from me, rather than the news. About five miles north of where you left your car, the local police found a big bonfire. It had a couple hundred laptop computers in it, and one human body. Hasn't been ID'ed yet, but safe bet it's Kadri Soner."

Only one human body. The girls all went home, and probably his players too. It was over. Except that Sheikh al-Karchi had gone back to Dubai, having experienced little more than a disappointing business venture. Surely, we haven't seen the last of him.

"When you get home, expect to see a scheduled appointment with a counselor in your inbox," he said. "Talk about this, Thom. Trust me. It'll help."

"Take care of Sondra," I said. "And Anton's family. Take care of them, too."

Bill shut the door. The driver sped away.

CHAPTER 36   Homecoming

My jet outpaced the sun in a race across the
Atlantic. This time, the chair across from mine sat empty
and upright. The dull roar of the engines resonated through
the long empty cabin, and somehow that made the chair
feel even emptier. I wondered how Sondra was doing, and
hoped she was recovering well.

The Arctic Ocean shined brightly below, the sun
reflecting off its choppy waves. How would it feel to be
sailing on such a sea? Bobbing up and down, waves
striking the hull and spraying the deck. Alone on the open
sea, squinting into the sun. Taking in the beauty,
adventure, and profound isolation. I could relate.

Bill hadn't discussed my future with Homeland
Security beyond this assignment. I didn't know whether
this would be a one-off, or if it would be the beginning of a
career in the clandestine services. Had I been nothing more
than an asset, used this once for a purpose specific to my
talents, and then tossed aside? Would I be sent back to the
salt mines of strategic analysis? Maybe that's where I
belonged, anyway.

In four years, my contract at Carnegie Mellon would end. I would surely be sent packing then, assuming Tucker Burgreen hadn't found an excuse to fire me sooner. Would I be a full-time analyst after that? A full-time something else? Wave after wave of self-doubt and uncertainty crashed against my hull.

I thought about the people I'd see back home. I'd have to call Dante when I had the chance, to let him know I was returning early, and to thank him for all his help. I looked forward to seeing McKenzie in the faculty lounge and trading good stories over bad coffee.

For most of the flight back, I thought about Marina.

I was still thinking about her when our wheels touched down at Andrews. The jet taxied a bit before finally stopping near a hangar. It was still late morning. It had been morning all day.

The co-pilot appeared and beckoned me forward as he opened the cabin door. I followed him down the short staircase to the tarmac.

"This way to the hangar, sir," he said.

"I was expecting a ride back to Pittsburgh."

"That's after the hangar, sir."

As we approached, a man in a blue suit and sunglasses stepped out. I walked up to him, and he put his hand out to shake mine. He was very tanned, blond, and had a medium build and stern jaw. He smelled of cheap aftershave and had worn but well-polished shoes.

"Dr. Vale? Avery Hamlin. CIA. Good to finally meet you."

We walked together toward a limousine. I didn't recognize the driver, who opened the cabin door for us as we approached and closed it behind us once we'd entered. Hamlin was a handler, and lately I was one of the horses in his stable. I'd worked dozens of strategic analyses for him over the last three years. We had never met in person until now.

"Gonna take a little detour on your way back to Pittsburgh," he said. "Drop me off at Langley. But let's you and me talk a little shop on the way, what'd'ya say?"

"That'd be fine."

"Driver, put the glass up, will you please?"

Tinted glass slid up, soundproofed surely. Hamlin took off his sunglasses and loosened his tie. He leaned forward and looked me directly in the eye.

"Help me out here, Thomas. Help me to help you."

"Sir?"

"I'm going to have a meeting with the Director sometime soon. Suppose he asks me why one of my analysts went cowboy, and directly confronted known al-Alrasid associates. What would you have me tell him?"

"Cowboy?"

"You were to have no confrontations with the opposition. None whatsoever. Was this not made clear to you?"

"It was...."

"Then what the hell were you thinking?!"

I cleared my throat and paused for a beat. "It was pretty clear to me, early on, that my partner had more aggressive orders, and I backed her up when she needed it. I helped her take down a terrorist money laundering scheme, and I got her the hell out of there when the walls were closing in. And you know what, Hamlin? Don't hold your fucking breath waiting for me to apologize!"

Hamlin stared at me for a few seconds, trying to be stone-faced. Soon one corner of his mouth curled up, and he could no longer stop himself from busting out in laughter. He thumped his chest with a fist a couple of times and slapped his knee.

"Alright, alright," he said, still laughing but calming down a little. "Let's hear it then. From the top."

We drove through start-and-stop traffic all around DC. The driver clearly had orders to circle around for a while. I retold the whole story. Unlike Bill, who was mostly interested in what we'd learned about Sheikh al-Karchi and al-Alrasid, Hamlin asked a lot of specific questions about our tradecraft.

We drove for nearly an hour before we turned off the George Washington Memorial Parkway and arrived at the Langley campus. The driver circled halfway around the campus until we reached the George Bush Center for Intelligence. We stopped at the curb, and Hamlin got out. He slapped the top of the car twice and leaned back in.

"Time to send you home now," he said, nodding toward the driver. "I like what I heard today, Thom. You got balls. You'll be hearing from me again soon. Keep fit."

He slapped the top of the car once more, closed the door, and stood watching us as we pulled away. A few minutes later, we were back on the highway.

The drive to Pittsburgh seemed to take an eternity. So near home, and so near the end. I wished I could will the miles away. Dusk was settling over the Monongahela by the time the lights of the city appeared. The streetlights were shining brightly over East Carson Street through a cold, misty rain. The soft glow of lights from The Buzz loomed ahead, calling me home. When we hit a red light one block away, I couldn't wait any longer.

"Here's good enough," I said, grabbing my army sack and getting out. The driver shrugged and drove off as the light turned green. I walked quickly through light rain, weaving around puddles and pedestrians. I stood in the light which poured from the front windows of The Buzz and looked inside.

She was there.

She was ringing up a coffee and dessert for one of the regulars. She still had her EMT uniform shirt on underneath her apron. She must have come in after a shift and immediately threw an apron on and started working.

I walked in the front door. Marina looked up, saw me, and did a double-take. She looked me up and down, inspecting my uniform, and covered her mouth with a hand to try to hold back a laugh. She flashed me one finger to indicate "just a minute." She gave her customer change and a receipt before bouncing over to see me by the back stairs.

"Did you get drafted?" she asked, giggling. "Is that where you've been for a week?"

I just smiled and shook my head. That was all the opening she needed to throw her arms around my waist and bury her head in my chest. Only this time I held her too. I felt her warmth against me and her fawn brown hair smelled like lavender. I kept holding her. Eventually, she looked up at me, her deep brown eyes meeting mine, but she didn't say anything.

"I missed you," I said. "And I'm sorry I've been so distant."

She smiled and gave me one more quick squeeze before letting go. She stepped back and leaned against a tall counter behind her, looking me up and down again.

"So, what's with the military drag? Halloween costume? Maybe you could make it work with some boots and a camo hat."

"It's a long story."

"Well, I can't wait to hear it. I'll even listen to you talk about math and stuff. Hey, is that a bruise on your face? You bump your head or something?"

"I'm actually not supposed to talk about it."

"Why's that?" she laughed. "You could tell me, but then you'd have to kill me? Well now I'm totally fascinated." She drifted back toward the coffee machines. "Want a hot buttered croissant and a latte? I'll put an extra shot in it. You look kinda tired tonight."

I stood there for a moment, watching her bustle about the machinery. And I thought, why the hell not?

"What time do you close up tonight?"

"Nine o'clock," she chirped. "Couple more hours."

"Why don't you come up afterward, and I'll tell you everything."

She looked up from her machines for a moment and nodded. I turned to head up the back stairs but paused in the doorway.

"Oh, and Marina? By any chance, do you have a swimsuit with you?"

"No."

"Perfect," I said.

I'm not sure which of us was wearing the bigger smirk as I turned and walked up the stairs. I couldn't wait to get out my olive drabs, still wet from the rain. Maybe light a few candles, chill a bottle of wine.

I was ready to not be alone anymore.

I unlocked the door and walked in, clicking on a light as the door shut behind me. I tossed the sack down on the floor, only then noticing that it landed near the feet of a man, who'd been standing alone in the dark, waiting for me.

Anton was holding my Glock-19, aiming it at my head.

I stared down the barrel of my own gun, with its fitted silencer, and froze.

I was unarmed, fifteen feet away, and Anton had the drop on me. But he didn't fire. I was as good as dead if he wanted me to be. It could only be that he needed something. Something only I could give him. He must have left Rozvadov well before Sondra and I were ambushed by the last tan guard. Flown commercial, probably. He could have gotten here a few hours before me, perhaps. But why?

"You went missing," I said. "We thought you were dead."

He didn't respond. He crouched down slowly, never taking his eye off me. He kept pointing the gun at me with his right hand, fishing for my army sack with his left. Once he'd managed to grab it, he stood up quickly. He looked uncomfortable, and his stance was awkward. His eyes were wide with panic, and his gun arm was trembling.

"You working for them now? For the sheikh? For al-Alrasid?"

"I'm working for me," he said. "Upstairs! Now! Touch nothing!"

I kept my hands at my sides and walked slowly to the iron spiral staircase. He followed me closely, but not closely enough to give me an opening. On the upper floor, the light of several computer screens was just enough to see by.

"You've been trying to get into my machines," I said. "You really thought you'd be able to do that?"

"Sit down and shut up!" Anton tossed my luggage sack to the ground beside him, his gun never wavering from me.

"What do you want with this stuff anyway? Do you really think they trust me with state secrets?"

"Yes," Anton said. "I think sometimes they do."

And he was right. Some of the analyses and problems I'd worked on over the years involved highly sensitive intelligence and information. Most of it had been deleted at the completion of the jobs, of course, as a standard security measure. But my machines contained plenty of valuable pieces of information at the moment, if you knew where to look.

"And you think you can sell them? To whom?"

Anton backed further away from me, with the gun still trained. He seemed to almost relax a bit, and the tense terror in his face was replaced by a smug sneer.

"You know, for years I looked after American agents, coming and going. They stayed at the casino hotel while recuperating. Meeting with people. Acquiring their assets. Making deals. Throwing a lot of money around. I always took care of them, no problems, no questions. And you paid me well. Enough to send my girls to college. Ivy League, like your Presidents and millionaires. All the advantages of the West. They're going to have it really good.

"Then one day Sheikh al-Karchi shows up. Takes the VIP suite, gambles like a whale, throws money around everywhere. He tips me ten thousand Euros a day, for nothing. For keeping his tea hot and driving him and his men around. Nothing."

Keeping the tea hot. Funny way to describe it. I thought about that for a moment, and something I hadn't realized before finally occurred to me.

"But this time he had more for you to do," I said. "Such as dressing up like Veronique when his personal bodyguard was too busy to do it. Keeping an eye on things for him."

"Very good," he said, nodding. "And I was keeping an eye on the two of you as well. It should have gone smoothly. You were supposed to just watch them and report. You were supposed to watch Kadri Soner and his stupid friends play poker like donkeys for a few weeks, get drunk at the bar every night, and leave town with those whores. And that would have been it."

"And you get paid by both sides and live happily ever after," I said. "I guess I should feel better knowing you're not a terrorist. Just a greedy backstabber."

"Backstabber?"

"You sold me out to terrorists!" I yelled. "My identity! Just coming here, you've burned me!"

"No," he said. "They don't know I came here. I only told them I could get U. S. intelligence secrets."

It took me a few seconds to realize he was probably telling the truth. He couldn't burn me because I'd spent a week posing with Sondra as a couple. If he gave me up, he'd be giving her up too. And that was something he could never do. He'd come here in the hope of stealing my files and leaving undetected. Selling them for millions, maybe. Only he didn't have the hacking skills.

"You must realize there's no way in hell I'll ever give you anything, right?"

"Not afraid to die for your country?" Anton said. "Good for you. But I don't think you understand your situation. Now that you've seen me here, you have to die. No matter what. After I empty this gun into you, I'm going to create a gas leak, and blow this whole building off the map."

He paused for a moment, to let it sink in.

"Give me all your files, and I'll do it when the building's empty."

I couldn't help but envision all the students downstairs, studying. Marina tending the counter. Mr. Sobczak. I looked at Anton and saw a scared, angry, desperate man who was in over his head. Could he really do it? Kill a dozen innocent people, just over money? Was this the man who had earned Sondra's complete trust?

"You win," I said. "You know, I'm almost glad Sondra isn't around to see this, you fucking snake."

"The files! Now! No sudden movements!"

I gestured at the army sack he was still holding.

"You had no hope of breaking in because a password isn't enough. It takes my thumbprint, and you have to plug in my common access card, which contains my specific decryption key. It never leaves my person. Actually, it's at the bottom of that bag you're holding."

Anton glanced at the bag and then back at me. He slowly crouched down again, set the sack on the floor, and loosened the drawstrings. He kept his eye on me as he reached in and fumbled. His eyes squinted in confusion for a moment. Then they widened and his nostrils flared as he stood back up, holding Sondra's wig.

"Explain this! Immediately!"

"I suppose she would have wanted you to have that," I said, with a somber voice.

"Explain!!"

"We thought she was OK, but there was hemorrhaging. We got her back to Ramstein. She laid down. And…it was peaceful. In her sleep."

"No! Liar!" he screamed, stepping closer to me, gun arm shaking spastically. His eyes were glassy and bloodshot. He looked like he could explode.

"How could you set her up like that?" I continued. "That morning, sending her to Pilsen after that girl, knowing what she was walking into."

"No! I didn't know! How could I have known?!"

From the room below, I heard the door opening, and then shutting again.

"Thom? Are you upstairs?"

Anton swiveled his head for a moment, distracted by Marina's voice, and I leapt at him. He was too startled to get a shot off before I tackled him hard near the top of the spiral staircase. He tried to aim the gun from on his back, but I clinched his hand and slammed it into the iron railing. The gun clattered over the edge and down the stairs. We both instinctively reached in its direction, and that was enough to send us both tumbling down the stairs, grappling with each other all the way down.

Marina gasped as she saw us. She pulled her arms in tight, as the food and drink she'd brought up fell to the floor with a splash.

We landed together on the hardwood floor. Anton tried to break away and reach for the gun. I used the opportunity to grab his shoulders from behind and slam him face down onto the floor. I straddled his back while he still struggled to reach the gun, but it was too far out of his reach.

I pounded on the back of his head with bare fists, one after the other, some of the blows bouncing his head off the hard floor with solid thumps. Ground and pound. He was no longer moving after ten or twelve blows, but I didn't stop. My eyes were blurry with rage and terror. I couldn't see Anton anymore. All I could see were the faces of the people he'd betrayed, and the people downstairs he would have killed. I kept pounding until his blood began pooling in a small puddle, just above his forehead.

And then finally I sat back, gasping to catch my breath, tears flowing, and still straddling his now lifeless body. Marina had fallen to her knees, glazed eyes staring through me, into space. Her mouth was open in a silent scream.

"Marina?"

"Thom. Oh my God. What the fuck?"

"Marina…it's going to be OK now…."

"Who the hell is that, Thom? And who the hell are YOU?!"

All I could do was shake my head. It was a good question.

CHAPTER 38   Cold Coffee

Around two thirty in the morning, the neon signs of the bar across the street flickered off. I watched their reflections in the pavement of East Carson Street, shiny from the hard rain still falling. Avery Hamlin stood in the doorway of The Buzz, lighting his tenth cigarette of the evening. He walked over to my table by the window and sat across from me.

"My associates will be finished with your loft soon. Is that what you call it? Loft? Apartment?"

"Studio, I guess." I didn't look at him. I was watching the ripples of the raindrops in a giant puddle by the curb.

Hamlin's associates were two muscular men in black sweatshirts, jeans, and hats. He sent them upstairs carrying leather tool bags and a large black tarp. They would make all traces of Anton disappear. I didn't want to know the details. They would turn my place upside-down, sweeping for bugs, hidden cameras, and explosives – and then put everything back in place and vanish. I would never have known they were there if I hadn't seen them myself.

"Good of you to come so quickly," I said. "Should I read anything into that?"

"I don't like it when my officers' ops follow them home. Can't have it."

I looked over at Marina, who was wiping down the counter. This café was her home as much as the studio was mine, and she'd been obsessively cleaning it for hours. She'd stayed close by me all night. I'd made all the necessary phone calls. Within ten minutes, Hamlin called me back, and within two hours, he arrived with his small crew. I could only guess a helicopter must have been involved.

"Nice set-up you got here," he said. "You own the café, too?"

I shook my head.

"Well, it's gonna be the cleanest café in town if your friend over there doesn't settle down."

"Try and understand why she might be a little worked up tonight," I said.

"She gonna be OK? You think maybe she's gonna be a problem?"

I looked up at him finally, and with one glare I made it clear that he'd better never, never, never ask me that question again.

Hamlin withered in his chair slightly, but quickly recomposed himself. Two pairs of heavy footfalls on the back stairs preceded the two men in black. They walked through the café together. One of them gave a quick nod to Hamlin just before they reached the front door. Hamlin gave them a thumbs-up signal in response, and the men left the café.

"Well, how do you feel, Thom?"

"Tired," I said. "Just tired and worn out."

"Sounds about right," he said. "I suppose you could use a little quiet time now, right? But how quiet is too quiet? That's what I'm wondering."

"What do you mean?"

"Are you going to be happy now if you go back to being just an analyst? Are you going to be happy just solving math and stats problems? Did we ruin you for that?"

My mind filled with images from the past week. The sleek Falcona shining on the Andrews tarmac. Sondra's fierce eyes. The gorgeous colors and designs of the casino halls. The girls in the jacuzzi. The car crash, and the dying face of the man I'd killed. The first man I killed, but not the last. Would Anton be the last?

I looked over at Marina, who had stopped cleaning. She leaned back against a wall, watching Hamlin and me. She only lived in my other world.

"I don't know," I said.

"That makes three of us," Hamlin said. "You, me, and Bill. You know, Bill was telling me once about this guy he knew, oh, about eight years ago. Went by 'Sean' for a while. Bill saw him jump off a third story roof once in the middle of a training exercise. Wish I could have seen that myself. I bet that was really something.

"He told me he knew it right then. You were absolutely wrong for The Farm. And at the same time, you were absolutely right. Now what do you suppose he meant by that?"

"I don't know," I said, looking down and shaking my head.

"I don't know either. Maybe you should take some time and figure it out."

Without another word, he turned and walked out of The Buzz, disappearing quickly into the night. I watched him walk away, and then my gaze turned back to the large puddle by the curb. The rain had stopped, and a distant streetlight now reflected off its placid surface.

Staring out the window, I saw the reflection of Marina's figure walking up behind me. I turned in my seat and watched as she pulled back the chair next to me and sat down.

It wasn't the same Marina.

The woman who threw her arms around me every chance she could get…was still and tentative. Her feather-in-the-wind energy lay grounded. Her warm, brown eyes weren't bright with joy, but pained and soulful. Disillusioned and hurt, she looked on me with uncertainty.

And yet, here she still was. She wasn't angry at me. She wasn't afraid.

She looked down at my bruised and swollen hand, set upon the table. She reached over and gently put her hand on mine. She took my hand carefully and tenderly and looked into my eyes. She didn't say a word. She didn't have to.

THE END

And now, a sneak preview of Book #2 in the Thomas Vale series…

CRYING CALL

CHAPTER 01 — Into the Fire

Our surveillance van sat upon a service road half a klick uphill from the target house. The sides of the van groaned from a stiff October wind. Four hours past sunset, a waxing crescent moon accompanied a clear sky of stars. Bright light shone from every window of the target house. Otherwise, it would be invisible against the dark West Virginia hills.

The surveillance techie brushed long curls of red hair from her face as she pulled up a new file. She and I huddled near the front of the van, studying and analyzing screen after screen of data and images. In the back of the van, FBI agent Jack Bonewitz held his hand to his ear, listening to reports from his team in the field.

A pair of headlights on a side screen caught my attention. I clicked the buttons that called up a full-spectrum scan of an incoming truck. What I saw made me sit bolt upright. I slapped my hand to my earpiece and yelled.

"Crosby! Get out of there! Now!"

The techie put her hand over her earpiece and turned abruptly to look at me, eyes wide, before looking toward Agent Bonewitz. It was Bonewitz's operation, a joint FBI/ATF sting, and in the briefing beforehand he'd made it damned clear his voice was the Absolute Word of God. With a finger point in my direction, and a swipe of that finger across his throat, Bonewitz signaled the techie to cut off my comms.

"Belay that order, Crosby," he said, glowering at me. "Malleus is incoming. Hold position. We've got him. We've finally got him."

We all wore earpieces with voice-activated microphones—all of us except Agent Crosby. His microphone and receiver were tiny, effectively invisible, planted deep in his ear canal by the same techie who'd just cut me off. He was inside the target house, undercover as a member of the Blue Panzer Militia, a secret cabal of police officers with ties to white supremacist groups. Ten Panzers were assembled for a war meeting inside the house and we had them surrounded. ATF agents were listening on laser microphones. They'd been recording the meeting for hours. We already had enough to put them all away for years, but we didn't have Malleus yet.

"What's wrong, Thom?" came the voice of Wendell "Dell" Nguyen in my earpiece. He was our NSA link, on loan to us for the operation to assist with research and intelligence.

"Dell, can you still hear me?" I asked.

"Yeah baby, still reading you," he responded, simultaneous with the techie looking my way and giving a thumb's up. She had only cut me off from the ATF and FBI agents.

"The heat signature from the incoming truck is all wrong. I can't tell if anyone's in it. Can you see it?"

Many screens were mounted inside our van. I pointed to the one synched to the discrete array of cameras we'd installed along the only approach to the house. It was reading infrared heat signatures and using real-time image processing and facial recognition to identify the incoming.

It was how we knew the identities of every Blue Panzer on site. Nearly everyone we expected had already shown up. Everyone except for Malleus, the one who called the meeting.

Now one more truck had just passed the array, with windows tinted so heavily we couldn't see its interior on the normal visual spectrum. Bonewitz believed it to be Malleus, which would ordinarily be a reasonable assumption. But while the engine block was registering red hot, there were no detectable body-shaped heat signatures inside the cabin. No sign whatsoever of a driver or passengers. Surely Dell could see the same thing back in his office.

Bonewitz paid no heed, not even looking at the screen. His withering glare was a reminder that he was tolerating my presence under protest. He leaned over my chair smugly, putting his face in mine until I had to look away. He snatched the ID badge off my breast pocket and read from it with a tone of condescension. "I've had just about enough of your bedwetting and false alarms for the night, Doctor Thomas fucking Vale. I don't know what analyst cubicle you crawled out of, but you better scurry back there before you get my boot up your ass!"

I scooted my chair back and turned away. Malleus. No one had ever seen him, at least not that we knew of, yet he'd been on the FBI's radar for years. This mythical organizer of militias and hate groups, using the dark web to organize domestic terrorism. I'd been working with Dell to track him. Months of exhaustive research and analysis. Tonight was the night where, for the first time, we were expecting him to show up somewhere in the flesh. And Bonewitz had jumped all over it, taking complete control and the glory of the collar.

"Ahem. I see what you mean, Thom," Dell interrupted. "That's really weird."

"If you can see it, then warn Crosby!"

"I can't do that, but…quickly for the record…run it all by me again?"

I repeated the quick version as Bonewitz turned toward a large screen showing the target house. The headlights of the approaching truck glimmered on the edge of the picture, already past the only other house within a mile.

"Teams, hold positions," Bonewitz ordered, commanding the two dozen ATF and FBI agents in the nearby woods, surrounding the house. "Do not move in until I give the order!" His agents were positioned in the woods, ready to pounce at a moment's notice. First with a power cut, then flash-bang grenades. The whole nine yards.

A confident sneer curled on Bonewitz's lips as we watched the car approach the house. But moments later, his jaw dropped.

The truck didn't slow down.

It sped up, screeching past several parked trucks, bouncing wildly on its axles. It swerved off the driveway, accelerated more as it clipped a garden lamppost, and finally crashed squarely into the front of the house. The truck left a gaping hole where the double door had been and disappeared inside.

Only a second later, the screen before us flashed brightly, the target house engulfed in light. A second-and-a-half after that, the sound of the explosion reached us. The van shook, and I wasn't sure if it was from the force of the blast or from all three of us instinctively crouching low.

The techie gingerly climbed back into her chair, her breathing fast and shallow. "Oh my God!" she gasped, her voice cracking. "Crosby!"

Bonewitz threw open the van door and stepped outside. In the distance, the sight seemed surreal. The target house was an inferno, white and yellow flames pouring out every window of both floors. He grabbed at his hair for a moment before slapping his hand over his earpiece.

"Agents, fall back! Fall back and hold! Report casualties! Backup is on the way!"

I stepped outside next and couldn't believe my eyes. A Biblical pillar of fire rose before us in the night, its flames quickly turning orange in hue and giving off billowing black smoke. I shivered from the cold wind, but more so from the sight.

"Am I seeing what I think I'm seeing?" Dell's voice in my earpiece snapped me out of a stunned stupor. "Was it a suicide bombing?"

"I don't know," I said, wringing my hands together. "Did anyone jump out of the truck?"

"Impossible to tell from that angle."

The air smelled of pine needles, and clouds of my breath floated before me. I was only distantly aware of my fingers picking open old cuts on my thumbs as I hyperfocused. It was stimming behavior, a side-effect of my autism. Self-inflicted pain that grounded me in the moment. What should I do? What are the variables? What's the problem? How do I solve it?

Solve it now. Solve it!

Bonewitz looked at me. His face was expressionless, except his cheeks just below his eyes were tense. One corner of his mouth twitched downward for the briefest moment. Anger and disdain.

"Stay here where it's safe," I told him, and his expression switched to confusion. I turned and ran down the slope, toward the flaming house, his curses in my earpiece.

"Dell, have you got a contour map of the area? Which direction would be downhill from the house?"

Thick trees seemed to spring up from the ground as I sped downhill. A thousand feet of Appalachian forest stood between me and the clearing around the house. But I grew up in the mountains. The moon was merely a sliver, but the light of the distant inferno helped, and it was all the light I needed. The occasional stray pine limb scratched my arms or face, but I was still making very good time.

"Downhill from the house would be southeast," Dell answered a minute later. "You think someone might be fleeing?"

"If someone jumped from the truck before impact, they'd try to escape. Downhill is easiest." I was huffing and gasping too much from my sprint to go into further detail. If a jumper knew the house was surrounded by agents, downhill would also be the best direction to minimize contact. Agents generally prefer surveilling from level or higher ground.

"Gotcha, baby. But you might want to circle around the perimeter, to avoid the ATF guys."

"Copy that," I said.

I changed my vector slightly outward and kept running, narrowly dodging tree after tree. The smell of the forest, the bobbing and weaving through the trees, the wavering light, and the feel of my heart pounding in my chest. I soon became disoriented, as though the trees were spinning around me.

"Southeast of the house," Dell continued. "It's not just downhill. A rain gully starts not far from the house. It twists around for about a mile and then leads to an old logging road. Might be a getaway route."

I spun around, lost. Tired and gasping for oxygen. The glow of the inferno gave me a sense of the distance and direction to the house, but I had lost track of my compass direction. The trees stood all around me, towering over me. They stared down menacingly, branches reaching out for me. Trying to stop me. Warning me.

I closed my eyes and took a deep breath. Reopening them, I noticed a break in the woods nearby and jogged that way. There was a clearing in the trees, and the night sky glittered above. I found my favorite constellation, Orion the Hunter. The rightmost star in his belt, Mintaka, rises almost exactly in the east. I fixated on that direction and made a few mental calculations, took another deep breath, and began running again.

Several more minutes passed as I completed circling around to the southeast of the house, and I found the long gully. I stopped for a moment, and only then realized I hadn't heard from Dell in a while. I was about to update him on my location when an odd crackling sounded in my ear, followed by a loud feedback squeak which made me wince and stopped me in my tracks.

"Jesus, Dell!"

"Thom! They cut me off from you and I had to hack my way back in! Bonewitz ordered his men to expand the perimeter and arrest anyone they see! Watch your back!"

I turned toward the house and saw the glow of the inferno bleeding through the trees. The forest was silent and still, as though waiting in anticipation. A subtle movement in the distant underbrush grabbed my attention.

At that moment, something very hard and very fast slammed into my abdomen. I staggered backward, gasping for breath, seeing no one around me. A high velocity bean bag, or rubber bullet? In the dark, it was hard to be sure.

"Wait! I'm on your..."

The next whatever-it-was struck me in the sternum with sledgehammer force. I finished that sentence lying flat on my back, looking dizzily up at the stars. What should have been words came out more like a bad case of whooping cough. Before I could fully register what was happening, camouflaged ATF agents were controlling me. My head was shoved down hard on the ground. A coarse rock scraped me under my left eye.

I was soon lying face down with my hands ziptied behind me, still gasping for breath. It didn't help that an agent was kneeling on my upper back, dangerously close to my neck. I heard Dell's concerned pleas for an update, but couldn't answer him. A flashlight was set on the ground, beaming directly into my face, at which point they finally noticed I had an earpiece like theirs. It was yanked unceremoniously from me and seemed to be the topic of a whispered conversation between a huddle of agents.

"One suspect subdued," reported an agent on his comms. "Armed with a handgun in a right-handed lower back holster. No other contacts." And then he paused, undoubtedly listening to a response that I couldn't hear.

The light in my eyes was too intense. My face shoved into the dirt. The cold. The noise. My body began to convulse involuntarily.

"Stop fighting me!" the agent yelled, kneeling on me harder. Additional flashlights in my face.

My eyes squinted closed, bright light still beating its way through the lids. Don't have a meltdown. Don't have a meltdown. My legs kicked the earth behind me. I couldn't stop them.

"Stop it, right now, or I'll mace you," the agent screamed in my ear. "Stop it now!!!"

Body out of control. Where am I? Shaking. Pain and pain and pain.

Suddenly the pain stopped. I was dimly aware of high-pitched screech. The agent on my back stood up quickly, cursing, and I was able to turn my head away from the lights. The agent threw his earpiece on the ground near my head. The fact that I could then hear the screech louder and more clearly told me that it was coming from the earpiece. The earpiece then spoke.

"The man you've detained is Thom Vale, of Homeland Security. He's the guy you heard trying to warn Agent Crosby. Stand down."

It was Dell's voice. I don't know how he'd managed to break into comms against Bonewitz's orders and against the techie's control, but I felt profoundly grateful. I tried to tell him I was OK, or thank him, or anything, but I was still coughing out my syllables, my mind too foggy to realize he wouldn't hear me anyway. I rolled onto my back and my lungs gulped the cold air. Breathe. Just breathe.

The sky and the treetops were spinning. Several ATF agents in camouflage stood around me, discussing me. I couldn't absorb their words. All I could do was remember the breathing exercises my therapist had taught me. Dr. Jasiri Stallworth. Just breathe. Calm. Focus. Don't have a meltdown.

"Attention! This is Jack Bonewitz! Do not release the suspect. He is wanted for questioning. You will disregard the rogue broadcast you just heard. Bring Vale to me!"

TO BE CONTINUED...

Acknowledgements

No writer is an island, not even writers on the spectrum, like me.

Like many autistic adults, I only realized I was on the spectrum after my eldest son was diagnosed. I began studying the literature on "high-functioning" autistic people and realized that it resolved most of the unanswered questions of my first forty-five years. This realization happened about the time of my divorce, and it influenced my writing and the development of the Thomas Vale character that had been slowly germinating in mind for decades.

The biggest influence on my writing was my father, John. After my mother, Shirley, passed away in 2016, Dad turned to reading as a way of passing all the empty time. He gravitated toward authors who wrote smart action heroes—his favorites were Lee Child and James Patterson. I read a few of their books on his recommendation and was impressed with their craft and vision. I've also always been inspired by the universe-building of Frank Herbert, and the clear dedication to research and character arc that makes Thomas Harris' books so intriguing. And I thought…I can do that. What's stopping me?

I set to creating a character and a universe that would please my father. My first reader. Dad passed away in 2023, but he and Mom continue to be my greatest influences. When I don't know what to do as a parent, I imagine what they would do. And when I don't know what to do as a writer, I think about what would impress them. The rest is easy.

Becka is my "first reader" now. And my copy editor. And my adviser on many other aspects of writing and publishing. Oh, and the love of my life, too. Thank you to the moon and back, sweet angel.

Additional gratitude is in order for numerous other beta-readers who gave me helpful feedback. Ed Alberts,

Jacqueline Clark, Dan DeCerbo, and Matt DeCerbo (the Matt Vale character is loosely based on him).

Michael Barry, Professor of English, not only gave feedback on my first draft, but offered up several bits of advice and anecdotes that were like writing prompts. He got me thinking along lines I hadn't considered before. I believe he improved my writing noticeably.

Mark Benvenuto gave me advice on some of the army stuff. He's written a few books, including the hysterical "Twisted Tales from VMI" which you should purchase and read immediately.

Authors Scott A. Clark and Anna Zabo gave me excellent advice on navigating the publishing market. Scott, in particular, taught me some things about self-publication, giving me the confidence to go on. Check out their websites for their latest titillating works of fiction.

Thanks to the handful of agents and acquisitions editors who gave me useful feedback despite not quite having the vision to sign me. Sorry we couldn't help each other.

Thank you to Richard C. MacCamy, Professor of Mathematics, without whose support I would certainly be "Mr. Boats" rather than "Dr. Boats." The Rick McKenzie character is an homage to him, and the Dante character an homage to my beginnings as a mathematician.

The team at Miblart.com is responsible for the terrific cover art. I highly recommend them to any other self-publishing author. Very prompt and professional.

Lastly, thank you to some of the other friends and artists I've known who've taught me, inspired me, entertained me, or just made me smile. Wayne Hwang, Pab Sungenis, Mike Vitale, Neil Simonetti, George Christopher, Russ Walker, Deborah Brandon, Charlotte Yano, Andrea Parks, Pete Kornblum, Jennifer Jeffery, Mike Juliano, Brian Robert, Lazaros Kikas, the Eclectic Studies Group at Carnegie Mellon, my brothers in Alpha Phi Omega, and the Ask the Professor crew at the University of Detroit Mercy.

About the Author

Dr. Jeffery John Boats grew up in Allegany, NY. He is currently a Professor of Mathematics at the University of Detroit Mercy.

"Blood Game" is Jeffe's debut fiction novel, the first in a series of action thrillers featuring heroes from marginalized and underrepresented backgrounds. The great Paul Erdos once said that a mathematician is a "machine that turns coffee into theorems." Jeffe, instead, turns coffee into stories with a diverse cast of heroes from every walk of life, because saving the world is a job for everyone.

When not writing or teaching, Jeffe enjoys spending time with his three children, often lovingly referred to as Chaos, Mayhem, and Havoc. He also plays poker well, chess badly, and baseball the best he can with the merry miscreants of the Detroit Men's Senior Baseball League.